GATLIN'S GATEWAY

A Novel of Gatlinburg

CATHERINE ASTL

MINDSTIR MEDIA

Published by Mindstir Media, LLC
45 Lafayette Rd | Suite 181| North Hampton, NH 03862 | USA
1.800.767.0531 | www.mindstirmedia.com

Printed in the United States of America
ISBN-13: 978-1-960142-64-1

DEDICATION

To the people of Gatlinburg

To my most beloved son, Dean, and to my most beloved
and supportive parents, Nick and Cathryn Abernathy

Also by Catherine Astl

Non-Fiction:

Behind the Bar—Inside the Paralegal Profession
Behind the Bar—From Intake to Trial

Fiction:

Three Gates
The Colonists

Historical Fiction:

Oliver's Crossing—A Novel of Cades Cove
Mountain Mulekick-A Novel of Moonshine
in Cades Cove and Chestnut Flats

AUTHOR'S NOTE AND ACKNOWLEDGEMENTS

WHEN I WROTE *Oliver's Crossing—A Novel of Cades Cove*, my first and only goal was to honor the people and its unique slice of American history. I have been visiting the cove my entire life, and in doing so, had mostly stayed in Gatlinburg. Fascinated by the history of these parts, I knew my next book would have to bring Gatlinburg, the Gateway to the Smokies, to life while always honoring the people, their heritage, and legacy. It's a town that has plenty of history, and I relied on many books, memoirs, histories, and sources to understand the flavor of these people and the place of the white oaks. Thank you to all of the historical and genealogy societies, archives of the University of Tennessee, Sevier County, Tennessee genealogy and history records, and the National Park Service for providing source materials.

Within these pages are historical facts and exact quotes taken from some of the best sources, some from the very memoirs of the people themselves. While this is a work of fiction, the people are real, as are all events. Being a work of fiction, I acknowledge that, while taking meticulous pride in conducting research, all errors, omissions, mistakes, and creative liberties are my own. Historical fiction novels do not include footnotes or citations; however, if any reader wishes to find out more about sources used, they are welcome to inquire.

Thank you to my beloved and wonderful son, Dean Astl, for patiently listening during the many days of reading drafts, writing, revising, and sifting through research. Thank you also to Caroline Fielding, Bryan and Steven Fielding, my wonderful extended family, and to my beloved parents, Nick and Cathryn Abernathy, for instilling a love of the mountains, a love of family, and the importance of honoring one's ancestry and heritage, while also looking toward the future. It's a fine balance, and they do that perfectly. I am ever so thankful for their lessons. And, I think this very balance of honoring the past while embracing the future is what makes Gatlinburg so interesting and allows us to learn from its people and experiences.

My highest hope is that this book honors those memories, and the futures, of the people of Gatlinburg, Tennessee, and their very special way of life, and that it inspires you to visit or return to the Gateway to the Smokies with a special sense of their unique legacy.

CHAPTER ONE

Late 1700s-1803

T HE DEER WALKED all day. Through the creeks and under the shade of many chestnuts and white birch, he chewed leaves and the woody parts of flora. The thick forest of white oak trees, however, provided the best and broadest vantage point to watch the men with reddish tones. Making his way over the moss and leaves, he kept his keen eyes on them. They had sticks with feathers attached and whooped loudly, usually right before hurling the sticks directly at rabbits and squirrels, but sometimes simply at random. One of the men locked eyes with him and threw a thin stick, directly at his very own furry body. But he had too many years of experience to fall for that trick.

Immediately, he darted his light brown torso nimbly through the brush, carrying his magnificent ten points with him. The stick fell quite far away, even from where he originally stood. No, he would make sure they would never hit him as their meal and prize. Never. The red-tinged men were too slow for his finely tuned animal instincts. He smelled them before they ever had a chance of glimpsing the huge animal who knew how to dodge life's obstacles. The deer would watch them though, for these two-legged beings had fascinated the stag for some time now. And sometimes, they had shiny metal L-shaped gadgets that fired and could kill instantly. He learned from watching other unfortunate deer that could not outrun the silvery metal bulbs striking their sides or traveling through their heads. Luckily though, these red men had very few of those alloy tools they called *unudana*. *Guns*. And luckily, when the shocking, loud crack came, death came instantly. No suffering; something the old stag couldn't bear to see. He had seen too much.

The animal peered at the muscular group, all of them walking back toward the stamped-down path. They called it a trail. A bit gravely in places but mostly the deer observed it was just a slash through the grass. The deer was very familiar with these men; both beast and being sharing the forest to live, eat, suffer, and love.

"We go to the Little Pigeon." One tall man said, leading his group of Cherokees.

"V-v. *Yes*, we will go the way of the u-s-di-g-a-nv-nv." *The Indian Gap Trail.* The younger ones in the group knew this trail was a favorite, due to frequent game found in the area and its connection to the Great Indian Warpath that followed the west fork of the Little Pigeon River. Much later, people would call this greater area Pigeon Forge, the Sugarlands, and Gatlinburg.

Gateways to the Smokies. But for now, the Cherokee hunters were the only inhabitants, along with the occasional but increasing presence of fur trappers and traders.

The men, a ragged, but strong group with a blend of mahogany, reddish and caramel skin tones, saw one of these trapper and trader groups down the valley. They were walking, no horses. But lots of furs were slung over their arms. Where was their wagon?

"Interesting…" the big Cherokee said with a hint of doubt. "They don't usually walk in this *shaconage*, land of the blue smoke. Not with skins to carry and all their gadgetry. Where's their wagon?" They were well aware of the white man's habits and *stuff.* This was a new sight, different. They always had their gear, their wagon, and their creature comforts—*nutsosedvna.* Food. Dried and canned. Extra clothes. Tools and paraphernalia for their animals. Tarps. Skillets hanging on hooks off the sides, or if hanging inside the wagon, one could hear the cast iron banging to the beat of wheels moving over holes and obstacles. Wagons could travel fifteen to twenty miles per day across plains, but significantly fewer in mountain terrain. Perhaps it *was* better on foot, given these steep slopes...one could cut a steep path and still cover twelve to twenty miles if on foot. On a good day. But they still needed a place to stash their things….

The big Cherokee frowned, stayed crouched behind thick brush, observed, and tried to sort it out.

Down in the valley, the trading and trapping group was also in the midst of a thought spiral, trying to sort things out, ever observant for a glimpse of an Indian. Each group familiar with the other, yet never outright asking intentions or plans; instead trying in vain to read each other's thoughts and reasons and intentions. Here, motivation and sheer commitment to this puzzling task always beat talent.

"There's definitely enough fur, but we can't get it all by ourselves." The men said, caps pulled low over their brows, and deerskin parkas pulled tight over their sinewy shoulders. "Them Cherokees, they just won't trap beavers and such. And what they do trap ain't enough."

"Wonder why they won't trap beavers? They bring the highest prices!"

"I thought this'd be easier." William Ogle lamented. "They was supposed to provide all the furs. Or at least most of 'em. And we'd just exchange with them for our guns and knives."

"And maybe some traps too." The others chimed in. The stag, far up the slope and back in the forest, watched this other group of men, the paler ones, slathered in furs and beards. Not as tall or sturdy; they made up for it with their collective ambitions.

"But no matter what we give 'em—guns, bullets, knives.... they can't trap fast enough. Or well enough."

"Maybe they're deliberately not doing it?"

"Why would they do that?"

"So they don't help us."

"Oh, I don't know about that. There's somethin' in it for them too. Why do that? And, we've been workin' together for a long time anyways. No, I think they just can't meet our demand."

⁓⊙⊚⊙⁓

The ragged group of bearded fur traders with no wagon walked through the thick brush of the forested slopes. In fact, their wagon was stashed away in an even thicker stand of trees, about three miles up a slope they knew well. All war is deception—even trade wars. Even wars of the mind. And they had to play the game better than the Indians, for they knew the red men were masters of the land and could track animals and other humans better than anyone. The arsenal of deception allowed for victories. And with victories, power.

It was the year 1800 and Tennessee had been a state since 1796, a mere four years ago. Not long at all, and it was certainly still establishing its identity. But it already had a few feathers in its cap. Previously known as the Territory south of the River Ohio, it was now named Tennessee, after a Cherokee village, *Tanasi*. And, it was the first territory admitted as a state under the Federal Constitution. Warm relations thus far, between Indians and Europeans; the natives even helped their English trader friends in the French and Indian wars of the 1750s and 60s. But it soon got a little too crowded.

Indian tribes—Cherokee in the east and Chickasaw in the west—European men, women and children, and a scattering of blacks, especially in the middle Tennessee farmlands, made up a mixture of cultures and people working, making a living, establishing homesteads, hunting, raising families, oppressing, taking land, encroaching on others' territory. Running out of space means running out of resources. And when that happens, conflict always ensues. A moderate amount of friction can be handled. But when the assets of land become more and more scarce, disputes escalate and the results cannot be stopped.

Both Indians and Europeans had been actively and willingly trading for years, but still gave each other a relatively wide berth. Even today, as the Indians were well aware of the white man's party of seven walking almost parallel to their own group, they watched before approaching. But then, relief, when the trader group came into view and the big Cherokee recognized one of the men almost immediately. He was the *Uwuyatanv ganohalidohi. The fur hunter.*

"Du-do-v". *Name.*

"There's the one named William."

The group of fur trappers and traders walked, kept to the trees for shade and cover, eyeing the Indians who they were sure didn't see them. Not warily; they knew one another well and were friendly toward one another. But still, the two peoples were worlds apart in their history, their culture, and their priorities. And they both were well aware of these differences. Never hurts to keep one eye open.

Rocky ground and slopes made for a tough walk. Tree roots crisscrossed the paths and road making for prime stumbling ground. They had to be careful. Though it was a well-worn path, there were still patches of uneven terrain and old rotten logs hidden beneath brush and if you happened to step on one, it usually led you downhill quite a ways until you were lucky enough to crash into a tree. *Careful now. There's a big boulder here. Slippery due to the rain last night. Walk around it. Grab hold of that tree... walk around the puddles of water...it can give way and make you slide. Or sink your boot and get you stuck....*

Finally, coming to a meadow, plain and spacious, red necks stood out amongst white-barked trees, fur caps appeared with blue eyes underneath, and multiple red bodies, feathers dancing in the nights of dark hair, walked to the middle, at ease, but also on guard. The two groups met and approached with waving hands, bowing their bodies in greeting.

William Ogle walked toward them, walked directly toward the big Cherokee. Nothing new here; he'd been walking his entire life. And always toward something better; friendly, sustaining...home. From New Castle County, Delaware where he was born in 1756 to his beloved land he had found in the south, still he walked. Smiling, his beard short but thick, his stature tall and a bit more wiry than the sturdy Indians, he remembered telling everyone he knew about how, when leaving the northeast, he had found the "land of paradise" here in the new state of Tennessee, while hunting, trapping and trading. He smiled at the memory, his long face beaming, ears slightly sticking out, but handsome in a clean, open way. William loved thinking about that first time he had seen the place where the soul knows it has found its heaven.

Heavily wooded with white oak trees, roaring creeks, and two hundred million-year-old mountains, ones softened by wind, ice and time, ones who shook boulders off their shoulders, sending them tumbling down their steady spines, yet carrying the weight of the riches of history on its backs. Wild, home to such diversity of life as to make it a place where certain animals had never evolved anywhere else; this place where the trees with the pale bark and the deer saw season after season nourish and punish, welcome and banish both man and beast. *This is my home. I hope I get to live a long life here...right here is where I want to be.* He closed his eyes, breathed in the freshest air, softening his chest from the weight of six furs on his shoulders. His soul knew it was home.

Releasing his breath and frowning now, he opened his eyes. Because whenever he'd dream of staying right here, in paradise, the vision got foggy. He couldn't quite picture it no matter how hard he tried to summon the scene. *It'll happen. It has to.* And then, to reassure himself, to tamp down a rising fretting, *I'll see it when the time is right....surely. I will live here and die here...right under that largest and broadest of white oaks.*

"William!" He heard his name crackle through the wide meadow.

Startled out of his dreams and worries, he saw the big Cherokee before him, bowing and holding out a large hand.

"O'siyo!" *Hello.* William relaxed, shrugging off the foggy visions, broke out into a smile. "So nice to see you!"

"Meet my friend, Wohali. His name means *eagle* in our language." the big Cherokee told William's group.

"How's the new year treatin' ya'll?" It was spring, 1800, the dawning of a new decade.

"Very well, very well." The large Cherokee replied, holding out his hand. They knew the white man's ways of shaking hands and the way they interpreted the time period for the new year.

"But for the Cherokee," he said with a smile. "Our new year is on the new moon of the autumn—the great moon. Because our Great Creator, a bit like your own God, made the Earth in seven days. Which was completed on the new moon of the autumn. And so, that's our new year. Some of our Cherokee tribes begin their new year during spring. Either way, it's been the new year for some time for us Cherokees, while your people just started yours!"

They laughed at that. The men murmured amongst themselves, furs slung over both shoulders. *How interesting. Same tradition. Just different ways and times. Wonder how that happens?*

లౠౚ

William took the big red hand and then placed his hands together, as in prayer. He knew that was the Indians' way of greeting. Both groups showing respect to one another.

Exchanging pleasantries, they spoke, each in rudimentary English and Cherokee—enough for basic communication, yet with the added language of hand gestures and facial expressions. Pointing, eyebrow-raising, smiling, frowning, and gesturing; most importantly, eye contact. One young Indian turned his back, arms folded, the universal sign of displeasure and hostility.

The big Cherokee noticed, feeling the need to explain such outward anger.

"He is the prophet of the group, the *a-de-lo-ho-s-gi*. He claims to see the future. Sees you men taking all the land. Every creek and river. All the furs. All the deer."

Another Cherokee chimed in. "But he's young. Not yet knowing if his power is real or just a strong young warrior's imagination."

The large stag directed his antlers ahead and watched. The young red-faced Indian male was making faces of severe anger. His tongue was even out, straight. Eyebrows down in the middle. That young male reeked of corn. And hate. But another, stronger, odor wafted on the wind—truth. The deer lowered his antlered head and backed up, retreated further into the forest, still watching.

Changing the subject, the big Cherokee sighed and asked, "Where you going on such fine day?"

William responded. "We're huntin'. And lookin' to trade. Probably just like you all?"

The Indian nodded. "Beaver. Skins. Clothes."

"Beaver? Thought you stayed away from those."

"No. Not stay away completely. But beavers are...whimsical...fun, *u-wo-tlv-di*. And the children love them. And the beaver dance, what we must perform prior to hunting them, is long and...complicated. Land harder to come by and we need to prioritize. Bear, deer, raccoons, rabbit. Much easier to hunt and trap. But we are seeking some beaver now...just did our beaver dance last night..."

William nodded in understanding and was excited about the prospect of extra beaver skins.

"Looks like we're gonna trade a bit then? See here…" making hand gestures, pointing the way. "Soon as we trap some 'coons and beaver, we can meet up at the Little Pigeon. Right before it comes to that big bend."

The Indian nodded, turning to his men, explaining the plan. They too nodded in understanding. They knew every speck of this land.

"Go trap. Meet at Pigeon in three days." The big Cherokee did not wait for a response instead waving his big hands and walking away. The hostile young man fell into step with the rest of his tribe, remaining silent, but with one last look back at the white men. He stuck out his tongue. One of the white men of William's group frowned and touched his rifle. The young Indian sneered, made a rude gesture, and continued walking. He knew it wasn't mature, deeply antagonizing these men. Showing anger. But he knew they were part of something that was taking away his people's land and way of life. *I'm the only one who sees it. Everyone else sees a resentful, wayward, difficult young man. But I know it's happening. They're taking our land. All of it. And it will be soon.* Anger turned to tears and he tasted the bitter helplessness as he walked away.

The deer observed from deep in the woods. Salty hate from that one young Indian male invaded his nostrils; much stronger than the whiffs of corn emanating from the rest of that group. He could almost see the misty ring of sniping the young, angry creature breathed out, coupling with the cold air. It hung there, like a murky omen. But then, the wind shifted. Smelling something different now. Anger yes, but also a briny sadness. Pushing his head down, with his immense antlers, he looked at the ground. Land. Solid. He could roam anywhere he liked; just had to be careful of predators and humans with their killing tools. Barring that, he was free to meander and wander at will.

Freedom. Promised land. Suddenly, lifting up his immense head, he saw what the young Indian had seen in his mind's eye. The deer took a deep sigh, breathing in the hopes of these two groups of men, but knowing they could not both be victors. Walking now, making his way through the forest, stepping on crunchy pine needles and soggy leaves, farther and farther away from that young creature that was filled with anger, and catching the white mens' conversation on the breezes of change:

"Gotta watch that one."

"He's trouble all the way around. Seen that type before."

"Yep. One in every crowd."

"At *least* one…"

"And they never change. Get worse as time chips 'em away."

"He don't like anyone who's not an Indian. Who's not his own kind. Well, he'd better get used to living with others. Gettin' more and more crowded 'round these parts every year. Gonna have to do somethin' about it. Eventually."

Trade was active and lucrative for all. Every man—because they were usually out in the elements more—and most women and children, needed numerous beaver hats every year. Rabbit was used as well, but beaver remained the staple fur of the times. Five million hats per year were sold in England, and they were in constant need of American pelts to replace the supply. Weather and the wear of living in the wilderness produced rips, tears, and general bald spots; they had to be replaced often. Every style from high-crowned to broad-brimmed, to the conically-shaped hat of the plain Puritans were sold. Firms from France, England and even Russia bought pelt after pelt from both white man and Indian.

Indians weren't forced to trade. Quite the contrary. They were the primary agents in the North American fur trade, and voluntarily hunted and transported and traded pelts. They raised their standard of living and actively sought out access to technologies to improve production and wealth. They had lots of practice in trade—before the white men even stepped foot on the North American arena, the native tribes engaged in extremely extensive trade practices amongst themselves for food such as beans, squash and the almighty corn, as well as decorations, but fur was their greatest ambition. When the white man arrived, the fur trade exploded and benefitted all.

Indians traded for more than just "beads and baubles, or even guns and alcohol." They certainly coveted "guns and shot and powder, but they also greatly desired knives, awls, twine, kettles, blankets, and tobacco." Fish hooks, buttons, trunks, and lace were also highly prized.

Cherokees would "immediately carve the thunderbird symbol into their newly acquired knives." Elders would tell the story to the children: "The thunderbird was the ruler of all the people of Earth." Wide-eyed youngsters would become mesmerized by the elder sitting by the fire at night, whittling away at a knife

13

handle and telling them "if a thunderbird beats its wings, they cause thunder and stir the wind. In turn, that very wind foretold victory in any war or conflict."

The angry young man scoffed at that. As a seer, he knew better and almost preached that all the thunderbirds in the world couldn't stop the white man's ambitious progress. But he didn't. Instead he recalled their friends, the Chickasaws', ancient story of hope: *Appealing to their wise hopayi, or prophet, for a solution, the prophet advised to place a stick in the ground and whichever direction it pointed—after spending the night in the wind—would be the direction to go. The Cherokee tried this while learning the land of the blue smoke. Where should they settle? Day after day, it leaned east, where the sun rose with every dawn. One day, it didn't lean in any direction at all, instead standing straight toward the sun. They knew then they had reached their homeland. The wind told them not to go east anymore. And the stick lay on the ground.*

"But" the young Indian muttered to himself, "While we were actually going toward the sun every day, toward the east, when it stood straight that one day...we made a mistake. We failed to place the stick in the ground again. I did though, every day, and in secret. And every day forevermore, it leaned west. Towards the sun, yes, but toward the *setting* sun." He sighed. He'd have to adapt. One way or another. But damn if he didn't want to.

It was during this changing, yet promising era that William Ogle, while working, trading, and roaming creeksides for beaver dams and pre-set nets and snares, came upon a perfect spot to build a home, an idea that had been brewing for quite a while.

Happening upon a clearing with beautiful views of the slopes, breezes sliding through his beard and then, his soul, he stood still for a moment. Breathed in the clear air and listened to the quiet woods full of life. *Yes. Here it is.*

Bending down, he ran the thick soil through his fingers. *Yes. This was it.* Fertile. Abundant. The mountains surrounding him, just the way he liked it, their leafy, strong faces always on watch. It was perfect.

These mountains have called me ever since I began coming to these parts. I know the terrain; this here is the most fertile soil I've ever touched, lots of beavers, rabbits and other game to keep my fur trade going, I have many Indian friends in the area, and... he paused his thoughts, felt his heart warming...*my soul knows it has found its heaven.* Familiar thoughts now...*felt this every time I've been around these parts. Spoken these very words to myself numerous times, always with a smile and always with an inner peace. My soul has found its heaven...A land of paradise.*

But just then, he stopped. Frowned, but not in angst or worry. He couldn't quite put this sudden interruption of his feelings into words, just knew he was somewhat entranced, his essence completely fulfilled. *It's beautiful here. Abundant. Fertile. But there's more. These mountains call me, telling me I'm in harmony with everything. God. Myself.* William Ogle gazed out as the softly sloped peaks melted into possibilities...the very peaks that pierced the very clouds of heaven above. And then, he closed his eyes and saw it clearly. *A Gateway.*

William flung his eyes open. Noticed the deer just then. It stared at him with its huge rack partially hidden through dozens of trees, but close enough to see the huge dark tan body standing stock still. *How long was I in that Gateway? How long has that deer been lookin' at me?* He smiled, chuckling to himself as he patted his rifle he had aptly named *Persuader.* Once named, a man's rifle brought good luck and *Persuader* always brought him luck. At the very least, it warded off bad luck.

He thought about taking a shot. They could all have a feast tonight...and many nights thereafter. That huge buck would feed all of them for weeks! Fawns were the most tender of course, but whether buck or doe, old or young, who could tell the difference in quality? All were tasty and essential to frontier life. Properly cooked, or preserved. Smoked, or salted, venison was never unwelcome. *And it'll give us something other than knives to trade with the Indians—food, deerskin, which, when tautly stretched, was great for making clothes, bags, drums...*

But somehow, as the two creatures eyed one another, William's instincts told him this buck was special, and as he stood there observing, *Persuader* at his side, thoughts began swirling. *That animal is a protector. A survivor. It will keep an eye out for Martha and the kids for when I can't be here.* He paused. Wondering at his thoughts and where these sudden and crazy forebodings were coming from. *But where will I be? I'll always be around...but perhaps I will be out hunting? Somewhere far away?* The strong premonition haunted for a moment or two. Remembering that young, scowling Indian, he vowed to always protect his family and to stay closer than perhaps he had wanted. After all, beavers only traveled five to six miles to find more suitable water and logs for their dams. That was far enough. *I will simply stay closer than I had planned.* Five or six miles was far enough. *Surely, it was far enough? And if I roam farther—perhaps I will have to find food to trade, to do something I hadn't thought of yet...* he looked at the animal staring at him with resolved eyes... *If I do roam far, this very deer will be there for my family.*

And the deer, smelling the ominous prediction and seeing the man's hand fall from the rifle, vowed to keep an eye out for this man's people. To be their protector. For the large and graceful animal knew William Ogle—this familiar human who saw and felt the soul of the mountains—would soon be very, very far away.

CHAPTER TWO

1802

THE TOWN OF Gatlinburg began as an area in the Smoky Mountains inhabited by Indians and seasonal fur traders. But it still had a while to go before it adopted that name. For now, it was known as White Oak Flats due to the plentiful white oaks reaching to the sky, like toothpicks stuck in every inch of land on every side of every mountain. The white oak bark isn't normally edible, too bitter, but the Cherokee Indians boiled the acorns and ate them. *Didanawisgi*—a Cherokee medicine man, would prepare the acorns with the young children helping and learning.

See here? You must soak for one or two days, mix with ashes from the wood fires to speed up the removal of bitter substances. Taste this... The children would screw up their faces at the taste. *See? Bitter! Don't ever just eat the bark. Unless you are completely starving. Yes, I had to eat the bark one time. During a snowstorm when I was stranded. It was the only thing that wasn't covered in white snow in the entire world.* He sighed at the memory. So hungry as to eat the bark right off of the trees... *Children: To take away the bitter taste, you may boil the acorns and let them cool. After taking the bitter tannin out, eat the acorns whole, so meaty! Or grind them into sweet flour for baking. You can even bake them until very dark and use them as a substitute for coffee. White oak can also work with stomach issues, and as an infusion for cough and sore throats. Children...come close and I will tell you a secret.* Big-eyed, they gathered around the medicine man. *Sometimes the spirits need a little help from witchcraft.* The children gasped; they never spoke of witchcraft! Shivers ran up their spines. *But there are times when those witch's brews are helpful. Listen. When you mix it with the corn whiskey, and you drink it, it helps your woman come back when she's run off. So, you mean it treats the woman who's gone off? Yes, young ones,* the medicine man replied. *And if it doesn't, enough of it wards off loneliness.* He smiled. *You forget she's even gone.*

Squirrels, turkey and pheasants gorged on the three-quarter-inch fruits of the white oaks that took but a season to mature. The large stag deer with the largest crown of antlers also ate the acorns as it watched the leaves sway to the music of the wind. Most of the white oaks were about 100 feet high, and hundreds of years old. Very slow growing; their broad leafy coverage has witnessed this particular deer's birth, growth, and wisdom. As the deer rubs or files his antlers on the bark, it peels off the bark, revealing a whiteness underneath. Every late winter, the antlers shed, and every spring and summer, they return, in full velvety glory.

Deer return to the same tree to rub each year. And despite the years and years of scrapes and rubs from the largest of deer, the largest of the white oaks still stood tall, strong.

എൟ

William Ogle ran his fingers across a medium-sized white oak. More manageable than the larger ones and sturdier than the smaller ones, this would make perfect logs. Such thickness! Cutting it would produce a mighty sturdy house. Flat but thick stones from the creek, at least four for each corner for the foundation. Maybe six? Not too far apart, but just enough to support the first boards. Then, lay rough-hewn planks from corner to corner. Next, lay boards across the other way to make a floor. Need some clay to plug it all together, and definitely lots of clay once the walls start stacking up. About six feet high because that's all a man can lift over his head. Once help came, they could build ladders or stand in the back of a wagon. Make an attic. A loft. Some additions can be made down the line, once saws and tools arrived so they could cut the logs and make holes into other rooms. More creek rocks to shore up the porch foundation, make it as even as possible, and as large as possible. *We'll be spendin' a lot of time on that porch. Resting from the hot fields at noon, eating a piece of cheese with biscuits and ham and butter. Shelling peas, sewing quilts, watching the children, rocking away a few glorious minutes while scanning the peaks and skies for eagles and the white oaks for deer. Mountain life was meant to be lived outside. It's where the soul is most at peace.*

Such a vision he had! William loved it here, smelling the piney aroma of creeks and slopes, the earthiness of that one large and majestic deer that always seemed to be nearby, the fertile land and leafy lushness decorating the slanted walls of the mountains. All the children running around, fetching, milking, hewing, helping; Martha sweeping the front porch and yelling at the youngins to remain outside or *I'll scootch ya'll outta here 'cause I just swept the floor for the millionth time just today! Want to keep it clean for at least a good hour!*

And indeed, it would all happen. But William Ogle would not be around to see it.

∾⊙⊙∾

The logs had been cut. All of them. They were stacked and ready to go, the whiteness of the trees' innards gleaming in the mountain sunlight. Stacked high, waiting patiently at the perfect farm and homesite for the future, while William walked home to South Carolina to pack up and plan his permanent return. Before embarking, he managed to lay the foundation, and even put up about the first few layers of walls with the help of his Cherokee friends. Everything else would have to wait.

∾⊙⊙∾

"I've found the land of paradise! And we're goin'!" He announced when he finally arrived home to the Edgefield District of South Carolina. It was early 1802 when he strode up the gravelly pathway where Martha stood staring at her husband. She hadn't seen him in two years, and she couldn't quite believe he was here, today, with his beard a bit longer, a bit sparser, a bit grayer than when he left. He'd managed to write a few scribbly letters these past years, stating he was okay, and still trading, and one recent one all about how he'd found a place amongst the white oaks he wanted to move to, its praises singing off of the rough and dirty letter.

"Your beard is so long! Ain't you able to cut it?" She smiled as she walked and embraced him.

"Woman!" he chuckled, "I sure ain't cutting it with a knife and that's all I had." He picked her up and spun her around. "Ah, it's good to see you, Martha. How're the kids?"

Seven people emerged from the house and the woods and the fields, five sons and two daughters, and all fourteen eyes grew wide as they ran and yelled "Pa!"

Pa's home!!

Where's the furs?

"Did ya see any Indians? Were they nice?"

"Do they really live in tepees?"

"What did you eat?"

"How much ya'll gettin' for them 'coon skins? How about beaver pelts?"

Bear skins? Really? But isn't that dangerous? Beavers and raccoons are so much easier to kill.

Were you scared? Did the bears try to claw you?

"Indeed, children! Let him answer!" He saw Martha eyeing him, not liking that he was so close to bears with their deadly claws and teeth, even with *Persuader* by his side and courage like a mountain lion.

"Bear isn't as highly sought after. Mostly for rugs and such thicker goods. And I did try to stay away." Martha's eyes narrowed ever so slightly as if to say, *did you really...?*

"Did you see any deer?" The littlest one asked. "They're my favorite animal..."

"I did. There was this one stag. Huge! Biggest one I ever seen. It was always around. Like it was watchin' out for me."

The littlest one said, "Oh, it *was* watching out for you! I know it." Such confidence lay in the air, heavy. And William felt something just then. A religious man, of course it must be God that was watching out for him. Surely, the deer, all on his own, wouldn't be consciously looking out for him? Surely, if it was, it was God's hand guiding the creature…

⚬⚬⚬

Later that night, after he was settled in, bathed, and fed a feast that Martha had put together, he told his family his plans. "We will move soon. After the harvest. We must grow the next crop—that's why I came home and why we're not going right away. We need supplies put away if we're going to move to the place of white oaks, and we need some more resources. This next and last crop will get us there."

The happy family embraced one another that night. They gathered around the fire, and William read from the Bible: *If time be of all things most precious, wasting time must be the greatest prodigality, since lost time is never found again.*

"Wait. That's not the Bible!" Martha exclaimed to her husband. The children sat on a quilt on the floor, stretched out in front of the fireplace, while she and William sat on chairs.

"Ah, you got me." He laughed. "Nope, no Bible. Ben Franklin."

"You and that Franklin again!"

"Well, it's almost like the Bible! Even better sometimes. There's truth in it. A practical truth. One we can understand. And I don't like to waste time." He sighed. "I don't have it to waste." Martha stared at him, opened her mouth, and then thought better of it. Remained silent. This plan was so important to William; it was like he was desperate to race to this land of paradise. Such urgency! She had to admit she couldn't wait to see it...the way he described it was vivid in her mind's eye. She could see it so clearly.

First though, hard work indeed lay ahead. But they were never afraid of that. In fact, they'd never known one day that was not about rising with the dawn, tending the animals and land, and then, sweating under a constant sun, only to share a meal with flaky biscuits and fruit pie, reading from the Bible and going to bed, listening to the mountains creaking in the night. And that's just the way they liked it.

William woke up with a fever on a late February day in 1803. The harvest was completed the previous fall and the banner crop sold in early winter. Resources were ready, and most of the packing and preparations were completed. They had simply to stand by for this latest icy snow storm to pass and for the world to fling off winter's heavy coat and bare its skin to spring's warming rays and gentle breezes. The new year had seen the young United States and France negotiating for a vast amount of land. It hadn't been finalized just yet, but there was already much anticipation about what was already being called the Louisiana Purchase. Napoleon continued the wars of the French Revolution and fought Britain for supremacy of Europe. And, in a tiny cabin in South Carolina, William Ogle felt awful and worried about his future.

In addition to the fever, he felt chills, a very bad headache that had not abated for days now, and general tiredness. "I feel like I just spent a week carrying beaver pelts. After being beat up. Through muddy ground. With no food or water." He tried to sit up, but couldn't summon the strength.

They tried alumroot for the fever and whiskey for the aches. A little gin they had was also offered to William. The drink helped. Eased both muscles and mind. "I sure wish we could get our hands on some quinine. But some doctor up in Missouri has it I heard...reckon we don't have any 'round here."

"Them Spanish knew about quinine since the 1500s!"

"I hear…" Martha whispered," …that mixing it with whiskey or gin 'specially does wonders." But they had no quinine. And their gin was now gone. The little whiskey they had left was saved for tomorrow.

The dawn came and William was worse. Sweating, he hadn't urinated for three days, and his eyes fixed on the ceiling every two hours or so. Seizures, Martha thought. "My God, what if he…" She didn't want to think it. Put her hand to her head. But she had to think of it, for her husband, her William, was fading fast. Too fast. *What else can I do? What will I do if the worst comes? Oh, I cannot think on it!! I can't...*

Somewhere, deep within the treed slopes of the Tennessee mountains where the white oaks stood guard, a large deer bowed its head, antlers brushing the leaves of the greatest of white oak. It stomped, sniffed the air, and then stood stock still as it lifted his head skyward, to see a lone cloud drift up to the heavens.

It was the night of March 1, 1803, and despite the most desperate and loving nursing by his wife, despite the drink and every home remedy they knew of, and despite the most fervent prayers to God to save one of the best of men, William Ogle died. Martha saw his eyes fix on the ceiling, then close, and then...nothing. No gasp. No breath. His hand still lay in hers. *Is he gone? Oh, please, don't let him be gone.* But she knew he never took another breath. She stared at him for a long time, an hour per-haps; never letting go of his hand. It was now warm, but not hot like it was. *My William. Husband. Father...he's really gone.* Neighbors showed up, her brother and his family appeared. Food piled up in the cabin, onto a rickety table on the front porch; so many brought whatever they could to deal with such a loss. Someone pried her hand off of his, gently, and led her outside. *No. No, I can do it.* The widow turned around and walked back inside her home. *I want to do it. Let me go get his church clothes. I can do it. Go let the church know...please, let everyone else know....*

Far away, the deer sensed a sudden intense ache and rose from the place where he bedded down, covered in thick branches, with his back to the wind. He stood, antlers tall, catching the sobbing wind in his eyes. He walked toward the stack of hope, a pile of white oak logs still intact and exactly like William Ogle, the man who had put his rifle down when they had locked eyes in the woods, the one who had stared at his huge tan body and knew instinctively that the animal would act as protector of Martha and the kids when he wasn't around had left it. And the deer knew then he must keep his vow to keep an eye out for this man's people, whenever they decided to come to the place of the White Oaks. Because they would come. Of that he was sure.

∽⊙∾

Martha prepared his body, while the bells tolled in the lone church, one chime for every year of his life. Forty-six chimes. Almost forty-seven if he would've lived a few months longer. A wooden coffin was quickly built by the Ogle boys, and neighbors brought still more food and walked behind the wagon to the Fruit Hill Church area where the preacher helped them say their final goodbyes.

"William Ogle. The man whose heart will always be with the White Oaks."

"So sad. He will never fulfill his biggest dream, of living out his years on his beloved land."

"What will you do Martha? Will you go to the place of the White Oaks? Or stay?

She sighed, drying her tears with her hand-embroidered handkerchief. "I honestly don't know. I just don't know. A part of me wants to just stay. I mean, we are settled here. Yet, he left that legacy…even started buildin' our home…" Martha said, thinking about what to do now. "He wanted to live there so much...he always said it was as close to God as one could get. He said *I feel like I am home.* Every single time he spoke about it." She laughed a little at the memory, a warming thought on this cold, empty day. "Every time he spoke about it..." she repeated, eyes glistening, "which was every single day."

As was custom, they buried him in the church graveyard, but many in Appalachia buried their dead right on their very own hillsides, forever nearby to their homes and fields. *Keep 'em close by. Always remember their lessons, and pass them on to your own kin. Memories. It keeps everyone alive, as long as just one person remembers. Just one.*

❧

They were surprised when one lone Cherokee appeared at the funeral. A big man. How had he known the man they called William was dying? Communication was limited; they didn't speak each others' language well enough, and news did not travel that quickly. How did he know? Puzzling, and certainly strange. But when the big Indian grasped a stick and drew a deer in the dirt alongside William's freshly dug grave, the Ogle family and friends opened their eyes wide in surprise.

"Here it is. The deer." Stick still in hand, the Indian looked into their astonished eyes.

"Oh. William always spoke about one deer that always seemed to hang around his land. Well it wasn't his land yet, but he wanted to build there."

The Cherokee nodded. "I helped chop logs for the cabin."

"You're the one that helped?"

The Indian nodded. "Yes. And the deer was always around. Watching."

"The biggest one, the stag, the very one William always spoke about?"

The Cherokee nodded. "V V." *Yes.*

"A-da-nv-do. A-wi-i-na-ge-e-hi." *Spirit Deer.*

And then, the big Cherokee spoke the best English he knew.

"William. His spirit animal is the deer. Magical ability to regenerate. If antlers fall off, they grow back. To be a deer is to be in touch with life's mysteries. King of the Forest. Protector. Messenger—an animal of power. Stands for sensitivity, intuition and gentleness. Fertility. I trust all my hunts from now on to the deer. In honor of William. Honorable man. Good hunter and trapper. Husband and Father."

But how did you know?

"I read it in the deer's eyes." They frowned. Didn't understand the spirit animals and what, exactly, Indians saw.

"That, and the deer looked up at a cloud in the sky. The only cloud. That was the sign. William had gone to the spirits. That's how I knew."

Murmurs erupted from the crowd. *How can this possibly be? There is no way a deer and a cloud forecast a man's death! He must've heard it from some traveler. But who? There's no one that travels these parts without us knowing! And we're in South Carolina! This Cherokee came all the way from Tennessee! Impossible...God had a hand in this. That must be it. God guided him here. That is the only explanation. Whenever life hands us a contradiction, or impossibility, or anything else we cannot figure out for the life of us, the answer is God.* But even with this fallback position that faith thrives upon, this very shaky answer troubled the Ogle family. *Trying to figure out how the Cherokee knew about William...there's got to be a reasonable explanation! We're just missing it...our God is good. Great, in fact. But growing up on the land, observing nature our whole lives, well, we know what we know. And this situation isn't acting like anything we know.*

The big Cherokee began walking home that day. To report to his people about William's funeral. To honor the trapper and trader he had worked with and would remember as a good and honest friend. He sniffed the air and bedded down for the night, somewhere in northwestern South Carolina. And amongst the white oaks in a beautiful bowl of the Tennessee mountains, a large stag also bedded down that night, within sight of a pile of logs gleaming in the dusky rays of the setting sun.

Practical matters took precedence in the coming days. On March 5, 1803, the last will and testament of William Ogle was read to a small gathering at a cabin in South Carolina:

'I give unto my son Hercules Ogle that hundred acres of land he now lives on. Also, the remainder of the land is to be divided among four boys except a child's share which I give unto my beloved wife Polly Ogle (Martha Huskey Ogle). Also, I give unto my beloved daughter Rebecca (Mc) Carter a cow and Calf, bed and furniture, Pot and Some other furniture. Also, I give unto my beloved grandson William (Mc) Carter a young sow. Also, the rest of the property to be equally divided among all the rest of my children except my beloved wife which draws a child's share."

"The will of William Ogle is hereby recorded in Edgefield County, South Carolina, Will Book 'A', box 22, #783."

❧❦❧

After the reading of the will, after deeds and paperwork were signed, and after everyone else had retired for the night, Martha Ogle sat alone with her thoughts. *Widow.* The fire was low, but she didn't bother with another log. Smells of savory stew and flaky biscuits lingered in the cabin, wafting upwards, toward the loft and out of the window opened just a crack, allowing inside, the night sounds of the mountains; squawks and howls humming on the empty winds. *He spoke of it every single day when he was alive. I couldn't wait to go with him. And we are pretty much packed up already. All plans are made and done. We were going to go as soon as the weather turned to spring. Within a week or two! When the daffodils began poking their yellow faces toward the sun. Oh, why did he have to die just when they were leaving for paradise on Earth? Answer me God. Why? I know you saved him, and he's now with you in heaven. But why couldn't you give him his season? One summer when he could live in his white oaked kingdom he loved so much?* She picked up her Bible, sighing. She needed words to comfort this profound loss. Needed to stir and poke at the dusty relics of William's life. *What should she do?* Genesis: *As long as the earth endures, seedtime and harvest, cold and heat, summer and winter, day and night will never cease.* She sighed. The Bible helped a bit. Managed to keep the deeply distressed feelings tamped down and, at least for a breath or two, to loosen the knot in her chest. But all of the most meaningful words in the world brought little comfort.

She didn't sleep at all that night. Which was just as well, because as dawn broke and nature's colors sifted themselves toward daylight, she had used those quiet, solitary hours to resolve to fulfill her husband's dreams as soon as possible. Trusting her husband's insistence that it was indeed paradise on Earth, she would go to White Oak Flats and settle her family there by the time the sweet harmonies of spring whispered through the woods.

It took four years.

CHAPTER THREE

1803-1807 (Transition Years)

MARTHA OGLE AND the large Ogle family packed up the rest of their belongings from their South Carolina home and moved in with relatives in Virginia. She was ready to go to William's place of the white oaks, but first, she had to plan a bit more. Sure, she *had* planned, but that was *with* William. She found it was another thing entirely to execute the move *without* him. *I am a widow, with seven children! Yes, some have grown, but I still have some smaller ones. And one grandchild even!* Custom said to marry again. Marry right away, as soon as possible. To the best man with the most to offer she could find. And one that wanted to, and that could move to Tennessee. But she had already had that best man with the most to offer. How could she possibly replace her William? Oh, they all had tried alright! A supper here, a meeting on a Saturday night porch there, a mention of a widower ten miles away, but none stood a chance. She wasn't interested in marrying ever again. *I am still married. Even if William isn't here.*

As she sat in the cold house in Virginia, she traced the foggy windows with her finger. It was now winter; spring, summer, and fall, for four years now, having been a time of activity, trepidation, changing of moods and plans, and temporary movement that always became too comfortable too fast. And so, she traced. A tree here, another one there. A "v" that symbolized a majestic stag deer. Then, she ran lines down the windowpane, down, down....

She stood up, chilly, wrapped a shawl around her shoulders. Walked around the room a few times. It was awfully frosty here in Virginia, and tracing foggy windows and going out for still more logs for the fire didn't help. *I am fretful today.* Wringing her hands. Chilly and restless. *A good combination,* she laughed. *Keep moving, you won't get as chilly.*

Turned back to the window and saw it. She sucked in her breath, realizing. Letting her breath escape, she almost laughed out loud. Wondering for the past four years about why she was paralyzed about going forward with her original plan. She never got her answer as to why, even in the depths of sleepless nights when the mountains called to her. But today, right now, she saw it in her tracing. *All lines pointed south.* Towards William's cherished land. She hadn't even consciously thought about it! But her fingers knew. They channeled her soul. Streaks of faint lines pointed down, offering the message she was waiting for. Martha smiled to herself, feeling hopeful for the first time since the funeral, since the move to Virginia, since her mind raced in ten thousand different directions for four years.

Slowly, the veil of sorrow lifted; every day a bit more focused. No, she didn't have to find *someone* else to make a new life, a new dream. As everyone kept pushing her to do, *no thank you!* She simply had to go *somewhere* else....and that place was obvious. She knew it all along, of course. *I just wasn't ready yet. I don't know why, don't even ask me! Don't know why it took me four long years. Wonder all you want about why I went to Virginia and not to William's land of paradise when we were all packed up, crops sold, and ready to go. I cannot tell you why! But I know I had to mourn. Settle things in my chest. Maybe have a bit of help with my younger ones, so they grew enough before setting off on my own. I always did things practically. Was never impulsive. Four years, it's been. Four long, hard years. But now it's time. The right time to go. To the area where the white oaks grow, where the soil is fertile, game is abundant, and William will be with me forever. Where the large, robust stag will look out for us.* Yes, it was time to return to life, return to the dream. Time to be in the right place to see it through. *Time to bring my William's dream to life.*

She sat down, gathering up her knitting needles and packing them away neatly in her sewing basket. Needed to get busy arranging the move; as usual, mind racing. *What made the place with the white oaks so important to him?* She thought back to her husband's quiet, deep-rooted history. He had come from Revolutionary War stock...*My goodness, he had come from a line traced back to 1085! Right after William the Conqueror took over England in 1066 at the Battle of Hastings, he had said. So very long ago...it's almost overwhelming to think at least one Ogle has seen medieval times, plagues, Shakespeare, the Inquisitions, Crusades, numerous eras of renaissance, and rises and falls of nations. Such lessons learned from those that came before*

us! The Ogles had soaked it all up and passed it all on...not only for them-selves, but to prove to others that they had lived and learned. They were the ones left behind to tell the stories, as plainly and honestly as possible, before the winter came to take them home to God.

This story of ancestry is now well-known amongst the Ogle family lore. But it did not stop there; history keeps itself moving. In 1664, an ancestor named John Ogle left his native England and went on an expedition to colonial America. He headed a bit south, which set in motion the Ogle family settling in the colonies and many moved even further south to a mountain region called the territory south of the River Ohio, now known as Tennessee. Letters were exchanged about grand opportuni-ties in the colonies and more Ogles came over to America and settled here and there, some in the mountains, and some in the northern colonies.

Then, on one fine day in 1756, William Ogle was born to Thomas Ogle and Elizabeth Robeson Ogle in New Castle, Delaware. Martha remembered her mother-in-law telling her William was a healthy and robust child, very curious and very strong. *That boy is gonna make a name for himself*, his mother always said, seeing a special potential and perseverance in her young son. As for Martha, she had loved him since her first sight of him—strong arms, strong jaw. Strong personality, yet car-ing and logical and reasonable at all times. They mixed very well, everyone said. Same temperament and same brains. Both were thinkers.

We met and married in 1778. Courting was quick, as usual. Why wait? Turned out to be a great provider; we never wanted for meat or food and his crops always grew tall and firm. Fur trapping was a particular specialty of his. Yes, he traveled often, and far, yet managed to stay close to us, sending messages and gifts with decent regularity. A great father to our seven children: Hercules, Rebecca, Thomas, John, Isaac, William, and Mary Ann. Five sons and two daughters. And now, a grandson. All hard workers, kind, and cherished. She chuckled as she remembered all of their sons had nicknames, a very common occurrence in the deep mountains of Appalachia: Hercules was "Hike", John was "Johnny", Isaac was "Shucky", and William was "Black Bill". Thomas was simply called "Tom".

There were so many Johns and Williams that they had to use nicknames to differentiate: Johns were "Big John" if he was the father, "Lil John" for a son, or even "Lyin' John" if he happened to have that particular personality flaw.

⌒⌒⌒

Sitting by an icy window in Virginia, Martha was jolted out of her thoughts. Smiling, she heard her children murmuring to themselves. Happy sounds. *My goodness, most of them are not even children anymore!*

So grown up now. They need to get on with their lives. Settle in one place; create some opportunities for the boys and open up some options for the girls. They are ready, she thought, sighing a happy sigh. *Oh, they've been ready for a long time. Four years. It's me that had to sit for a while.* Smiling to herself, and gathering up the rest of her knitting—a fine scarf and thick booties for the grandbaby, she threw her shawl off and placed her hands on her hips. A deep breath. And no knot in her chest. *Yes. I've mourned long enough. It's time to go.*

✦✦✦

Martha's brother, Peter Huskey, and his family agreed to accompany her and the children on their journey. *Truth be told, I feel as if I am moving closer to my own roots as well,* something she hadn't expected to feel because she hadn't ever thought about it before. It was always William's roots she was seeking to re-plant, but she had some deep roots of her own. Born in Wake County, North Carolina, daughter of John Frederick Huskey and Rebecca Washington Huskey, Martha was part Cherokee Indian. She always liked to hear about William's adventures and meetings with the Cherokee in his letters and when he returned from trapping and trading.

They had gotten along well. And William had always told her how he liked *the mix that makes you up, Martha. Makes for an interesting woman,* he said, winking.

I've got my one-of-a-kind woman right here.

The Ogle family set out with their two wagons full of supplies—skillets, jars, seeds, tools, furniture, and dried food, and headed south, the image of the foggy streaks on the windows pointing the way. Rickety and rough, the journey took three weeks.

And when she stepped off the wagon, still swaying a bit from the long days of traveling, dirty and sweaty from the dusty trail, Martha Ogle looked out and stared in amazement. Trees danced in the gentle breeze and layers of mountains stood there, strong, asking *what took you so long?* Sunlight smiled through the clouds and sprinkled the slopes with dots of peace; even the shadows gleamed in the afternoon sky. *My God. It's beautiful. Perfect.* She felt her soul settling.

Your efforts were not in vain, she spoke to her husband as the bumpy journey came to an end and she had finally arrived at his beloved land. *You were right.* Her boots crunched the pine needles as she walked over to a large white oak. Stopping, she looked out at the beckoning landscape; bending backward a bit to stretch out her back. Then, from somewhere deep inside, Martha Ogle closed her eyes, put her hands together in prayer and reached for William. *I will live your life, and mine, the way you intended. Right here. In your— in our—land of paradise.*

CHAPTER FOUR

1807—Fulfilling the Dream

T HE DEER PICKED up his large antlered head and saw the woman. Truth be told, he had smelled her way before his keen eyesight had caught up. Plain brown hair swept back into a low bun, simple but clean cotton dress, sturdy shoes. A round, pleasant face and strong spirit. The man they called William—this was his wife and offspring. He knew it by their scent, their essence. Here they were. Finally! Feeling an immediate sense of protectiveness, the deer stepped forward, cautiously, catching sight of the wagons. A couple of horses were trailing behind carrying two girls. Sturdy boys followed along by foot.

Most deer live about five to six years, but some can live ten or more, like himself. However, as strong as he was, even he knew his time was running short. Seeing his own offspring far into the woods on the other side of the forest, he was glad he had taught them, even briefly, to recognize the particular scent of this band of humans. Nudging their noses down on the pile of logs, he repeated it again and again and communicated in a deer's unique way that this scent was special. *Protect them. Whoever carries this scent.* He had instilled this in his offspring before they pranced away, full of energy and life. Stags don't typically tend to their young; he'd mated with many a doe and had many offspring moving amongst the pleats of the mountains. But he took the time to teach all of them the scent. They all could recognize the special sturdy aroma of the Ogle family. One of his male offspring paid particular attention; returned to the pile of logs and sniffed for a long time. *Yes, he will be the one to carry on the protection when I'm gone.* The large old stag walked slowly toward a thick stand of white oaks, circled around, acutely aware of everything. Feeling content about his immediate environment and satisfied his legacy and purpose could safely live on, he bedded down in the softest of pine needles and watched as his male offspring, now with its own magnificent crown of antlers, inched closer and closer in sharp observance.

Martha, holding a piece of paper in her hands, and with Peter's help, walked until she found the exact plot of land her husband had obtained at the "mouth of Walden's Creek" in White Oak Flats.

"My God!" She exclaimed upon seeing a stack of logs on the property, and even a few logs already starting to make up a large square foundation. "The beginnings of the floor. Walls! Look at this...he prepared so well." Sadness enveloped her, thinking of William's labors and efforts. "He had already started building his dream..."

Oh, he had told her he did some preliminary work on the house, cut the logs and even began "putting things together," as he put it, but to see it in person...*these logs he touched*...it flooded her with tenderness. Well-hewn timber sat in large piles, ready to be hoisted above his head and notched into place. *He really was going to build us a wonderful home...I can see that. The outline, the starting of the walls.* She ran her fingers over the felled wood, looking out through the trees, toward mountains pruned by wind and time, its peaks nailed to the bluest of skies.

"These are well-done," Peter said, running his hands across the logs, scrutinizing their condition. "They're still rough, but well-done."

"He had the Cherokee help him," Martha answered.

"Is that right? Hmm...well, they made a good team."

"Indeed. William told me the Indians helped him...cuttin' logs all day long for weeks. In between trapping furs and such." Martha sighed, watching her children explore the immediate area, wondering where to put her garden, where, exactly, to situate the barns and other buildings in relation to the house.

There was a loud crash in the woods just then, and she gave a little yelp, turning quickly. A huge stag came into view, prancing majestically, locking eyes. William had told her about the large stag many times—how he felt a connection to the animal and how it was almost like a protector. "Don't us ever kill that particular deer," he had said, "because it's special. You'll know it when you see 'im. Big guy. Wise. He'll be around even if I'm not. Always poppin' into view when you least expect it. But not in a frightening way...in a comforting manner. You'll know 'im, Martha."

Martha wasn't sure she believed him...how could a deer be comforting? How could he know who she was, and why to protect one human out of so many? Animals were respected of course, but because they provided food, labor on the farms, and were part of nature, one of God's own. *They're not people, William!* She had admonished her husband. *It's just a deer. Like any other one. And they only live...what, 5, 7 years? Maybe 10 years or so at best...how do you know the same one will be around? And they roam around the entire mountains don't they? This one'll be long gone by the time we get there...*

But William never made it. She lowered her eyes and bowed her head. And, a second later, the deer did the same. *Did he just bow his head? It seems like he did...* Shocked, Martha began to see perhaps William's affection for the deer wasn't crazy. In fact, she began to think this was the actual stag he spoke about! *Am I the one who's crazy?* She chuckled to herself.

Then, she sank into serious thought. *But I think we could use all the help we could get. There's no one around, this land is beautiful but remote, and there's going to be a long time before other folks would join us in the place of the white oaks. What's the harm in a little believin' that a large stag would stand watch over us?* She was a widow, had seven children, and a brother and his family in tow, and a house to build. And a garden to plant. And barns and corn cribs and roots and herbs to gather. Berries to pick. Nuts to gather. Hunting. *Goodness, there's a lot to do.* Indeed, Martha Ogle would need all the believin' she could hold.

Situated perfectly on this land, the 1807 springtime proved luscious and fruitful. A perfect time to settle a homestead. One and all chipped in with hard work, determination, and the young but strong American spirit to build the house William Ogle dreamed of. The logs, already felled and waiting in neat piles, proved excellent for their cabin, which was "near the confluence of Baskins Creek and the west fork of the Little Pigeon River." Notching each end so they would fit together snugly, the Ogle boys and their uncle continued to add onto the floor and four corners that William and the Cherokees laid out years ago, replacing some of them, as needed, for strength and stability. One log across, then another, all supported on flat stones from the creek. No nails or pegs mind you; these logs were laid one by one, higher and higher, until the one-room cabin rose to the heavens. Or at least until about six feet...that's about the maximum height a man could push a log over his head without fear of it slipping out of his hands and crashing down on himself or someone else. One side was cut out—they had good tools. A stone and mud and stick chimney was constructed. The girls gathered mud from the creek banks and walked bucketsful up to the homesite where they slapped handfuls into the cracks and crevices.

"Nice and tight this cabin is. There's another few cracks here." Uncle Peter pointed out a few more gaps in the logs. "We don't want waterfalls down our necks while in bed."

"Or, waking up to an inch of snow on top of our quilts in the wintertime!" The youngest girl exclaimed, shivering at just the thought.

"This here chimney and hearth are both higher and larger than usual...see here," Peter pointed at the opening where logs were already crackling. "I jammed some wooden dowels in there for you, Martha, to hang your pots and pans. Skillets and such."

"Thank ya, Peter." She stood back and put her hands on her hips. Looked up at the sturdy home. *William's home. Finally, his dream is a reality.* Martha was proud, but an intense sadness also threatened...*William...my dear William never got to see this.* Did he though? Oh, she knew he had this very reality in his mind...how many nights had he described the home he would soon build! *He would have loved the house. It's exactly as he described. He had even wanted an extra-large chimney and hearth. Said it would heat the house better and cook food more evenly. Peter must've remembered her speaking of it.* She sighed. Deeply religious, raised as a Presbyterian, who believed only those with faith can be baptized, yet practicing as Baptists, whose beliefs did not include adding infants into the mix of those who can be baptized. After all, the Bible doesn't teach that, and if it doesn't say it in the Bible, the Baptists don't follow it. Martha looked up at the sky toward her God. No matter the differences in beliefs, or the varying ways people went about their lives, she knew her God was there.

The mountains were barely visible above the white oaks, but their peaks winked at her in the sunlight, as she walked outside, staring up at her newly completed home. Pleats of rock folded raggedly into its hollows, trees standing tall, many of them leaning right and left as if pointing to each other across its valleys. *William, I hope you are proud of us. We did it. Together.* She smiled with tears, one chasing the other down her cheeks. For William *was* there, and always would be. Her God would make sure of that.

Wiping her eyes, she turned and walked toward the creek, a wide pathway already created and tamped down from hundreds of trips back and forth for water. *Thirsty.* As she crouched and scooped up clear, cold creek water, she also patted her face, taking the hem of her dress to dry her forehead and her tears of remembrance. Standing, sighing one more time, she turned back to the cabin. *Oh, there's that stag.* That huge animal peered at her through the trees. Not too close, yet close enough for her to see the dark brown fur, the eyes staring at her with something like affection. She saw it blinking and then bowing its head. Strange. *Was it really possible the deer remembered? Recognized? Maybe I'm not the only one missing William...* She took a breath, wondering if the rest of the family noticed this huge animal hovering around, never threatening, but acting like a protector. *Cherokee Indians, whom she herself was descended from, indeed most all Indians believed in the spirits of ancestors. Of course, her God taught her something a bit different—loved ones went to heaven, and those left on Earth honored their ancestors' spirits with remembrances, flowers on the grave, stories told around the firesides at night. The Bible led them through death and all aspects of living: "He will wipe away every tear from their eyes, and death shall be no more, neither shall there be mourning, nor crying, nor pain anymore, for the former things have passed away." But faith is faith, no matter the details. And to the Cherokees, when loved ones died, their souls lived on in spirits, in trees, the wind and in animals. A deer? Could it be...?*

"Ma!" She jerked her head toward her daughters, a bit sorry to leave her private trance. "Ma, d'ya want the peas in the front, or the beans?"

Ah, they were laying the seeds in the garden. *Time to get going. Remembrance and wonder and prayer must wait. Now, there was work to do.*

Walking back toward the cabin, she saw her family busily clearing land for a garden. They were certainly well-prepared. They'd brought hogs, chickens, a mule, two cows, and two horses, along with their two wagons; thus, they were also hard at work building a much needed shelter for the chickens. And a hog pen. Not to mention getting ready for the main corn crop. Her brother Peter was particularly adept at burning small patches of vegetation, which yielded ash fertilizer; great for their crops of corn and grains. They would plant corn, mostly, as their main large crop, as farming was to be their livelihood. *Clear land, get it ready, make sure it all gets done. Keep moving. So much to do! And I should start preparing something for supper...make some biscuits...they'll all be starvin' soon...*

Too, a barn needed to be built right away. And so, the sons of Martha and William, along with Peter's sons set to work building a cantilever barn, the roof hanging over the lower portion, better to protect the animals from the elements. Peter explained as he left the fields burning, readying them for planting, "When it rains, or snows, and when it gets too hot, the overhead level hangs over and shades 'em. Really keeps the animals warm and dry. Upper loft is bigger than the base. That upper's for storin' hay, the cows and horses are down below, with plenty of room and air flows nicely through."

Within a couple of weeks, hog pens and chicken coops rounded out the smaller buildings and areas of the homestead. Inside the cabin, it was cozy and comfortable. Beds for each person, many up in the loft, a table, and cane-backed chairs furnished the simple cabin. Seeds, quilts, a bolt of cloth, sacks of sugar, coffee, and salt were staples now stashed in storage areas in the house. Safe, dry and away from the bears and other curious and hungry critters. Skillets, pots, and kettles hung on the thick wooden dowels sticking out of the hearth; light smoke from a kettle of stew rising up through the chimney, the meaty aroma could be caught by the wind, even from the middle of the cornfield. A split rail fence kept it all enclosed together: the cabin, garden, and outbuildings; animals, humans, and the memory and spirit of William Ogle whose soul now rested happily in his land of paradise. A large stag deer ever watching.

CHAPTER FIVE

The Land Of Paradise

FOUR MORE YEARS went by. The children married
and had their own children. Crops grew. Bounties of
harvests were reaped and sold; gardens fed the sturdy
boys and girls. Snows quieted the mountains for a time every
year. The cycles of seasons kept their pace; spring emerging
time and time again to waken the world. The original stag
now part of the soul of the mountains, its male offspring made
his appearance every week or two, standing guard just like his
father, watching the busy humans as they picked at the ground
with metal tools, led their animals this way and that, and sniffed
the plants sprouting out of their rows and rows of fields every
single day. The boys of this family even sniffed the ground. Got
on their hands and knees and scooped up dirt, holding piles to
their noses, caressing it with knowing fingers. Were they deter-
mining ripeness? If the ground had enough water? Sniffing for
the right mix of minerals? The deer didn't know exactly, but
he did know these Ogle men and women were dedicated and

determined, and they had ways of doing things that simply *worked*. They'd changed this landscape in no time at all. Cleared so much land for their corn crop that grew tall and sturdy every season, that the breezes now had many places to go, minimal obstacles in their way while wandering the slopes and valleys. The cabin, corncrib, smokehouse, barn, garden, chicken shelter, and a split rail fence hemmed it all in; an established and cheerful homestead.

Actually, there were many more than just the Ogle homestead now; lots more people. Some had come to White Oak Flats shortly after Martha, her children, and Peter's family arrived, and some family members and friends had come a bit later. *Let's see here*, Martha Ogle chuckled to herself, for keeping her clan straight was a Herculean task! Perhaps she foreshadowed her large and strong family; her first son was named Hercules after all. Growing up quickly, as they did in the south, Hercules had married Elizabeth Haggard, and now had a couple of Ogle grandchildren to raise. Rebecca had married James McCarter. Thomas married Sophia Bosley. John, Isaac, William and Mary Ann were doting siblings, sons and daughters, aunts and uncles. Peter's family, he and his wife, Mary, boasted their own large clan of seven children who were quickly marrying and expanding the Huskey presence in White Oak Flats.

"It's like a roll call!" Martha happily and regularly exclaimed, as her beloved brood plodded up the porch steps, the adults with boots, the kids barefoot. At the end of the day, oftentimes, the crowd would all gather at Martha's to wash up and to share a dinner of stew, biscuits, and corn grits, with a blueberry pie or two for dessert. The grown young adults had their own cabins by now, weaner cabins. Right next door, or very nearby, young couples would move into such a house, which they called weaner houses; they could stay nearby for assistance setting up a homestead, yet still have that much-needed privacy of newlyweds. Growing up fast in these parts, young adults still needed help to learn all they needed and to gain experience. Having parents around, ones who've been through hardships was crucial. They still needed to learn so much—repairs to farm equipment, tending animals and husbandry, what it really took to maintain a house in the mountains - constant sweeping! And a myriad of other chores they were familiar with, but didn't do all on their own. *Besides, you need time to mix together, the adults said. See how you do runnin' as a team. You in the kitchen gardens and keeping an eye on the children, and he's out in the fields most of the day or tending the animals. You will likely milk the cows, but when the kids are older, they can do that. See also about them fetchin' water from the creek. And he'll go out hunting too. But sometimes, if you see a rabbit, you go grab a rifle. There's always one in the house and get that rabbit to put in the pot for dinner. Keep the skin for a hat.*

Though Martha Ogle and her brother's families came to an uninhabited and isolated white oaked valley as the very first settlers in 1807, they arrived, in fact, as a crowd of well over twenty people, all relying on one another, while at the same time, one and all being extremely self-sufficient. Now, many others had joined them, including forty-two people forming a wagon train consisting mostly of two other large families, the McCarter family and more branches of Peter and Martha's own Huskey family. *Martha Huskey Ogle, first settler of White Oak Flats.* She wore that distinction proudly, humbly, honoring William always. She had written to her relatives of the beauty, fertile land, and endless mountain peaks showing off the colors and wisdom of their seasons, and they had finally decided to join her. As such, the population now swelled to over sixty, and they brought with them livestock, household belongings, food supplies, tools and seeds. They made a grand but cumbersome spectacle upon their arrival to the flats, wagons swaying, a menagerie of animals spread out for half a mile, children tagging along, every item imaginable swinging from arms and backs and shoulders.

But when they finally arrived, when they had all caught up with one another and gathered again as one, they fell silent. For as the crowd stepped off wagons, horses, or merely stopped where they had just been walking, one and all stared at the majestic beauty of the mountains. Breathed in the freshest piney air, easing any knots of trepidation or worry. *You were right, Martha. The mountains do have a personality. Look at them! They're standing there, without a sound, but telling you that you're finally home. Be careful, respect our power, they say, but indeed, if you do, this is the most wonderful home on Earth. Don't you feel it in your deepest soul? Keep looking! Now close your eyes and listen. We will wink at you in the afternoon sun, embrace you in the night. Wake you up in the morning with a soft touch...get ready for another day tucked into God's country. Our icy brows come and go, our rosy cheeks often turn to gray, yet we don't intervene. Never intervene. It's up to you and you alone. We simply stand witness to it all. A land of paradise.*

Enough time had passed now in White Oak Flats that children were growing up, marrying and beginning their own lives. One of the Ogle children, Rebecca Ogle, had married James McCarter, and they now had their homestead about six miles away from her mother's cabin. Farms were vast and homesteads were far apart. No town or store was nearby. *Life is hard,* Rebecca often said, but with a heartiness and softness that belied the everyday toils. For she loved it here, enveloped by the breezes spilling down the spines of the mountains, the scent of pine and earthiness of the gardens and fields, and the aromas of her own hearth cooking up venison or rabbit meat, with cabbage, potatoes and radishes to feed her family. *Pa's land of paradise* she often recalled as she stood in her garden, walked by the creek in the early afternoons, or sat on the porch watching the sunset below the crests. She had always understood why her father felt this way. *Look at this place! It is so beautiful when the rains come over the mountains like thin sheets of paper catching a breeze. The rain would tease you, and either appear immediately to soak one and all, or magically wave its goodbyes and move to another peak. Or when the bluest of skies blended with green grasses and yellow crops to make a fertile bowl of plenty, God's hand lifting the slopes of white oaks to the heavens. Sure, they were on their own out here. Tougher life than city folk for sure. Thank goodness James' brother, Joseph, had come too. After all, they had to build their own cabin, plant gardens and crops, tend their animals and in general, survive. Oh, and I also have a toddler, an infant, and another on the way now. But nothing could tear me from this place, the place where Pa knew he had found his soul.*

Martha and William Ogle's grown daughter lingered in her own thoughts for just a minute more. *A beautiful place yes, but still a remote and wild environment.* Sighing, she ran her sweaty palms down the front of her simple cotton dress and got back to work. Squatting down to pull weeds from the radishes in the garden, a smile formed on her face. And one lone deer, heavy with new antlers, watched.

⁂

The residents of White Oak Flats were settled and the corn was growing nicely. Everyone was healthy, babies thrived, and when good health and enough food is had, humans begin thinking beyond just their basic needs.

At night, when the day's work was done, Martha prayed in her warm cabin, read her Bible, and felt her God. But she longed for a more permanent house of worship. Praying around the hearth at night, and worshipping in their own ways sufficed for the time being, but a church of their own would mean a richer life, a gathering place, a hub, specially designated for weddings, funerals, and celebrations. A place they could wrap their arms around one another in grief and comfort, to pray together, to hold hands and sing, and to exchange happenings.

Martha had been putting feelers out to her own family and some neighbors, totaling almost eighty people now. *Would you be willing to build a church? Would you want it here in our own community? Where could we build it?* Enthusiasm was great; their very own church meant so much! And so, Martha adopted her newest plan. Picking up her pen one late afternoon, as the open doors of the cabin allowed in a cool breeze, she sat at the table and wrote a letter to "Fork of Little Pigeon Church" to see if she and the residents of White Oak Flats could establish their own church. *"We wish to establish ourselves 'as an arm of the Fork of Little Pigeon in Sevierville'."*

She signed her name, not without some difficulty, for she, like most people in that time and place, had sparse literacy. However, she was able to write a basic, short, but sufficient, letter like the ones she wrote to relatives, and signed it with a flourish, ending with the date: December, 1817. *It's been ten years since I've first set foot on this land of paradise.* Martha stared into the fire for a long time that night. Rebecca had just left with her family and she was alone. *How far we've come in ten years.* The fire crackled, thanks to old and dry logs that fell onto one another as they burned in the hearth. She breathed deeply. *Thank you, William.* And as she climbed into bed later that night, thoughts of William and God filling her chest, she felt at peace. *Building our community, opening our own church, everyone happy and healthy.* All is as it should be. All is well.

෴

"They said yes!"

"Whooee!" They sure did!" Peter said, snatching the letter from Martha's hands, reading the good news for himself. "They done give us our own church!"

"Now we can pray all formal-like and in our own house of God. Praise the Lord."

"Amen."

One and all gathered at the news. Sharing the joy they would have their own church! Oh, they knew they could pray anywhere and God would hear them, and they had done so for a decade now. Under white oaks, beside creeks, in the woods, in bed at night under colorful, warm quilts made with loving hands, or even rocking on the front porch as twilight sifted its final colors over the gently curved peaks. But nothing was the same as having a completely separate and designated building where they could pray together, celebrate births and weddings, picnics in the spring and summer, and grieve with strong shoulders nearby for support. They cleared land right next to where they laid the flattest and largest of rocks for the foundation of the church building. "That'll be for our cemetery. Our loved ones will stay with us forever."

They all nodded. Indeed, no grave was ever without flowers and small stones for mementos. Mountain people did not forget their dead. Ever. They remained alive in memories, folk songs, mountain lore, and tales. Who knew which ones were real stories? Who cared? *There's something about a tale of grandpa eatin' a watermelon straight outta the pig trough when he was a boy. Tickin' off his mama who was always screamin' at him to get serious or he'd live like a pig the rest'a his life. And Grandpa said, "Well if I'm gonna be a pig, I better start practicin'." Oh, his mama was hot. 'Especially when he kept eatin' right outta the trough. The pigs themselves wouldn't even get near him! He had to sleep on the porch that night. And for a few nights after that I heard. Or the story of grandma hollering at a tree swearin' that it's a ghost. Swingin' her chicken thighs at its trunk, and rubbing the soles of her feet on the chicken...don't know which was scarier...a possible ghost or grandma swingin' her chicken rubbed feet up and down the mountainside.* They laughed at their shared upbringings.

Onions hung in our home. Oh, they stunk up the place! Never knew what that was all about until Mama told us it's to ward off the typhoid fever.

You know, that really works. We never got typhoid.

These stories, they're funny...but they sure hold wisdom.

Indeed. That's how we learned some of the best advice of life.

All the wisdom we'll ever need.

Think on it...we all survived. Must be somethin' to it.

The older folks would smile at the young ones' conversations and feel a warm heart because they knew they'd raised these kids well. Respectful, hard-working, helpful, loyal, God-fearing, and kind. They would be the next generations to carry on family traditions, hard work, and the soul of the mountains deep within their cores.

And, there were so many more people to raise now! The seasons passed, white oak leaves of dark and bluish-green became showy and boastfully wine-red in the fall. As they fell from the branches, more and more settlers came to White Oak Flats, many of which were Revolutionary War veterans from North Carolina. Most had received fifty-acre tracts for their war service, which they then converted into land deeds, creating large homesteads of their own.

Who were these people with large families coming to White Oak Flats? Among these early settlers was Timothy Reagan, born deep in the woods of the Smokies shortly after his parents emigrated from Ireland. Made of tough stock, he served in the 2nd Regiment of Maryland troops during the American Revolution and was injured at the Battle of Brandywine. After the war, he and his wife, Elizabeth, and twelve children decided to take the land deed for Timothy's service and go to the place of the white oaks.

Another was Henry Bohanan. One day, a wagon pulled up with Henry and his family in tow. Also an American Revolution war veteran, he served as a private in the 1st Virginia Regiment, Continental Line, Light Dragoon commanded by Captain Robert Boling. Through three years of skirmishes from July 6, 1778 until June 1781, Henry fought the British for continued independence. For those efforts, he was issued: "Land Warrant 1390 on July 17, 1783, as a soldier on the Continental Line." But he never laid claim to that land, instead heading to the place of the white oaks.

"How'd that work out?" Peter Huskey asked the newcomer Henry, whose homestead was about two miles away from his own.

"Well, see here. Tennessee became a state in 1796." They all nodded, the families of both men listening as they went about their chores. "In Section 31...let's see here..." he pulled out a piece of paper and began laboriously reading his official papers. "Section 31 of the Bill of Rights adopted with the Constitution says that 'the people residing south of the French Broad and Holston between the Rivers Tennessee and the big Pigeon are entitled to that right of pre-emption and occupancy in that tract.'"

"Ah, I see. So it kind of...transfers to this land."

"Yessir. It goes on...the framers of the Constitution say that in consideration of the value of the county of these settlements, these brave pioneers had extended themselves as a barrier between the older settlements and the Indians, maintaining their ground without titles to their land from 1783 to 1790."

"Sure took a lot of us a long time to get here. The 1770s, 1780s...Tennessee becomin' a state in 1796. And here we are in the early 1800s...a new decade. New days ahead."

"Yessir. Sometimes takes a while." Henry sighed at the haunting memories of war but then brightened at what he saw in front of him—his future. "My cousin William has land 'round these parts too. I like it here."

"Well, we're sure glad you're here. Got a large family," he said, pointing to the crowd and laughing and slapping his shoulder. "Gonna need that 'round here."

"Oh yes, I got 150 and three-quarter acres on the east prong of the Pigeon River. Gonna need all the hands I can get."

"Well, if ya'll need any help, there's a bunch of us here and one and all willin' to lend a hand."

"Thank you so very much. Makes us feel better for sure."

What did these newcomers find when they arrived? Well over a hundred people now. Mostly farms of corn, but there was a scattering of wheat and other grain crops. In the Smokies, some kind of crop always grew or was always tended to, not just in spring and summer. Pruning fruit trees occurred in the winter, and when an ice storm threatened, farmers turned over fields to allow the freezes to break up the soil. Burning during thaws helped control insects and rid the fields of old weeds and vegetation. Come spring, cold-tolerant crops were planted: onions, mustard greens, turnips, potatoes and cabbage. When the oak leaves were the size of a squirrel's ear, it was time to plant the major crop—corn. Planting lore abounded and as deeply religious as they were, they were also practical and had their own superstitions and legends that even involved astrology. Of the twelve astrological signs, all are associated with parts of the body and each day of the month corresponds to one of the signs.

"Plant corn when the Aries sign is in the head, so there will be more ears. Around April 10th."

In addition to the Bible, farmers had that now-famous Poor Richard's Almanac started way back in 1732. "Benjamin Franklin didn't even put his name on it 'til later. Published it under the name, "Richard Saunders," the men and their sons stated as they discussed their crops.

"Man, what a bunch of information. But really, his sayings and funnies are what makes it worth readin'!"

"Like, red-headed persons have the best luck with peppers."

"Why? Does their inner fire transfer outta their fingers into the peppers?"

"Reagan, he's from Ireland, they've got a spitfire couple of girls in that family, all with red hair. Hoo weee, I only wanna eat those peppers on Saturday nights!"

The boys ragged each other with bawdy teasing.

"But don't laugh while planting corn. The grains will fall apart on the cob."

"That is true. One time, that summer we laughed at the girls and teased them as they washed in the creek...the corn wasn't as good that year, remember?"

"Yeah, I remember that. Here's another: plant turnips thirty-nine days after Easter Sunday, known as Ascension Day, for abundant foliage and large turnips."

"Tomatoes should be planted in Gemini or the scales..."

"Don't plant cucumbers on Saturdays. They will be bitter. Also, if you plant cucumbers during the full moon, you'll have all vines and will not bear."

"Hunger is the best pickle—that's what he said in the Almanac!"

"Well, let's not make a big dill about it…" At that, they lost it, holding their sides until they doubled over.

"Seems Poor Richard is rubbing off on us…we're makin' our own funnies now. *A big dill!* Ha! Now that was funny."

Indeed, the new settlers found a wise, fun-loving, and amiable crowd, consisting of many people, but still from just a few families. No businesses save for their farms and the revenues that came with selling crops. Their lifestyle was early to bed, early to rise, hard work all day, every day, tending crops and animals and children and then, themselves. God came first. Neighbors and families were close-knit and both kept to themselves and gossiped every Saturday night and Sunday morning now that they had their church, which was growing and prospering. There were few disputes, no bullies, no formal schools, yet children learned practical and wise things just by doing and from the Bible and from what their parents taught them. They learned to sense danger and protection. Fetching water from the creek while watching and listening for bears, seeing calves born and keeping coyotes away, watching the eagles soar and that one lone stag deer that was always around, watching, safeguarding over everything.

CHAPTER SIX

1818

THE ENTIRETY OF the Smoky Mountains of North Carolina and Tennessee were seeing population booms. People were on the move. Just about thirty miles or so to the west, the community of Cades Cove was forming as John and Lucretia Oliver had barely survived their first winter of 1817-1818. They were but a day's horse ride away from one another, provided the horse was healthy and spry. Even if the horse was old and slow, they were just a few days apart at most. But they may as well have been a million miles away, for mountain communities were very isolated. Of course, they rode wagons and horses to trade in Maryville and Happy Valley once or twice per year, but mostly, they stuck to their homesteads and roamed all of a circular few miles or so. Usually no more than five to ten miles made up their entire world. But sometimes, that small world could suffer greatly.

It was on the afternoon of March 30, 1818. Peter Huskey, Martha's brother who had graciously moved his entire family with hers to William's land of paradise, died. It was sudden. Yesterday, he'd been out in his fields, as usual, feeling the spring air in his bones, those little hints of hopeful warmth. His wife, Mollie, had been hoeing and preparing the entire garden and it looked wonderfully ready for planting. That night, they prayed and went to bed. The next day he felt "funny" he said. And stayed in bed. Very unusual for him, or any mountain man, to stay in bed past dawn. Mollie frowned.

"I'm gonna get you some warm broth. Get that sickness right outta you."

"Thank ya." He replied, taking her hand and smiling at her. Strange, she thought. He never does that. A practical man, a very good man, but not an affectionate one. Felt his forehead for any fever. There was none. But his voice was raspy. And he said his left arm felt heavy. She eyed him and smiled back and stepped outside while the broth heated up. Chickens ran around. She grabbed an egg or two to scramble in a skillet later on and shooed them back in the coop. It was going to be a warmer day than normal for this time of year. A good day to plant a garden. *And the peas and beans and...oh....! My goodness!* She put her hand to her heart, startled at the sight. *There's that big stag.* The biggest she'd ever seen in all her years. The one everyone sees hanging around and the one everyone says watches everything. It moved so quietly, she hadn't noticed its approach from the east. *He sure is big. And he's looking straight at me. Such sad eyes it has. And he is bowing his head. Standing still as a white oak on a windless day.* Mollie Huskey's eyes held the beast's for many moments.

A feeling came over her. Not fear, but a sort of resolute peace. Then, the deer broke the spell, dropped his eyes, and retreated a few steps away, turned around a few times and bedded down in a comforting watch.

When she went back inside, Peter was gone. The smile was still lightly playing on his lips. Somehow, she wasn't shocked. But a deep sadness enveloped her, very slowly at first. She sat for a moment, wondering what had happened. *His heart,* she thought. *Was that it? Must've been his heart just gave out. Sixty-five years old. Worked like he would live the next hundred years, but always prayed like he'd die any day. And today was that day.* The reality set in quickly, as it tends to do in this wild environment. She was now a widow. Have to plan a burial. Get help preparing Peter. *God took him this afternoon. He is with our Lord now.* Comforting perhaps, but still, almost unbearable. The children and grandchildren would miss him terribly! Always tellin' those fishin' stories! How to break the news to them? To everyone? Sighing, she'd have to get moving. Grief waited for no one. Standing up, she hugged Peter for the last time. *A good husband you were. A great provider. We had a good life together. Thank you, my love, for bringing me here, for our children and for our land. Thank you for sharing my life.* Tears streaming down her cheeks, she caressed his cheek, still warm. So content he looked! She dried her face with the corner of her apron, looked out of the open doorway just then to see the stag very close by, peering inside the open cabin door at her with sad eyes.

"Still standing watch, I see." She chuckled just a little bit at her talking to a deer. But just then the animal tilted its crowned head upwards and watched the lone cloud in the sky drift higher and higher. After a few moments, when the cloud had gone to the heavens, the large deer began walking again. It knew the way; here, follow the garden's rickety wooden gate; there, follow along the banks of the cold creek, stepping around the thorns of the roses that are so easy for all of us to miss, moving in the direction of the sun, into the hills of the afternoon, disappearing into the deep embrace of the white oaks.

∽∾

The entire community came together to honor the steadfast and loyal patriarch, Peter Huskey. He had arrived in 1807 with Martha, his widowed sister, to honor her husband's wish to settle in his beloved land of paradise. Had helped her build, get settled, find her way again.

Following Martha and her family to this land was the honor of his life, he often said. Never looked back, never regretted one day of living in the flattened valley where the white oaks soared to the bluest of skies. So long ago. They were the very first ones.

His coffin was made free of charge, smooth pine board fit to his slim and reedy body. Lined with white cloth, softened and lovingly draped inside. Saying goodbye to a beloved leader was never easy, but Peter's death was felt profoundly by all.

"We will read from Peter 1:7...very fitting I think, to honor Peter Huskey," said the preacher. "So that the tested genuineness of your faith—more precious than gold that perishes though it is tested by fire—may be found to result in praise and glory and honor...."

The preacher spoke about honoring and praising and finding glory in the life of Peter…*brother, husband, father, son, neighbor, friend…*

They nodded, feeling the grief sink in, yet that special peace of a life well lived mixed well with their sorrow, bringing solace in this time of need.

"And now, a passage from Genesis. 'And the gold of that land is good…' Indeed, our Peter was the gold of our land. A good man. The best. Faith, family, farm. The gold standard of men."

Martha sat on the wooden pew and prayed and thanked her brother for accompanying her to this unknown land. *I am so glad you came with me. Goodness knows it would not have been possible without you. I am sad you left us, but look at the legacy!* She looked around at the crowded pews and still more people outside, listening through the windows. *So many people! Children, grandchildren…I dare say there will be a Huskey and an Ogle in these parts forever. And it was all because you came with me. My dearest brother.*

Deep in the mixture of grief and faithful gratitude, Martha Huskey Ogle walked home alone after the services. Visiting would come later of course, but for now, she wanted to be alone with her thoughts and prayers, with her own golden memories of a dear, dear brother. Her shoes crunched the leaves as she walked, hearing the whispering voices of the entire community behind her. Holding a handkerchief, she dabbed her eyes and walked toward her cabin. The sun was so bright, little flecks of gold appeared in the creek as she walked its banks in the shade of the white oak trees.

The deer watched from behind a stand of trees swaying in the wind as if they were expressing their own goodbyes. Life has cycles; even his own was in its waning hours. He knew it. And that man who'd just been tending his fields a day or so ago—the one they called Peter—he had known it too. The deer had smelled it on his breath, as he stopped for a long time in his fields, holding his left arm and breathing harder than ever before. His eyes closed and his breath blew out, catching a journey on the last wind. Yes, the man had known it then, though he continued to work and went home to his wife like nothing had happened. But the man knew. Knew, just like the deer, how to recognize and detect life's cycles. And most importantly, how to accept them.

A sweet decay; the odor of a life well lived and ready for the next phase permeated the deer's nostrils and the mountain valley where wildflowers chose where they would grow, and nature would, at her discretion, take care of man's unfinished tasks. An aroma of peace, knowing their offspring were in good hands, ready to take over the torch of progress, melted into the last rays of the setting sun. *Take your time,* the mountains cried out. *Grief is its own season. Turn your back on me if you need to. But there will be a day again, soon, where you will turn again toward life, and then I will see you smile.*

The stag walked to his secluded bed and lay down, the sun's final rays capturing the large unbridled deer, free and at peace, bathed in gold.

CHAPTER SEVEN

1820s
Life in the Flats/ Trail of Tears

1820'S AMERICA BOASTED over nine and a half million people. James Monroe was re-elected president on December 6, 1820—it took that long to tally and deliver the ballots—with the biggest landslide in history: beating John Quincy Adams 231 to 1. But not to worry. Perseverance and grit pays off and Quincy Adams would get his chance and be elected president five years later. July 10, 1821 saw the territory of Florida bought from Spain, and on August 4, 1821, most of America sat around their fires and hearths and living rooms with the very first *Saturday Evening Post*.

The United States was booming. The Erie Canal, the internal combustion engine, and the Smithsonian Institution were all founded or begun during these roaring '20s. A reward of one cent was offered for the return of Kit Carson, a fourteen-year-old boy who ran away from his apprenticeship to a saddle maker and who would later play a large role in America's expansion of

00087963504

Sell your books at World of Books!
Go to sell.worldofbooks.com and get an instant price quote. We even pay the shipping - see what your old books are worth today!

the west, and man known as William Austin Burt invents and patents the typographer, later known as the typewriter.

Despite such profound progress, little of it arrived on the doorstep of White Oak Flats. The Appalachian mountain people were still very isolated and lived simple lives. Rustic cabins, no creature comforts save for a warm hearth and quilts on the bed. They were nonetheless certainly aware of outside events, marveled at them even, but remained tending children, homesteads, fields and animals. The thing they didn't deal with as often these days were the Indians.

The Cherokee Indians were seen less and less. Sure, they themselves gave up millions of acres of their own land; they were paid for it and some even created small plantations and had African slaves working for them. And yes, they relished being able to trade and adopt some of the European settlers' ways when it came to money, wealth, and different, better ways of growing crops and farming techniques. Many even converted to Christianity, their own traditions filtered, to the dismay of many elders. And those elders, though fewer in number now, worked very hard to "retain their cultural identity operating on a basis of harmony, consensus, and community, with a distaste for hierarchy and individual power."

That distaste was in direct opposition to the emerging American culture of individual wealth and power. And these two views would always clash. Funny isn't it? All men strove for harmony, community, and tried to tamp down power in others. Yet, all men also strove for power for themselves. Shakespeare often wrote of this two-faced flaw: *Few love to hear the sins they love to act.* No matter the hypocrisy though, we won't listen. Individual wealth and power will always win. Look at any instance of this in history and this fact of human nature will emerge every time.

Watching their way of life withering away, the 1820s saw increasing numbers of Cherokee moving west to the Arkansas territory. Martha Ogle, herself part Cherokee, along with the people of the community of White Oak Flats were friends with the Cherokee tribe. After all, they had helped William cut down trees and even helped him with the start of building the cabin. They had trapped and traded with each other for decades, if not longer, and few skirmishes occurred, although violence did erupt now and then. But these two peoples did not truly inter-act beyond trading and trapping. They did not visit each other's homes, did not celebrate holidays and did not interact on a daily basis. They did not farm together and never shared more than a meal or two by a creek while taking a rest. They were separate and that is how both cultures felt it should be.

Yet, the residents of the Flats were still sad to see the increas-ing effects on the Cherokees. More and more skirmishes erupted and there was more and more talk about getting them "out of the way". Both sides wanted to live in peace and have it all settle down. Surely there was enough land for that to happen?

Georgia was one of the first to strike as they "began increas-ing pressure for the federal government to release Cherokee lands for white settlement. They undertook the issue, pon-dered and discussed it, but some settlers did not wait around for approval. They simply moved in and began surveying and claiming territory for themselves."

And of course, the Cherokee began fighting back; all of this tug-of-war over land and rights and cultures created a situation that could not be sustained.

No, there will never be enough land for our desire for power and no, things did not settle down.

༺ঔৣঔ༻

Martha Ogle sat in her chair, reading her Bible, just about the only book she had ever read. It was enough. "Every story one needs to know is in that good book," she had taught her children and now, her grandchildren. So many of them now! And in the short hours of the evenings, her eyes would skip over the words and she would get lost in memories. *I miss you, William.* She found herself thinking this more and more. She had never remarried, never even thought of it. "Too old," she kept telling herself. *I've already had my children. Had my husband. Got everythin' I need right here. Love too. I still have love...it don't go away just because someone dies. Now look here. If I needed a husband to tend the land or to have more children with, I woulda done it. But all that was had with my William. And that was enough.*

Some understood, most, in fact understood where her mind was. Martha Ogle certainly wasn't lonely. Or bored. Was there ever boredom on a farm? How? There was always something to do! But now though she wasn't bored and was most definitely filled with faith, love, and warm memories, Martha knew she was also very tired.

Summer was her favorite time. It was a lull in the mountains, but not in life. Oh, the smell of berries ripening under the sun! The pigs and calves are growing, abundant greens in the garden—the land of plenty. Land of paradise. Martha was seventy years old and she went to bed that summer night feeling happy. Reflective.

William and I had a dream. William's land of paradise was even more magical than he'd described. More than I thought it could be. No, we never got to enjoy it together. We were destined to enjoy it separately, but weren't we together all along, William? In a special way that perhaps actually being together never could've allowed? Husband and wife we were, even after you were gone. And here we are each of us had our days to embrace this special place, the divine, fertile soil, the magic of the white oaks. Thank you for it all. For a wonderful life and family. My dear William…

She went to bed and dreamed of a lone white cloud drifting up the sky, while a majestic stag deer watched in silent honor.

Martha Huskey Ogle died that summer night, in June of 1827. Early in the morning, a granddaughter noticed her grandmother hadn't been seen that morning. The cows stood, unmilked. No smoke came from the chimney; well, maybe a wisp, but certainly not the roaring clouds of a morning fire that usually accompanied the smell of eggs and bacon. The air that morning was piney, earthy and nothing like the usual aromas wafting out of her grandmother's cabin. The door was closed as she called out…Granny Martha?

Running back to her own home, she told everyone, already busy on the farm, that Granny Martha's cabin was quiet.

The entirety of White Oak Flats came out to pay their respects to the brave pioneering woman who followed her husband's dream and came here as the area's first permanent settler to the welcoming embrace of the Great Smoky Mountains.

"And here," the preacher said to the packed church, people spilling outside, all quietly listening, "she will remain for eternity. Let us honor William and Martha Ogle. We are all here because of them. The beloved Ogle's land of paradise."

They placed their hands together, bowed their heads, and prayed. Sang hymns. Remembered.

One of a kind. She will have a blessed place in Heaven. Finally reunited with William, who was watching her all these years.

He's proud of her. I know it.

"I'll miss Granny Martha." The many grandchildren declared. "Her blueberry pies. The way she yelled at us to git outta the house 'cause she just swept."

They laughed. "Or, when she scrubbed our hands raw to get the blackberry stains out. The berries got under our nails and made us look like we'd dug dirt all day!"

"I loved when she pulled the quilts up to our necks and kissed us all good night. After our prayers of course. The way she looked down at all of us in our beds before goin' down the loft stairs to sew or wring out rags or store food…."

"She sure took care of all of us."

Martha Huskey Ogle, daughter, wife, sister, mother, grandmother, and pioneer was buried in White Oak Flats Cemetery, surrounded by the family and community that she began. Flowers piled high so by the time the last visitor left, the newly carved headstone was completely covered.

That night, when everyone had gone home to pray by their fires, and remember the kind, tough, spirited Martha Ogle, the large stag came out of the woods and stood by her grave. Unseen to anyone, he bowed his head and sniffed the air. All was quiet, at peace. Nothing stirred. Love, and be loved. If that occurred even once during a human life, all was as it should be. Walking slowly now, knowing the sadness of this summer season would slowly shift toward another, nature continuing its cycles no matter what any creature hopes for, the deer said his final goodbyes to that wise man's wife. Letting out a breath, he soon arrived at his bed and lay down in his safe and secluded spot. Now, he'd be sure to keep watch over the rest of them, the ever-growing descendants of William and Martha Ogle.

Death has a way of pausing the issues of life, but only temporarily. And the matter of the Indian lands and culture clashing with America's expansion was not going away. For centuries, the Indians were the only human inhabitants of the area of White Oak Flats. They did not permanently settle here though. Instead moving around as seasons and opportunities changed. When the white men came and remained in one place, both groups tried to live in peace and indeed, did so for a long while.

As is the case with humans though, in the long run, living together proved impossible. Why is that? Tribes, clans, and civilizations rarely overtly go out and say, "Kill other people" without any reason at all. Yet, ninety percent of all people that ever were, have made war on other people, some very frequently and oftentimes, brutally. In some cultures, a full quarter of all men die in combat. Reasons are many. The need for resources, more territory, labor, goods, and prime river lands fuel the need to make war. Or at least the need to run the others out. Plunder's treasures, security and defense, and power, spark that fuel even more. These are but some of the reasons. At other times though, it's just a matter of differing opinions; so incompatible they cannot be tolerated. Oftentimes, it's a lethal combination of these factors, a mix and match global game that invariably leads to fighting where one must win and the other must lose.

One side: *Why do those pale men worship only one God?*

The other side: *Why do those red and brown people have to see spirits in the trees and animals? How do they see that? Do they really see spirits? They must be mad. Call themselves tribes. Instead of towns and cities. Instead of communities and White Oak Flats. Smoke too much Gatunlati they do...they call it the 'teaching plant', but they just claim to see ghosts and fall asleep and laugh all night.*

One side: *Those whites call it cannabis, but they can't see the spirits like we can. All they do is try to push us off this land. Further and further west. Why can't they just live on their plots and let us be? What makes them owners of this land?*

The other side: *Owners? Why, we **are** owners. We have our land deeds to prove it, and you people never even planted any crops! Too, you took the money for that land...you sold it to us! Just like an owner would. We paid you, fair and square.*

One side: *Not all of the land. We didn't sell all of it. And, your clothes are strange.*

The other side: *You don't even wear clothes! You want this country to be different from what the Constitution, our Constitution, says.*

One side: *It's not our Constitution. We need no such thing. We listen to the land.*

The other side: *Those people have no law and order! Those people raise their children all wrong. Spirits in the trees! I never heard of such a thing. Don't they know there is only one God!*

And so it was. The human tradition of conflict, intolerance and the wasted potential for problem-solving was kept alive, and as virtually all human groups who have ever lived have done, one set about conquering the other once and for all.

Almost a decade ago now, back in 1819, the Calhoun Treaty was signed. This treaty between the Cherokee Indians and the government transferred land to the State of Tennessee, rendering the state much bigger. John Calhoun, the secretary of war at the time, and later vice president, negotiated the deal, paying the Cherokees for their land. Willingly sold, the Cherokees figured that since there were already some white men on their land—land they claimed could never be owned by anyone— they may as well get paid for it. And they basked in it; they'd never had money like this before. And, they were able to still grow and cultivate their crops on the now-sold property: *"The United States, in order to afford the Cherokees who reside on the lands ceded by this treaty, [shall grant] time to cultivate their crop next summer..."*

Seems like a good deal for everyone.

Then, why couldn't this be sustained?

It was late in 1828, and Andrew Jackson had just been elected president of the United States. He wasted no time in passing the Indian Removal Act in 1830, because he wanted expansion and because of one other happening that occurred which sealed the Cherokees' fate. Something was found on their lands. Something that would change the course of history.

Gold. That rare element that never corrodes, never rusts or tarnishes, and always shines even when being worked into wires and jewelry and coins.

Gold is here, in these lands. And we need to access it without fear of attack. We need the gold. And there is no holding us back.

Scores of southerners, everyone from Georgians, Carolinians, Virginians and Alabamians sought instant wealth held within the great mountains. Georgia even "held lotteries to give Cherokee land and gold rights to whites." Further, the "already declared laws of the Cherokee Nation were declared null and void after June 1, 1830, and also prohibited Cherokees from conducting tribal business, contracting, testifying against whites in court, or mining for gold. Cherokee leaders successfully challenged Georgia in the U.S. Supreme Court, but President Jackson refused to enforce the Court's decision."

An old man from the Cherokees, Chief Womankiller, "summed up their angry and sad views":

"My sun of existence is now fast approaching its setting, and my aged bones will soon be laid underground, and I wish them laid in the bosom of this earth we have received from our fathers who had it from the Great Being above."

Can we at least make a new treaty? Get paid for our land? They tried. And President Jackson did respond, with an offer of $5 million dollars for their land and for compensation:

"My Friends: I have long viewed your condition with great interest. For many years I have been acquainted with your people and under all variety of circumstances in peace and war. You are now placed in the midst of a white population. Your peculiar customs, which regulated your intercourse with one another, have been abrogated by the great political community among which you live; and you are now subject to the same laws which govern the other citizens of Georgia and Alabama."

"I have no motive, my friends, to deceive you. I am sincerely desirous to promote your welfare. Listen to me, therefore, while I tell you that you cannot remain where you now are. Circumstances that cannot be controlled, and which are beyond the reach of human laws, render it impossible that you can flourish in the midst of a civilized community. You have but one remedy within your reach. And that is, to remove to the west and join your countrymen, who are already established there. And the sooner you do this the sooner you will commence your career of improvement and prosperity."

It was over. Five million dollars wasn't enough. Nothing was. They were being moved...*all* of them. Besides, they saw in the sky and looming clouds these negotiators were sitting on the devil's cushion. Or at least, the *Uyaga's* cushion. *White men said devil. We say Uyaga, the spirit opposed to forces of right and light.* Either way, it's a malevolent spirit, out to do harm. *These powerful men had already broken every deal they ever made...would they really pay us the five million? At least we should get something from this horrific deal?* And so, a final plea went out to their very own people to accept their fate:

"I am one of the native sons of these wild woods. I have hunted the deer and turkey here, more than fifty years. I have fought your battles, defended your truth and honesty, and fair trading. The Georgians have shown a grasping spirit lately; they have extended their laws, to which we are unaccustomed, which harass our braves and make the children suffer and cry.

I know the Indians have an older title than theirs. We obtained the land from the living Great Being above. They got their title from the British. Yet they are strong and we are weak. We are few, they are many. We cannot remain here in safety and comfort. I know we love the graves of our fathers. We can never forget these homes, but an unbending, iron necessity tells us we must leave them. I would willingly die to preserve them, but any forcible effort to keep them will cost us our lands, our lives and the lives of our children. There is but one path of safety, one road to future existence as a Nation. That path is open before you. Make a treaty of cession. Give up these lands and go over beyond the great Father of Waters."

The day came, too quickly, when they were ordered out: "Every Cherokee man, woman or child must be in motion…"

One young Indian was especially affected by the events of today. Long ago, before Martha Ogle had come to live in this area, he was scowling and angry and sticking his tongue out at the group of bearded traders and trappers because he had the uncanny feeling his people were being conquered, slowly, but definitively. As the seer of the tribe, those visions only became stronger as he aged, and the anger had turned into a mature mind that knew when to fight and when to adapt. Still angry, he knew now that it was time to move to try to find a better life, wherever they were taking them. Because staying here was to have no life at all. "Every Cherokee man, woman or child must be in motion…"

And so they moved. But not fast enough for the federal troops and state militias who began to push the Cherokees into stockades. "And, in spite of warnings to troops to treat them kindly, the roundup proved harrowing."

Along a dusty road, they sat. *We're nearly all prisoners. Dragged us from our homes, no time to take anything except the clothes we had on! They strip us of all we have on Earth and force us out. At the tips of rifles no less!*

And along a creekside in White Oak Flats, residents talked of the events that forced out the Indians.

"I heard John Oliver, over at Cades Cove, was part of the militia roundin' up them Indians."

"Yeah, he was part of the militia, so he must obey orders."

"True. But I heard they saved his life during that first winter when he and his wife and little baby girl were starving. They brought dried pumpkin and such...it's really too bad we can't all live in peace."

"It really is too bad. They are our good friends. Even helped William Ogle begin buildin' here. Trapped and traded with us folk for a long time."

"Well. History is over and done with. Time to move on and make our own history. Life's Instruction Book they say of history—it's not the Bible, but history books are the real manuals people never seem to read or heed. Yet, it's filled with every single viewpoint and all possible events. Indians have one view. John Oliver has his. And we have ours."

Shaking their heads, they got back to the business of making history and working a farm.

August of 1830 saw a severe summer drought. There was no water in the springs and creeks and the Cherokee pleaded to stop their westward crawl until fall. In a rare display of mercy, this was granted by the militia tasked with pushing them westward. Feeling emboldened, they asked for control over their own removal. *We will go. As soon as fall comes 'round. Just don't force us with rifles at our backs.*

The militia also agreed to this request. And even provided "wagons, horses, and oxen; made arrangements for food and other essential items."

And so, in October and November, "twelve detachments of 1,000 men, women, and children, including more than 100 slaves, set off on an 800 mile-journey overland to the west. Five thousand horses, and 654 wagons, each drawn by six horses or mules, went along. Each group was led by a respected Cherokee leader and accompanied by a doctor, and sometimes a missionary. Those riding in the wagons were usually only the sick, the aged, children, and nursing mothers with infants."

The elders cried alone at night, hiding their wet faces and trying to stay strong, but they soon realized that everyone else shed tears under the starry, cold nights. And they quickly saw these could be very teachable moments for the youth, for everyone. Because it is not only what terrible afflictions occur in life, it's the sometimes costly way in which you must handle them. *Didanilvisdi.* To accept. And so, they gathered at night and shared their journeys.

"Long time we travel on way to new land. People feel bad when they leave old nation. Women cry and make sad wails. Children cry and many men cry, and all look sad like when friends die, but they say nothing and just put heads down and keep on going toward the west. Many days pass and people die very much."

"Let me tell you this. My grandmother was a little girl in Georgia when the soldiers came to her house to take her family away. The soldiers were pushing her family away from their land as fast as they could. She ran back into the house before a soldier could catch her and grabbed her pet goose and hid it in her apron. Her parents knew she had the goose and let her keep it. When she had bread, she would dip a little in water and slip it to the goose in her apron. Well, they walked a long time, you know. A long time. Some of my relatives didn't make it. It was a bad winter and it got really cold. But my grandmother kept her goose alive. One day they walked down a deep icy gulch and my grandmother could see down below her a long white road. No one wanted to go over the road, but the soldiers made them go, so they headed across. When my grandmother and her parents were in the middle of the road, a great black snake started hissing down the river, roaring toward the Cherokees. The road rose up in front of her in a thunder and came down again, and when it came down all of the people in front of her were gone, including her parents. My grandmother said she didn't remember getting to camp that night, but she was with her aunt and uncle. Out on the white road she had been so terrified, she squeezed her goose hard and suffocated it in her apron, but her aunt and uncle let her keep it until she fell asleep. During the night they took it out of her apron."

One fifth of the Cherokees died on the way to Oklahoma. Many were women, children and the elderly, the ones who had the most wisdom to share, all gone while on the *Nunna daul Tsuny.* The Trail where they cried. The U.S. government never paid the five million dollars promised to the Cherokees.

CHAPTER EIGHT

1835-1837

R ELIGION WAS, AND will always be, a crucial and integral part of mountain life. The people of White Oak Flats already had a church due to the efforts of Martha Ogle, still a beloved, revered, and remembered figure of the community.

But now, in 1837, White Oak Flats had grown even more, and parishioners constructed a new, bigger church naming it White Oak Flats Baptist. The settlers were convinced by Baptist missionaries to create a Baptist church before any other. They did not need much convincing however for even the Protestants and Presbyterians went to Baptist churches and believed in the sanctity of the Bible, that "churches should be self-governing bodies run by believers only", with "no human founder, no human authority and no human creed."

No one really governed the people of the flats; the church was the closest thing to the rule of law. The actual government's pacts and dealings did not have much of an impact on the rural parts of Appalachia. If conflicts or issues erupted, the church would solve one and all. Even if not a perfect outcome, most everyone accepted a church decision. And if not, a decision to point a rifle at an errant head made for a very quick reconsidering to accept the word of God. The rifle wasn't fired of course, maybe just a warning shot, perhaps just waved around to scare off particularly stubborn bullies…God wants us to keep peace. He had us invent rifles after all. And so, between the church and rifles, they were able to be good and orderly. God was ever watching and sometimes, He gave us extra tools besides words to preach and teach.

The building was perfect as a church, and every Sunday saw people sitting on the smooth wooden pews to listen to the sermon, then walking out into the sunshine to picnic and trade news, filled with goodwill and resolve. It was beautifully situated and nestled in the woods, a long gravel pathway leading up to the door and floorboards swept clean. Windows let in light and gave a view of the graveyard holding their loved ones in permanent peace.

But they also had other plans for the steepled building. Shortly after its opening, the residents of the flats began using the building as a school—something they hadn't had time to establish yet. Schooling did take place in White Oak Flats; only it had thus far occurred within the confines of log homes, under trees near the front porch and in front of the hearth in the afternoons—*we must be able to at least write our names and read*; in the mornings in the fields—*see here, these seeds should be planted deep, these ones though, should just be scattered because they grow better at random…now count them up…use your arithmetic*; and shockingly, if it was the first time experiencing such a thing, in the warm barns where horses produced foals and cows birthed their calves in a flinching, yet miraculous way.

Children's schooling was practical and involved skills needed to make it in the wilderness, yet was also adaptive and broad enough so that young adults could seek other opportunities in the world and still be able to navigate their lives. For now though, the church was still mostly reserved for worship and community meetings, school being held just a few times a month. Fields and chores kept everyone close to home. Sparing an hour or two to read a primer or draw figures and add sums in the dirt was all they could manage most days.

"I don't have time to walk to school, what with the fields nearly ripe and all. Wait 'til after the harvest. Then we'll get there."

"During the long winter months, we'll have plenty of time to read, write, and learn to add the price of a good corn crop."

By June 1, 1840, America's population had grown to over seventeen million people. White Oak Flats held a couple hundred, still members of just a few families. In 1841, the shortest presidency in history occurred when William Henry Harrison contracted pneumonia and died one month after he took office. There was still not one mile of railway in the entire state of Tennessee, yet the young state was the largest corn producer in the nation. Some Cherokee, who refused to leave, hid and lived in the thick wilderness of the Smoky Mountains. Oh, they knew all the places; had known them for decades, centuries. Dens, caves and nooks and crannies way up high that no one would ever find.

And every Tennessean now told story after story of what happened four years ago, back in 1836, when their very own David Crockett and Sam Houston led the fight for Texan independence. Of course, Crockett had died at the Alamo, but Houston then led the Texans to victory at San Jacinto and later became president of the Republic of Texas, which everyone called The Lone Star Republic. Legends they were, and young children were wide-eyed at their growing celebrity, wanting to wear felt hats just like Crockett. But they couldn't just buy a copy of the famous hat at a store. There was no store, the closest one being a day's ride away. And they didn't have any felt to ask their mothers to make a hat. And anyway, their mothers would've crafted coonskin or beaver hats as they were warmer and more durable.

The younger boys had circled around their mothers' statements of durability and had asked their fathers to figure out how they could manage to look like David Crockett from Tennessee. But they didn't know either. "Heck, if there was a store, maybe we can get some of the 'shine while we get you the Davy Crockett hats," the fathers laughed, and then, realizing what they'd said, held fingers to their lips. "Oh, don't tell that to your mothers."

"Don't worry, Pa. We know all about the 'shine." They giggled, poking each other like young boys do. "Most of the folks over in Chestnut Flats make the stuff. Stern stuff we hear. Corn from a jar."

"Oh, they're just trying to make a livin'." The fathers deflected and wondered the extent of their children's knowledge of the world. How did they know? How did they always manage to find out about such things?

"And many of them folks over at Chestnut Flats aren't really lazy either. Some are quite God-fearin' and just happen to live in a place where there's a few folks that bring 'em down. But they should, as a community, put their efforts into their fields. Never make a livin' offa illegal product. Always runnin' for their lives. Hiding. What kind of life is that? It's not like they can sell it in a store. Well, maybe one day in America, we can." *Imagine a store with corn whiskey lining the shelves? Legally?* They didn't even have *one* store that sold anything at all, much less the drink they tried to stay away from, for the most part. Definitely never on Sundays. A store here? They just couldn't imagine it.

Life moves slowly in the mountains. Familiarity is a source of joy and security, and mountain folk naturally fall into a rhythm of cycles. Spring, summer, fall, winter. Ice, snow, thaws, rain, dryness, humidity, and breezes. Nature's energy and strength keeps humans busy; so busy, there is little time for innovation. Little time to start something new. How could they? Crops never took a break, and neither did animals or children who fetched water and milked cows and swept floors and pulled weeds from gardens and shooed away snakes and learned to read under the summer trees and played in the creeks until the sun fell behind the mountains and then at night, listened to their fathers telling their mothers that a store would be awful nice around here, but nobody's got time for that, but if they did, wouldn't it be nice to buy some hats for the boys and even a bit of 'shine? And their mothers would frown and read from the Bible and then sneak a sip, their fathers laughing and saying *I keep tellin' ya. It eases the mind and body don't it? But don't worry, dear. God understands. And, after all, it's not Sunday.*

Noah Ogle, a member of the firmly entrenched Ogle family of White Oak Flats, listened to all the talk about not being able to imagine a store, as he grew tall and strong. He had always listened and wondered, why not start one? We've got plenty of hands on the farm, we're a huge family, and surely a store doesn't have to be manned all the time. Surely, I could situate it so I can see my neighbors coming, or they can ring a bell, and I can run in from the fields, sell them what they need, and run back again.

And in 1850, Noah Ogle did just that. He began a small store, the first one in the White Oak Flats area and though, of course, there was no 'shine or other illegal products, he did sell meal, flour, sugar, coffee, hairpins, and even threshing machines. And he was the contact man to order tools and other farm items. Sometimes there was some candy that the children came from far and wide to buy with their meager coins.

The town was excited and immediately embraced Noah's store; soon, they hardly remembered the small community without it. A neat gravel walkway with shrubbery on each side led to the small building boasting a larger porch than normal, and where the residents tended to congregate in the afternoons, while taking a break from the harsh summer sun. Inside was an open room with wooden shelves stocked with goods behind the counter, bolts of cloth, skillets, kettles, some farming tools and barrels of foodstuffs, safe from animals and critters large and small. A large bell hung outside where anyone could ring it and Noah would appear from his fields to satisfy his customers.

We still forget we can walk right here to get supplies, instead of takin' a horse and wagon ride for a few days! Or instead of making it ourselves. Or finding it or hunting it. Or simply doing without. This store has made all our lives easier.

Indeed, having a store, even a small rural one with limited supplies, was very convenient, and they could never imagine anything bigger and better coming into their lives anytime soon.

But that was all about to change.

CHAPTER NINE

1854—Gatlin comes to Town

WHITE OAK FLATS prospered and lived in peace. Most everyone thought in the same vein, religious and political views were shared by most. If they weren't, those outliers mostly kept it to themselves and kept it by their own hearths. Too busy for that nonsense. When a farm needs tending to, the rest of the world falls away. Sure, the rest of the country was spitting fire with this and that and plantations were complaining about industry and power and whispers of civil war were growing louder, but here in Tennessee, the larger issues hadn't made their way inside. Not in these parts anyhow. Not yet. No industry competed or interfered with their crops, they did not grow cotton or tobacco—at least not on a large scale—and the federal government couldn't quite reach their expanding tendrils through the thick white oaks enough to affect their lives. Governance still occurred within the parameters of the church and good old-fashioned neighbor to neighbor mediation. Maybe a rifle aimed every so often to get a particular point across. Also, there were no slaves. None were needed. *We tend our own land*, and they had such large families, that there really wasn't a need for them.

Need is a large factor in slavery—every civilization, ancient or otherwise, was built using slaves. Irish, Jews, whites, blacks, browns, children, women, Egyptians, Greeks, Romans, Indians, Asians, Europeans…all slaves. No one was immune from slavery, or even being the enslaver. No, it is not confined to one race or people. It is common to all; a repeated state of human affairs. And lest we demonize us humans, we're not the only ones… other animals practice slavery. Ants, and certain bees, beetles, and crickets force others to do their work or trick them to do their labor. Many biologists insist all parasitic relationships are deemed to be slavery. Think tapeworms and fleas. The algae species *cyanobacteria* force other algae to produce what they want. There's even evidence of slave revolts within the ant colonies. Some of them even worked out, resulting in freedom for those lucky ants. But mostly, the enslaved state of affairs continues for ants; for us humans too, albeit less so as the world gains technology. Machines can now replace hard labor. We simply don't need flesh and blood laborers as much as we used to.

"There's that rich white family who has a Negro butler they say, but he's like family."

"No one's like family if they owned."

They thought about that. And most agreed, at least here in the isolated area of eastern Tennessee.

"But those Negros...the ones over yonder, they done brought us the banjo! And for that alone, we are thankful. Don't see a lot of 'em around these parts though. Wish we did...I love that pickin' sound when it gets flying through their thick fingers..."

"Banjos, ya'll know, came with the slaves from West Africa... imagine that! They came all the way from that exotic land and now, we're all pickin' and grinnin' on our front porches."

'Yep, from the wilds of the savannah to the front porches of Appalachia."

"Two different worlds."

"But we recognize both of 'em."

"You wouldn't think so, but that banjo from another world fits perfectly within our misty mountains and white oaks. It's like one heart beatin' across the oceans."

"You know, it was a gourd they used. Yessir, they made them *banjars* out of gourds at first. Hollowed 'em right out and then stretched animal skin—leather—across. They put strings across it...humidity ain't good for it. Causes the head to loosen. Sound is horrible like a cat's claw got your skin. But we shape ours outta wood and it sounds better. Kind of follow the gourd shape, but wood's better. Lasts longer and you can shape it easier. When the Negros came here, through the Caribbean first, and then here to America, we went from callin' it a banjar to a banjo. Just sounds better—the banjo."

"Yeah, and just a couple years ago, 1848 it was, that Stephen Foster wrote *Oh Susanna!*"

"Hey, let's sing that right now..."

On the porch that night sat much of the Ogle family, along with the Huskeys, Reagans, Whaleys, Trenthams, and

McCarters; they were all dressed in their homespun clothes—simple plaid wool dresses for the women and girls, and woolen trousers and shirts for the men and boys. All handmade, mind you, and Appalachian women had perfected how to make a very tedious and never-ending chore fun. Sitting at their looms, often outside, since it was too large for the house, women relished the quiet time, singing, daydreaming, as their fingers danced over their work. From there, "beautiful and interesting coverlets took shape, and turning chores and tasks into opportunities for self-expression; they made 'pretties'—different patterns in their quilts." They also wove practicality and adaptation into their work. Their skirts got shorter and shorter, for example, because tending the fireplace for hours every day was dangerous in billowing skirts. Closer to the ankles and raised up a bit...that was safer. And easier in the gardens. Lasted longer with less blackened and dirty hems all the time.

Such a large crowd they were! They spilled out from the porch and onto the gravel walkways and under the trees, but the rustic, yet sturdy wood cabin supported the backs of the older folks' rocking chairs and cane back chairs as they talked and sang.

"Ya'll know Stephen Foster—he was only 21 years old at the time he wrote that!"

"Is that so? Maybe I'll be doin' some song writin' myself...we sure have a lot to sing about."

"Sure do. Creeks and corn and bears and rifles and ladies fit well into the beat."

"True. Think on it. Anything fits well into a banjo beat. It's kind of polka-like. Like the polka dance type music."

Slapping their thighs, they began:

I came from Alabama,
Wid my banjo on my knee,
I'm gwyne to Louisiana,
My true love for to see;
It rain'd all night the day I left,
The weather it was dry,
The sun so hot I froze to death,
Susannah, don't you cry.
Oh! Susannah, Oh don't you cry for me,
I've come from Alabama
Wid my banjo on my knee.
I jumped aboard the telegraph
And trabbled down de ribber...

"Dang, I don't know the rest of this verse... But now, there's some music! I heard from some of our kinfolk visitors a while back that the goldminers—rush of 1849—you know, those 49ers outta California, said they done changed some of the lyrics:

I come from Salem City with a washpan on my knee.
I'm going to California the gold dust for to see.

They laughed. "A washpan on my knee? What kinda noise would that make?"

"A mighty racket!" they laughed.

"Well, let's keep singin' it our way. We like our *banjos* on our knees. And we're not diggin gold...we're growing corn! And children!" Noah Ogle smiled, pulling a squirming youngster close.

I had a dream de odder night
When ebery ting was still,
I thought I saw Susannah
A coming down de hill;
The buck-wheat cake was in her mouth,
The tear was in her eye;
Says I, "I'm coming from de south,
Susannah, don't you cry."
Oh! Susannah....
I soon will be in New Orleans,
And den I'll look all round,
And when I find Susannah,
I will fall upon de ground.
And if I do not find her,
Dis darkie'l surely die,
And when I'm dead and buried,
Susannah, don't you cry.
Oh! Susannah!

Unbeknownst to the revelers that Saturday night, there was a large, gentle stag with a crown of antlers just up the slope from the cabin and homestead. The deer listened and thought of the happiness that William Ogle had begun with just an idea and a dream. That Martha Ogle had begun by fulfilling that wish. Wished so hard that both could've seen all of this! The people they had produced! The beautifully maintained homestead. Animals, crops. A wonderful strong cabin, the one built with William's carefully stacked logs that he worked so hard to fell and accumulate. These jolly songs and traditions that knit his people together! *I will see it for him;* the deer felt a sudden responsibility in his bones. Somehow, the best of one's inheritance, legends, and dreams are passed on in whatever vessel that nature deems will best keep them safe and alive. *I am one of those vessels*, the deer thought, proud to be chosen. *So is that song, those banjos, all those people telling stories. So is their can-do pioneering spirit and the folklore of these majestic mountains. Pass it down. Keep it alive. The deer's upper lip curled up, and a warmth enveloped its heart. Granny's recipes are still made. Church is attended. School, seasons and holidays. Fresh flowers on every grave. Great-grandpa's stories are still told. He's still alive that way. And always will be. Those legends and tales. Getting taller and taller every time we tell 'em. Just like they ought to be.*

The first day of the summer of 1854 dawned bright and festive. For that was when the berry picking occurred. Summer was all about berries...bears fattened up on their beloved blackberries and children's fingers were stained from now until the end of July. As usual, anything chore-like was turned into a social event. Children ran ahead, up the slopes to the best patches, swinging their buckets, and the women hung back, rifles in hand just in case of a bear, especially a mother bear with three or four cubs, and everyone stopped to drink and cool off in the creek, munching on cornbread stashed in cool cotton pockets. Soon, all the buckets were full.

"This is a banner crop this year. So many blackberries! Even the bears can't eat 'em all. We need more buckets."

"Yes, let's go get another one or two."

They made their way to the general store to see what buckets they had in stock, and were surprised to see Mr. Gatlin himself. Radford Gatlin was a name familiar in White Oak Flats by now. He had just opened the town's second general store, but did not actually live in the area. Noah Ogle's small store still provided basic goods and was much loved, but Gatlin had opened another fuller and bigger general store, situated more centrally and carrying what seemed to be everything and anything. And now, on this first day of the summer, here he was, and rumor had it, sightings were more and more frequent these days.

"Just checkin' up on your stores?" The women asked, as the children roamed around inside, marveling at the stocked shelves full of treasures.

"Actually, I am settling here now. The post office has established itself within my general store here, so being that I have numerous business interests here, I think I'll be staying." He said, pointing to the newly painted sign that indicated the post office.

"Ah, I see. We had heard about the post office but weren't sure it would come to pass. Or when, though we heard rumors the mail was coming here, and soon. And here it is! Well, be mighty nice to have you settled for good here in White Oak Flats."

Tipping his hat, he replied, "Hmm...White Oak Flats. Seems we need more of an identifying name..." Gatlin said almost to himself and walked away.

Word got around.

He's staying!

How'd you hear that?

News travels faster than green grass through a goose.

He's slicker than manure on a hoe handle. And, now, he's staying! Gonna settle here in town!

A store, a post office. Also a preacher. Like he's takin' over the whole town of White Oak Flats...

Known immediately to be flamboyant and controversial, residents at first greeted and welcomed Radford Gatlin to the Flats. Even embraced him as a character and even laughed at naming him a spade when he was really a shovel, especially the young teenagers who had picked up their grandparents' pithy and proverbial sayings with ever-added relish. *Slicker than shit on a shovel,* they'd jest amongst themselves about the newcomer who was cockier than anyone they'd ever met. But that initial curiosity and welcome of Mr. Gatlin was short-lived. Especially once he moved in permanently and got into mixes with, well, just about everyone.

⌒⌒⌒

"Dang, that Radford Gatlin sure is a pistol."

"I'd like to train mine on him. My rifle, *Big Iron*, would set him straight."

"*Persuader* is still in our family...was my Grandpa William Ogle's rifle. Still works mighty well to persuade ones like his type."

"The grandpa you were named after?"

"Yessir that's the one. The one who trapped and traded here with the Cherokees and who wanted to live here, but never did. Died before he could make it. Grandma Martha—she was the one who made it here. The first one."

They nodded, knowing full well the story of the first settlers of this area. Martha. The Ogles.

"*Persuader.* May set him straight. But then again, maybe not..."

Some of the younger children needed to know more. You know kids' tendencies to ask "why" on just about everything? Well, one young man of the Ogle family asked that very question. "Why's he a pistol? Why get *Persuader* to stare 'im down?'"

The adults thought he was old enough to know. After all, children grew up fast in the mountains. They had to learn the land, dodge wild animals, help hunt their food, tend crops, watch and assist births in the barns and fields, and were never far away when their own mothers had another brother or sister.

"Awright, kids. Here it is. Radford's a dang Democrat. And he's sympathetic to the south."

"The south? What's wrong with them? And what's a Democrat? What's the difference? We're the south aren't we? Tennessee's south ain't it?"

"Well now....one thing at a time. First, he's a democrat. This year, 1854, the Republican Party, or the GOP—the Grand Old Party—was founded. Started. Don't want slavery to expand out west."

"GOP eh? Never heard of 'em."

"They're new."

"But I have heard of the Whigs." one young boy exclaimed. "Makes me think of a lady's blonde helmet of hair." They laughed at that. Why these funny names for something so serious?

"Whigs. Free Soil Party...I hearda them."

"And the American (Know Nothing) parties. Now there's a stupid name. Why name yourself the Know Nothin's?"

"You just can't find logic in politics." All nodded their heads and pondered why this was so. "Good intentions, most of them have, when it comes to politics. At first. But then they get up there, in the white government buildings, and something happens. It always becomes a war. Contentious."

"That's a big word."

"So what? Can't he use a big word?"

Sighing, Ogle continued. "Anyways, there was that Kansas-Nebraska Act. Permittin' slavery out west. Well, the Whigs, Free Soilers, Know Nothin's...they all got together and began the Republican Party to fight it. Oh they really don't want to abolish slavery per se; they just don't want it to move west."

"Why? Why does that matter?"

"Well, they think it will lead to slaveholders and their interests to dominate politics. So... that Horace Greeley began the Republican Party. And it came out in the New York papers, and now, here we are."

Indeed, the newspaper magnate, Horace Greeley printed in June 1854, his mission:

We should not care much whether those thus united (against slavery) were designated 'Whig,' 'Free Democrat' or something else; though we think some simple name like 'Republican' would more fitly designate those who had united to restore the Union to its true mission of champion and promulgator of liberty rather than propagandist of slavery.

"Now, about the north-south thing. Gatlin's a southerner, and yep, we are in Tennessee, but we all side with the north. Don't like slavery. Workers, yes. Slaves, no."

"It also ain't no major concern of ours, you see. Here in Tennessee, that is. Or our surrounding areas. I mean, most of us don't own slaves—never did—can't afford 'em. And, besides, we do our own work on our own land."

"To be honest, most of us would love to own a plantation and have workers to run it. But slaves, now that's somethin' we just can't abide. Feel sympathy for 'em. But then again, Tennessee is in the south...our neighbor states have lots of slaves. Got those big plantations. How're they supposed to work their land without workers? So, I can see their way of life would be ruined if they didn't have slaves. On the other hand, they are part of the United States. And their economy is different down here. They grow and tend land. Up north, they make things. Factories. Industries. Railroads are up an' comin."

The young peoples' heads were spinning. Such problems in the world!

"Oh, but these problems have been around forever. There's always been slavery. Always been illogic in politics. Always been divides between people, especially in big countries. Too many minds." He sighed. "It's all in how we solve these things that makes the difference."

"But you just said they've been around forever, these problems. And we still have them. So...they've never been solved. Why not?"

The adults raised their eyebrows. They knew all too well that there was no good answer to that one.

Mr. Gatlin continued to raise eyebrows and tempers. One bright sunny day, when the mountains stood straight up, proud peaks grasping the sky, a huge stag was walking amongst soft pine needles, deep in the woods. Coming to a clearing, he saw two men. One of them was one of that Ogle family, the ones he protected. The other was the hothead they sometimes called Radford Gatlin, and other times called him other words he couldn't understand, but that always came with a frown and often, was accompanied by spitting on the ground.

"Gatlin! What're you doin' with the road?

Gatlin smiled back, tipped his hat and said nothing. Kept walking.

Nothing angers a man more than indifference.

"See here. You done established that Gatlinite Baptist Church. You done told us you lean toward the south and slavery. Now, you dispute with us about the road. Our road!"

Gatlin turned. "You keep talking about 'you'. Seems here that this is my town. My road. Remember? The town's called Gatlinburg now. Has been for a while now. My gateway to richness and legacy. It's 1856. Time to move forward, Ogle."

"Don't care what it's called. Could be Ogletown, White Oak Flats, or no name at all. Only bears your name just because you own the store and the post office is in your store, and you brought some money here."

"Exactly. I brought jobs. Opportunity. Another church. And a different way to look at things. Why is that so bad?"

It didn't sound bad at all. In fact, it all made sense. Which was why it was so unsettling that a man who was truly trying to do well and impact his community was so hated. How? Why?

"He don't drink. Don't show up late to his store. It's always open. Post Office runs smooth. Has some manners awright... thinks they're better than our manners. But manners are manners. Tippin' a hat. Sayin' hi or hello or howdy is all the same. Still a greetin'. Well, most of the time he greets you. Other times, when he don't want to hash it out, he's silent. Which ticks me off more than anythin'."

They all agreed with the assessment, still figuring out why a responsible man with what seemed to be good intentions was so despised. "He's even a preacher! Imagine a preacher who nobody respects or listens to!"

"Seems he's mixing with everyone. In church. In his stores. In the fields. But we're used to that. Mixing is what we do..." he laughed. "Some 'round here are just unfriendly. Just a few. But we know to let them be. But his kind of mixing is foreign to us. He puts it in our faces."

"A mixin' man can't have any friendly neighbors. But that's not the only thing wrong with him..."

"Why do we call it Gatlinburg if we don't like the man?" a little one asked.

"I hear some folks along with some remainin' Cherokees— the ones always hiding—told 'im we'd name the town after 'im if he'd just up and leave!" they all laughed at that, but knowing that mere talk and even some vanity sprinkled into the mix would never sway a man like Gatlin.

"In all seriousness, sometimes we do things for practical reasons. So other people will know where to go for a store, a post office..."

"It's not really named for the man, but for what you can find here in these parts," the little one's mother answered. Part of the Ogle clan they were. "White Oak Flats don't say anything about where we are exactly. But Gatlinburg, now everyone knows where that is. Even outsiders are using Gatlinburg...no matter how we fight it, it seems to have been adopted. Love 'im or hate 'im, everyone knows Radford Gatlin and where his store and post office is. So you see it's just for practical reasons." But as she said it, sadness crept in and she wasn't quite sure whether she believed her own words.

Many a conversation and plenty of gossip surrounded those very questions of why Radford Gatlin, with suspected decent intentions, and even some good ideas, managed to get the whole town named after him, yet also to get the whole town to despise him. No one could put a finger on it, except finally, one day under the trees and under the bluest of skies, when the peaks tilted their faces to smile at the sun, the grandson of William Ogle spoke a simple truth to the others that made everybody understand.

"He wants to take care of all of us in this town. Thinks he's the savior who'll do us all some good. But we just wanna take care of ourselves. Just like we been doing."

Gatlin's presence continued to rankle one and all in the mountain town of Gatlinburg. Running a useful general store, the busy post office, and working hard to put his stamp on the community, he was still party to many local disputes, had confederate leanings in a pro-union area, which he didn't keep quiet about, and was overall a very contentious figure. He managed to continue to mix with everyone.

"How did he even get here in the first place?" the women questioned during a bean breaking session on the front porch of the Ogle cabin. Chores had to be done, but they were a lot more fun if completed with company.

"It's like one minute, he opened his store and such but kept his distance, and the next, he's livin' here and wreaking havoc! Needs to spend some time in the sugar orchard and honey stands. To learn 'im some idea of what we're all about!"

The town started digging into his background. After all, mountain folk cherished family ties and knew what families were what. *Stay away from that family. They drink the 'shine too often. And on Sundays too! That's why they miss church sometimes. She's a nice girl and their family's been here forever. An Ogle match is always a good one. That McCarter boy can trap just like his grandpa. Seems to snare the best skins. He'll make a good husband in a few more years. Wonder who's gonna snatch him up? That grandma never works. Never moves. Her girls are always sweepin' and weedin' while she rocks away the day on the porch. The Reagan young'uns sometimes go over there and help them with the milkin', while she just sits there, smiling like an otter in the creek. She keeps a little bottle in her Bible. I seen it.*

Over the course of the summer, while talking at their frequent quilting parties where the women pieced together old rags and clothes for every young woman soon getting married, they also pieced together the puzzle of Radford Gatlin.

"He was born in 1798. I heard this from the young man who pulls the wagon, deliverin' goods to the two stores—Noah

Ogle's and Gatlin's. That and the postmaster swings by for some refreshment sometimes. He has all the news. And he reports that anyone who knows the man don't like him either. Always mixin' they say. Rude. Anyways, his background is vague. Can't get a whole lot...."

"Strange for us mountain folk to not be able to find information on this Radford Gatlin. There's only so many people and families around."

"Well, he did marry a girl named Elizabeth, and so far, has no children."

"No wonder! I'd stay away from him as much as possible!"

"I'd be 'tired' every night." They laughed together.

"Yessir. I get a headache just from thinkin' about him!" The women exchanged crimson smiles.

"Well, hear this. For a man with such a difficult personality that don't back down, I got surprisin' news the other day. He taught at an old Field School in the Paw Paw Hollow community near Strawberry Fields, and was preacher there at a Baptist church."

"But he sure don't talk like no preacher! Nor act like one."

"Indeed! Now, listen to this...." The women's hands were pushing their thick needles through the fabric and keeping their stitching small for a tidy effect. Steadying their softened cotton, they methodically formed the wedding ring pattern for yet another young girl getting married soon. Appalachian quilts combined Scottish, Irish and German influences, with a sprinkling of inspirations from Native American, Amish and Quaker cultures. Oftentimes, the quilts would express family history or local events, and women took good care to create the very best of their handiwork.

"One hot summer day when Gatlin returned home and found his cow out of the pasture field, he had to chase it down and wrangle it back in. Well, Mr. Gatlin done yelled to his wife—'Elizabeth!" he yelled to her. "You damned old hellion, head that cow off!'"

"My goodness! What did his wife say? I mean, our men yell sometimes, but you know they're just mad at the cow."

"And they don't call us names! Boy if they did, *Persuader* or his brothers would be starin' 'em down right quick..."

"Yessir, there's different types of yellin' alright...and that kind ain't right."

"Why would she marry a man like that?"

"Good question. Well, she answered him after he yelled, and done said back to him—and she was supposedly verrrry sharp when she said this....

"What did you say, Mr. Gatlin?'"

"Well, he must've marked her tone, and he answered her. "I said, *Mrs. Gatlin*, will you please head that cow off?"

"Hmmph!!" The women threw their heads back in laughter, slapping their thighs through their cotton dresses, but then exchanged concerned glances, eyebrows raised. Oh, they knew a few men who were mean, even evil. Sometimes it was the moonshine, sometimes it was just their nature. *A bad egg. Wired up bad.* But most of their men were God-fearing, good, family men. Any sign of misuse was quickly taken care of by the rest of the close-knit families. No father or brother would sit by and watch as his daughter or sister was mishandled. Sometimes a rifle or two had to be called in, but most situations settled down and were worked out. Rarely, the young girl simply moved back home, her husband moving to another town. Chestnut Flats perhaps, where there were few morals and religion was always optional.

"Paw Paw Baptist Church says he and Elizabeth became members of the church in September 1841, following a revival. Within a year, the Church ordained Gatlin as a regular minister, and almost immediately after joinin' the church, he became assistant clerk. Wrote the minutes in a very legible and beautiful hand, they say. And his spelling, punctuation and grammar were almost perfect."

Indeed, this was unusual in an era of atrocious spelling and poor English composition in East Tennessee, as well as many other places.

"Well, church seems to not have had a calming influence, because the postmaster tol' me that "on December 9, 1843—back some time ago, but people still recall it like yesterday—Gatlin was the major actor in a big church dispute that resulted in a split of the Paw Paw Hollow Church.""

"What happened?"

It was now well into the afternoon, but the quilting bee was long ago forgotten. Needles remained idle and all the women were at the edges of their cane-backed chairs or logs or boulders. Vegetable dye for dying the scraps sat in bowls under the hot sun, the rags within becoming deeper and deeper orange and red. Still, the women talked. They had to figure this man out. Their men just wanted to wave their rifles around like sleek wood and engraved metal peacock feathers, but the women knew there would need to be more than just *Persuader* or *Big Iron to* scare this type of man. This here was a different breed and only through observation does one understand. Once understood, they could then take action.

"Well, Gatlin struck again. Stirrin' up trouble. Sometime previously, Gatlin had written a letter to the local Baptist Association "condemning the Tennessee Baptist Convention for adopting a missionary program at Jonesborough."

"When was this?"

"This was around 1842, the delivery boy said. Apparently, Gatlin's position in this bitter Baptist missionary controversy was neither the anti-missionary Baptists nor the pro missionary Baptists should be denied 'fellowship' in the Church. But the Association interpreted Gatlin's letter as 'offensive' and sent a committee of their leaders to investigate the trouble at Paw Paw Hollow. Gatlin refused to let them use the Church, and the visiting committee reported him most 'rude and uncivil'."

"That he is. Sounds just like him." They nodded their heads. The cool late afternoon breezes held them to their chairs and logs and rocks for a while longer, but then, as it always does in mountain life, duty called. Yet they didn't want to leave their topic of study just yet; they were on a mission with figuring out Radford Gatlin and wanted to keep it going.

"The men'll be here soon. And the kids. They'll be wanting their supper. Why'nt we take what we have in our kettles and bread baskets and meet in the middle and have us a picnic for dinner? I have some ham and biscuits leftover from today's dinner."

"Love that idea! And I've got some pork loins and a cake."

The women caught their men coming in from the fields and children were rounded up and told to get ready quickly. *Go get washed up! We're seein' the whole town tonight and it won't get dark for a while now. Scrub at the creek...get under your fingernails and wash those faces. Behind the ears don't forget.* Once plans were relayed to everyone and they had gathered back together within the hour, the conversation continued. And one lone massive stag moved closer to listen.

"Two days later the committee made the second attempt to use the church and met with the same treatment from Gatlin. The committee's report sounds like there may have even been fistfights right there in the church yard!"

Gasps erupted. "Oh, Lord. Fightin' right in the shadow of God's house?"

"A witness said they "fought for half a day in the Paw Paw Hollow church yard." After being told by Gatlin they could only use the church if they would not discuss the subject which brought them to blows and if they would make up their minds in ten minutes, the committee with part of the Church members said *forget it* and thereafter met in a shed attached to the church. Here they proceeded to prefer 'Articles of Complaint against Radford Gatlin' and voted 'forthwith to exclude Gatlin' from the church."

Thrown outta his own church! That's something I've never heard of before...

And though they shook their heads, kicked dirt and spat at the ground as they relayed story after story they'd heard about Radford Gatlin, they thought seriously about the troubled background of this man who had come to their town. White Oak Flats. Now, Gatlinburg.

"What about his land? He sure does own a lot."

"Our neighbor county, Jefferson County, saw Radford Gatlin as early as 1825, I heard. Man, that postmaster hears everything and news ain't safe with him. Anyways, Gatlin seemed to be a gatherer of land, they said. Seventy acres on Blue Springs Creek in the Strawberry Plains section of Jefferson County, fifty-five acres in the same vicinity, and in 1838, another one hundred acres nearby—all a bit over fifty miles from White Oak Flats. Was he a different man at that time? It seems he wasn't. Engaged in 'many petty lawsuits with his neighbors in Jefferson County, and lost most of them.' Everyone who's ever met the man says he's just a very difficult person. May mean well, but he just don't know which way is up."

Funny thing about people. It's all in the lens. Look through one lens and you see something unseemly; look through another and you may see promise. If someone knows another to be difficult or stubborn, somebody else could view that same person as confident, or even determined. More often, these lenses tend to merge creating an uncomfortable, yet lively contrast. And so, though Mr. Radford Gatlin was known to be stubborn, unfriendly, and head-strong, he did earn a scattering of praise and respect, even to the point of it being reported in a news article:

Mr. Gatlin demonstrates qualities of leadership by serving as captain of a militia company for a few years. He also served as a juror and road overseer. He first showed up in Sevier County in 1842, when he bought yet another one hundred twenty-five acres not far from his home on Blue Springs

Creek. In 1849, he "enlarged his farm by purchasing another tract on Tuckahoe Creek". Known as Gatlin Place, here is where he also exemplified leadership, representing the Twelfth Civil District in Sevier County Court.

"Well, it may say that in a small newspaper piece that the postmaster showed us—maybe to make us all feel better about his being here in town…to give us a little hope that things may get better…"

"Guess it does say he's a leader. I mean…I see that a bit… he did open the store, brought some opportunity to this place… his store is always open. Ya'll never have to wait for him or go 'round the fields looking for him."

"Seems to want to do good, but he don't know how."

"But we've all been talkin' about the man…yet we still don't know how'd he get here in the first place? In William Ogle's *land of paradise?*"

⁊◎◌

"Whew! What a day!" The women were growing tired from the day, and they were sitting on soft quilts under a stand of trees right in the middle of the small town. The crowd had grown larger, picnic foods and drinks were shared and children ran around, loving the freedom of a surprise evening with no chores. With most of the town present, talk would usually lean toward crops, corn, horses, how much the cows were milking, children, the weather, rifles, hunting, and *do you have a bit of the drink with you?* But as the sun nodded below the tips of the peaks, and the temperature dropped just enough to give off a sharp chill, everyone spoke of one thing and one thing only. Radford

Gatlin. Who wasn't there by the way. Because he wasn't invited. The younger children ran around the trees playing *Soup Pot*— teams were made and if you were tagged, you must go to the circle drawn on the ground with a stick—the soup pot. While some of the older children retreated to the creek where they did what young adults do: teased, splashed, played, walked off in pairs and tried to see which ones they'd match up with in another year or so.

And the adults were watching the evening sky brushed with color while still sorting out their neighbor.

"Neighbor? More like intruder!" One of the Ogles spat out.

"Alright. Alright. Let's keep a cool head. Figure this out." A calmer head prevailed in the form of a grown member of the Reagan family. "So, here we are...1856 and Gatlin's here a couple years now. Ya'll know he bought his fifty acres from Elisha Ogle. Paid him thirty dollars. Land joins up with Thomas Ogle, Sr. and Thomas Ogle, Jr., Gatlin's being on the east side of the west fork of the Little Pigeon, starting at the river bank 'twenty poles below the mouth of Roaring Fork Creek.'"

"And we know he opened his store before he even moved here permanently."

"Yep. You're right 'bout that. He would take his horse and go to Sevierville and load up on foodstuffs: coffee, salt, sugar, and other necessary goods for our way of life: guns, rifles, ammunition and axes. He even sold cowbells that, let's face it, we all wanted. I mean, he does do us *some* good..."

They grudgingly admitted Radford Gatlin did bring some good things to the town. "If we can hear our cattle, we can keep track of them, determine if they were roaming too far away, or if there was any danger to them. Cowbells clanging as our cows ran; well, it sent everyone here in the flats running. Probably saved a lot of cows from roamin' off, or if a wild animal was threatenin', we knew it right away and then *Persuader* could do its job..."

Commodities trading—things that can be bought or sold—began in the 1800s, and cattle, grains, butter and eggs were top on that list. Thus, cows were very valuable, and they had to admit their lives were now much more profitable when they were able to bring most of their animals from the calm and busy fields of Gatlinburg to the trading floor, and the cow bells of Gatlin's General Store made that happen.

"Those cowbells sell just about as well as coffee, salt and sugar." The men agreed as they listened to the nightfall, the calm clanging of the faraway cow bells singing as the sun winked its final goodbye and dipped behind the surrounding summits.

The next week, the residents got a bigger—and more shocking—part of the story as to how Gatlin had obtained all of his land and how it came to be *here*, in their own land of paradise, when the newspaper boy excitedly hurried up to the Ogle's large porch and told his latest information.

"Not two days later!" the boy began, breathless. He sat down on the porch and was glad because he knew he'd get a ham slice and some sweet bread with honey from Mrs. Ogle. Always got a nice meal and these people were so hungry for news! Especially about Gatlin. Seems he makes his mark everywhere he goes, and never in a good way.

Upon seeing the delivery boy hurry into the area, it was always noticed by someone and young ones were dispatched to others' fields and homesteads. And now, the newspaper boy looked out as he rested his elbows on his knees and hung his feet off the porch and saw a crowd walking toward the cabin. News travels fast in these parts. Why, there's even some folk coming up on horseback! Swallowing his salted ham and honeyed bread, he stood, with most of Gatlinburg surrounding him standing in a haphazard circle, sitting on logs, or even on the ground. They were ready to listen.

"On September 4, 1854...remember September 2, he done bought from Elisha those fifty acres? ...we all know that. It was a couple of years ago now." They nodded.

"Yep, we all know that...Elisha's one of our own. We thought, heck, sell 'im some land and Elisha can make some money. Didn't think much on it. Men making business is all."

"Well, not two days later," the boy continued, "on the 4th, he entered 5,000 acres in a Tennessee land grant...which was now over 100,000 acres—pretty much all of White Oak Flats country! Yep, White Oak Flats...don't care what they call it these days. Gatlinburg ain't the proper name in my eye." He stood up and kicked around some dirt. "It's White Oak Flats to me! Always will be." One and all looked around at one another with concerned looks.

"Wait. What? 5,000 acres became 100,000? Two years ago?"

"Yessir. Gatlin only 'claimed 5000 acres', but he really got control of 100,000. Don't ask me...I really don't know all the specifics and legal language. But I know he tried to keep it secret. Never told no one. And no reporter ever reported it. Strange ain't it?"

The Ogles were standing now, pacing, agitated. "Wait a minute. Let me get this right. With this here...this here news you're tellin' us...well, there's nothin' else to think but that 'Gatlin intends to dispossess us from our lands!' "

"For the past two *years*!"

The crowd gasped, nodded. "Damn! I'm as mad as a crow and sad as a shallow creek all at the same time."

"I heard..." the delivery boy almost whispered now, "that thousands of acres of settled lands were included in this grant."

"Settled lands? Why...that could be *our* lands!"

They gasped louder. Could it be? Could their land be taken from them by this savvy, complicated, and dangerously ambitious man? Was this scheme hidden for two years, giving him all that time to solidify his claims? They could not believe this news. Tempers exploded.

"Not on our watch!"

The women had to rise suddenly and wrest rifles out of their men's hands and restrain them and talk them down to their senses, or else the Ogle, Reagan, McCarter and Huskey men would've marched over to Gatlin's place and shot him dead right then and there.

When people are threatened with the loss of land, loss of resources, and loss of livelihood, they tend not to simply say "Yes, here you go", and give it all up without a fight. No, they tend to strike back. And when other people see an opportunity to gain land, resources, and livelihood, they also strike hard and fast, knowing they must fight for it. Such an age-old story! And here, that same story had arrived in the middle of the Smoky Mountains of Appalachia. Each side has its own views of what is best and what is just. The only variable ever-present in this tired plot: *which side will win?*

Gatlin disguised his true ambitions, but not on purpose. It was the way he operated. He truly thought he would build his own town and, in doing so, help everyone in it, including himself. And why was that so bad? He had the money; why not use it for his own benefit? Why couldn't he buy more land if he wanted? Isn't that what America was founded on? *I can build more roads and attract businesses. Build my own legacy, land and holdings. Develop my land. And with it, more and more people can access our town, it will grow, everyone will profit, and our resources can be shared. We will be on the map. Who wouldn't want that?*

For mountain folk though, they didn't want that. These actions by Gatlin were shocking and bitter and overbearing. And the one, very easy thing that could've changed everything, Gatlin never even thought of, much less did.

"Ask! Ask us! If Gatlin had just *asked* us what we wanted instead of just assumin' we wanted more roads and stores and inns for travelers, we could've had a conversation 'bout it! Could've changed everything if he just asked! But he's thinkin' for all of us. Thinks we want the same things. But we don't."

"Yessir. We may've been able to compromise. Still can if he just talks to us. Sit down together see what we can all do to better our lives. But nothin' us folk hate worse than others tryin' to think for us. We got our own minds!"

Strike one for Gatlin.

"But is it a strike against him? Or *for* him?" The delivery boy asked. Hearing a collective groan and then a sigh from the people, there was no answer for a long while.

"Cause, you may think it's against him, but seems every time he strikes, he's the one comin' out on top."

At that, the people of the small, rural town of Gatlinburg, still comprised mostly of only the few established and original families, dispersed and walked back to their own cabins, lost in thought while the mountains stood watch over history, never taking sides, simply sitting there, stoic, while the human inhabitants fretted over who owned which tiny slice of their backbones and what to do with their own bountiful slopes and valleys.

Saturday tub baths in Appalachia were pretty much mandatory. Had to look nice for visiting on the porches that night and for church in the morning. Washing the week's sweat from working the hot fields, the animal smells in hair and clothing fibers, and dirt underneath nails, was something to look forward to all week. Wash rags were no longer stiff from last week's drying by the fire; a week's worth of sitting there, folded on a shelf in a dry, warm cabin made them pliable again. Sitting "Indian style", legs crossed, knees hitting the sides of the tub, mothers poured water over little ones' heads, while the older children poured hot water over themselves. Soap was made from lye, ashes, tallow, lard and milk, and all families had a bar or two at all times. But making soap was tough. It came out different every time! Different textures—everything from crumbly dry cakes to rubbery goop with barely a lather. Different smells—earthy or dusty or just plain awful, like you were holding a burnt hunk of biscuit in your hand that had fallen into the pigpen. Sometimes, adding more milk or honey made it lather up rather nicely. They all wished they could make soap like Luraney Oliver over in Cades Cove.

It had reached Gatlinburg that Luraney Oliver's soap was the best around. Maybe the best in America. Lathery, and soft, she had put crushed nuts, honey, and pumpkin into her mixtures.

"That soap of Mrs. Oliver's is the best I ever smelled or held in my hands. Once, when I was on my way to Happy Valley to sell corn, I stayed with them in the cove and washed with it. So soft and lathery. Gets all the grime off your hands. That, and she makes the best pumpkin butter too."

The Oliver family was the very first ones to settle in Cades Cove in late 1817—early 1818, and had barely survived that first winter, but had made it through and were now thriving in that little isolated mountain bowl west of White Oak Flats. They were known to be a kind, hardworking and industrious family. Too bad they hardly ever had any contact. Sometimes, news or a letter came through, but mostly, these mountains held their own tightly and close to home, embracing them on their own lands and farms, barely relaxing their loving grip to travel beyond a few miles here and there.

It was right after Saturday bath time when the wash-tubs were turned over to drain and dry, and twilight beamed off of everyone's gleaming clean skin when Mr. Gatlin's latest plan soiled everything all over again. This time, there was no amount of soap or cleanser or anything at all that could clean up the mess.

"I propose to change the main road through White Oak Flats."

"I knew it! You gonna change our town! Don't even ask us what we want on our own land!" They grumbled.

"Why?" asked one young man, recently married, who had a mind to keep calm and rationally sort this all out. They had met at the Ogle's homestead, on the large porch, where banjos were leaning against the doorway, readying for Saturday night music and singing. Chairs were brought out and quilts were draped to cover chilly knees and just a touch of moonshine made its way around the happy and thus far content crowd. Mr. Gatlin wasn't exactly invited, but he had shown up and they made room for him anyway, in an act of neighborly spirit, when he began talking of his latest plans.

"I'm going to court to see about it. Hear me out, gentlemen. And ladies." He tipped his hat. The ladies, lips pursed and eyes narrowed, poured just a bit more from the flasks into their mugs and tin cups. Not too much now. There's church in the morning.

Thomas Ogle, Sr. sighed and kept quiet. He knew if he spoke, he'd throw punches on that smooth face of Radford Gatlin. *Don't trust that man as far as you can throw him.*

"See here folks. The road will be good for everyone. It's 1857. Time to move forward. I propose…" And he whipped out a paper he'd filed in court, standing up and reading it to the small gathering. Whispers on the side of the porch: *Lord Almighty. He always has a dang court paper. Always running to the damn court. How does he ever get anything else done?*

"I propose an 'alteration in the road to run immediately from the north bank of Roaring Fork up Pigeon River along the eastern bank to the corner of mine—Radford Gatlin's—field opposite the farm occupied by Caleb Ogle, thence along the south side of said Gatlin's field so as to intersect the old road again at the fork of the road which leads to the Glades'.'"

"Good for everyone? Hell! That road will go right up to your store!"

"So? Isn't that good? For a road to lead to the Gatlinburg store?"

"Yes...but...but...it'll..." Thomas Ogle Sr. didn't know what to say. "It will change the town," was all he could think of. Maybe he couldn't quite put it into words, but he knew the feeling and knew with all his being that such change was chipping away at their isolation, their land, their very way of life.

The ladies exchanged glances they didn't even try to hide. One brave Ogle girl spoke up, "Dang! Strike two against you, Mr. Gatlin. It's happenin' before our very eyes!"

"Strikes? What do you mean?"

"Oh, you know that Knickerbocker team? In 1845—just a few years ago—they took... baseball is what they call it...and made it all formal. Rules and such. Diamond-shaped infield. Foul Lines. And the three strike rule. Three strikes and you're out. And you can't throw the ball at players anymore. Too many injuries, 'specially on the head. Now, they catch it in a mitt—a glove kind of—and they tag the player. They just need to touch the player. And then they're out. Three strikes and your time is up. Baseball has it as their rules, and now lots of people are sayin' 'three strikes' to say that your time is also up."

Gatlin, shrewd as always, smiled at the girl. "Indeed, Strike two." Under his breath, he muttered, "Unlike baseball players who have three, I play my own game. And I've got one hundred more strikes to go."

Later that same week, the town was not only continuing the thick simmer of angst and anger, it had finally reached a truly decisive boiling point.

It was a fine day, the 10th of June, 1857, when the birds circled and fields swayed in the gentle winds. The deer smelled the increasing stench of rage and envy and walked closer for a better view. He still instinctively watched over the family of that man they had called William. *What was happening? How long would they need protection?* The man with the dream of living in a smoky mountain paradise was long gone, but his kin was all around these parts. Numbering now in the hundreds, and spread all over Gatlinburg, the Ogle family, along with the other established families, were respected, tight-knit, strong, and settled in their farmlands and homes. Good thing too, for on that fine afternoon, they'd all need each other, and then some, because today, and continuing through the next couple of years, there would be very few days of peace between the residents of Gatlinburg and Mr. and Mrs. Radford Gatlin.

No one knew exactly how the fight began. Either no one talked or no one talked about the correct version of events. But they all saw what happened in the aftermath. In small rural communities, fields are wide open. Sure, there are trees here and there, but most land has been cleared for crops, cabins, buildings, barns, general stores, and roads. Entire families tended their own fields and were busy from sunrise to sunset, but there was always one eye on others' homesteads, others' fields. *What was going on over there? What were the Ogles doing? They enlarged their corncrib. The McCarters repaired their fence. Over there, the Huskeys and Reagans had two more calves...lots of calves out of their barns this year. And those Gatlins. They're building roads and encroaching on us. Do they mean well? Some of us—just a few, mind you—think they do mean well and are okay folks. Heck, if we had opportunities and money like Radford Gatlin and his wife, wouldn't we jump at that chance too? Would we?* Sometimes the answer was no. Most other times, it was not answered at all. Too uncomfortable to admit. Even to one's self.

"Come quick!" The young Ogle boy ran around the fields, announcing the fight.

"Elizabeth Gatlin struck Thomas Ogle, Sr.!"

"What?!" Residents grabbed rifles and ran with the boy toward the Gatlin homestead.

"Yessir!" he panted as he ran. "She struck him in the hand with a stick that she had been strikin' the cattle with. He was over there, tryin' to talk to her about something or other. More like, he walked over there tryin' to talk to Radford, but she was the one who he saw first. When she came up from strikin' the cattle, she hit him in the hand with a big ol' pine stick. Oh, but it was on purpose, don't you know! Didn't even get a word in to ask to speak to Radford when she just hit him! Well, Thomas caught hold of her stick and jerked her on the ground and that Elizabeth struck 'im several times. She hit him in the hand! Head! Jerkin' her stick all over!"

Charity Ogle, the daughter-in-law of Thomas, married to his son, Levi, had joined them and yelled that she saw a bit of what happened too. "I was turning the cattle into the road by the house of Mrs. Gatlin and saw Elizabeth Gatlin strike Thomas Ogle!"

"Then, Mr. Gatlin intervened and yelled at all of us: What the hell is going on here?! He done yelled at everyone. Boy, was he mad!"

"Then, he took his wife's arm and dragged her into the house. Dragged! Poor woman. I'd bash his head with the Bible while he was sleepin'."

"Charity! Such a thought! God is watching…"

"Well, I *would*. And I think God would forgive me. Why'd he make the Bible so heavy then? When the words within the Book won't do the trick, I think He would want us to close it up and use it. That way, his entire message will be received."

They chuckled; none argued.

"Then, Gatlin ordered us to get out and get home. He'd deal with Elizabeth himself, and Thomas too—he said, he'd retribute or somehow pay Thomas back. Make amends to him for his wife attackin' him. But you know he won't do that. He fights everything if he don't wanna do somethin'. Now, he ain't a true fightin' man, as we know. Not the physical fist fightin' anyways. A gentleman he thinks he is...they all do their fightin' and defendin' in court."

"Right so. We're like to see 'im defending his wife in court. And fightin' like hell to keep from payin'. You watch. He ain't gonna pay up or make amends to nobody."

A trial was held and Elizabeth Gatlin was convicted and fined one dollar." Gatlin's fine was also one dollar, but he fought this conviction, saying he, himself, had nothing to do with the fight, and "took both he and his wife's cases all the way to the Tennessee Supreme Court."

"No way in Hell I'm paying a dollar, or even one penny, for something that ain't right."

"One dollar, Mr. Gatlin." His lawyer admonished him. "It's not even that much money! And your wife did attack Mr. Ogle…"

"Don't matter the money. Or the amount. It's the principle. Man's got a right to defend his property and principles. And so does his wife."

"What was she defending? Thomas wasn't doing anything! He even testified he did nothing and Mrs. Gatlin just came at him. For no reason! She said she was mad that day—but remember? She wouldn't say what she was mad at."

"Probably her husband!" Charity spat out. "She's never friendly, you notice. Always mad at the cows, her fields, the weather, a chicken, her chimney or anyone walking close by. Mad at her life, truly. Thomas was just too close by that day."

Radford Gatlin dug in. *I'm not paying anything.* But the Supreme Court agreed with the verdicts and upheld those fines.

"But I hear that 'further' never paid it yet. And ain't gonna."

"Further?"

"Yessir. Gatlin's a 'further'. Came from far away—further away from our parts. In any case, far away enough that he ain't no neighbor of ours."

∽❀∾

Another Saturday late afternoon, after a washtub bath for every-one, the women covered baskets of biscuits and pies with cloth to bring across the fields toward the Ogle porch. Banjos were already in hand, slices of pie on plates and a little moonshine in jugs and jars—just a little, there's church in the morning—as the community of Gatlinburg gathered for the weekly highlight of their social life. Coming together, gossiping, trading news, eating and drinking together and a bit of stomping dance to accompany the banjo's popping and snappy sounds, rounded out their special brand of Appalachian culture.

As the late afternoon turned toward evening, they knew the general store stayed open a bit later on Saturday nights. Charity Ogle told her husband, Levi, and the children: "Maybe go down to the store and get some sugar. We're runnin' low and I want to make some extra sweets lately. Springtime always brings out my sweet tooth!"

The residents, as much as they resented Radford Gatlin, had come to rely on the general store. Times past, they would hoard sugar and buy enough for months, if not the entire year. Noah Ogle's general store had made that better; he had made sure that sugar and such was available quite often. Now though, with the steadfast Gatlin's General Store, it was readily available at all times, and in abundance, and if one ran low, there was no need to preserve it, or plan a three-day trip to another town to stock up for months. No, now they could get sugar any day of the week.

Some members of the other families joined the Ogles as they diverted from the front porch, walked down the path toward the general store, continuing the conversation. The children skipped ahead, relishing Saturday night visiting. And now, an unexpected trip to the store! Maybe they could get a piece of candy.

"And he just waltzes in here, tryin' to change roads and such. We've been here since the beginning! Us Ogles and McCarters, Huskeys and Reagans. We should be the ones trying to change the roads. Or not, if we don't want to. We should be the ones to make the decisions."

"So why didn't you?" Gatlin suddenly came upon the crowd, appearing from around the corner of his store.

Startled at his sudden appearance, Levi growled, "Were you eavesdropping?"

"It's my store. You were the ones talking, saying everything you want to say, behind my back, mind you. I don't eavesdrop. Don't say things behind your backs. I say things out loud." And then, repeated his thoughts. "Not behind one's back."

"Look here. We don't want trouble. Wanna be neighbors. But could ya ask us, or consult with us before you go around changin' our town? Our way of life? We've asked before, but we ain't never get anywhere with you."

"Gentlemen. And ladies. I am not changing your way of life. What I'm doing is making your way of life better. And mine too. It's the American way. What's the harm in the road? You should be happy! It opens up trading, routes, the ability for others to visit. To settle here. To grow the town. Buy more of your crops. What's the harm?"

Softening just a bit, both sides realized there are other ways of looking at this situation.

"Well, Rome wasn't built in a day. Recall that sayin' from somewhere. Maybe we can just remember to talk to one another. Not just do something...tell us about it. And we will do the same." Even though under his breath, Levi Ogle mumbled *though we'd never have just done something without consulting others.* But he knew this request to communicate was a way of keeping the peace with a man like Gatlin.

"Agreed. Still, there's no harm in what I'm doing." Gatlin smiled, which was met with silence and the start of frowns.

Levi and the others didn't trust him one bit. But they also had a strong desire to keep the peace and try to make things work. And they were used to the store with its sugar and coffee and convenient goods all within easy reach. For his part, Radford Gatlin shared that strong desire to make things work, perhaps even more so.

"After all, I have a lot to lose if we cannot live in harmony. Look here," he waved his hand over his storefront. "I have this store, property, land. I've made a life here. I rely on you for my business. Truly, I want the best for all of us. For myself *and* for your families. Both sides of a conflict usually want peace; they just have different ideas on what that peace looks like. Isn't that always the case?" he smiled and watched as the crowd, for the most part, nodded and grudgingly agreed. "So, let's work and see if we can have the same vision of what peace looks like. What do you say?"

Shaking hands, they talked a bit more small talk, bought the sugar, and parted ways. But all was not well. Walking back

in silence toward the Ogle porch where the rest of the community was catching up with one another and growing louder
with ever-loosened tongues, Levi's voice pierced the revelry as
they walked down a pathway, past the large kitchen garden and
approached the tangle of families.

"There is something very maddening about someone you
don't like making perfect sense."

It was a cold, icy night in November 1857. The fall harvest
had been bountiful, summer had set in fast this year and the
warmth had fueled a banner crop of corn. Well-fed and healthy,
Gatlinburg was now quiet and its robust animals hunkered
down in corners of barns trying to keep warm. The large stag
deer nuzzled its ground nest, airing out its bed of grass and pine
needles. If he stayed there just a few more minutes, his body
heat would melt the remaining ice and alleviate the chill in his
bones. He was ready to sleep in his nook of the mountains. But
just then, his nose picked up the smell of smoke. And it was getting stronger. He stood up to his full height and it was then that
he saw the flames.

"Fire!"

The entirety of the Ogle family and the other familiar humans were roused from their own warm beds, running
toward the smoke, clearly visible now, even in the darkness.
The deer thought about walking and watching the action from
a better vantage point. Or even laying back down to view the
rising chaos. A tough decision, being his bed was still warm,

comfortable by now, but by remaining at his full height, he'd already be on his feet if this fire spread closer to his warm bed of dense pine needles and grass. And it did look like it was spreading quickly, despite the iciness of the night.

"Fire! You goddamned Ogles! You did this!" Gatlin yelled, running around his homestead with a quilt he had flung around his shoulders flapping in the wind cape-like. He pushed his wife up a steep slope and told her to keep going, lest she be burnt to a crisp. The deer, still on his feet, and now, climbing higher on the mountain, watched the worn woman run and stop, cling to a tree, and watch in horror the people running around, flinging water everywhere, covering small flames with dirt, and then, eventually, simply standing still. The woman, dirty and with no shoes, cried, watching the scene unfold. *How did I ever get into this mess? This life with Radford...it never works out! Never makes any sense! I'm angry all the time. Never any peace!* She sat down and cried and cried and cried while the deer stood witness.

The fire was so large now that buckets of water from the creek and shovels of dirt were doing little to stem the flames. Soon, there was nothing to do but let it all burn.

Gatlin brought the arson charge. He knew exactly who to blame.

"Levi and Thomas Ogle. They set the fire to kill me! They didn't though, did they?" He spat his words out with a sneer.

"But my barns and stables were burned. My grain and cattle...all killed in the woods."

The Ogles couldn't believe the charges leveled against two of their own. They were all holed up at home that night. Nobody was around! It was freezing outside! *And we are not the kind that seeks revenge with fire. We've got Persuader and Big Iron and the rest and all of 'em look men right in the eye. Not sneaking around at night setting fires like cowards.*

Yet a proposed indictment ensued.

"Arson charges against Levi and Thomas Ogle." the headlines blared.

Gatlinburg was in an uproar. The vast majority sided with the Ogles—they knew that any member of that esteemed family would never do such a thing! How dare Radford Gatlin accuse them of setting fire to his farm! And trying to kill him! They were God-fearing people, these Ogles, for goodness sakes!

Then, there were those few who, while siding with them knew all about the bitter history with the Ogles and the Gatlins, and secretly wondered. Did they do this? Would they? But no, setting fire to any barn would put everyone in danger. There was no way to control a fire at night, in icy, but dry conditions. Sure, they'd set fires to clear land—they did that all the time. But that was different. They'd prepared the land for that, were ready, and the fires were small and controlled. No one was ever threatened when they cleared land on purpose to prepare the soil.

Those same people whispered their truest thoughts, whispering so perhaps even God would understand: *even if Levi and Thomas did do it, Gatlin deserved it. Been nothin' but trouble ever since he came here. Runnin' all over our lands and doin' whatever he wants. You can say that he's been burnin' us for years.*

In the Tennessee court, it was noted that "witnesses who appeared were Isaac T. Ogle, Elisha Ogle, William R. King, Hercules Ogle, Serena Ogle, Margaret Huskey and Mary Huskey", all testifying they had seen nothing, heard nothing, had heard of no plans for arson, and were all sleeping or "at least in bed because the night was so icy...colder than a mother-in-law's kiss."

Five days later, after an investigation that yielded no proof, no clear witnesses and no evidence, the Sevier County grand jury brought no formal indictments.

This did not end the ongoing feud, however. The icy conditions set in with both man and nature and barely a month later, on December 14, 1857, Radford Gatlin was at it again, fighting it out in court.

"Mr. Radford Gatlin appeared before Phillip S. Shults, a justice of the peace, and swore out a peace warrant against 'Thomas Ogle Senr, William Ogle known as the son of said Thomas Ogle Senr, Isaac Ogle Senr, Elisha Ogle and a certain Aaron Onsley. Gatlin made oath that he was afraid that these men would 'burn his dwelling and other buildings and perhaps destroy the lives of him... and his wife or that they will procure or cause the same to be done by putting into circulation false reports, by making misrepresentations respecting said deponent and wife, by suppressing the evidence of the late burning of Said deponent's stables, barn and property, thereby giving encouragement and inciting incendiaries to further acts of felony on the buildings and property of said deponent."

With this, another trial ensued.

Gatlinburg was in a tangle of anger, bitterness, sadness, and resolve. The deer sensed it all as he was making his daily walks, through ice, early snowfall, and crunchy leaves long fallen from the dead branches. Whiffs of rage knelt on strong breezes and a violent uneasiness settled down until the mountains held the totality of human emotions. Mostly, an eerie need for some kind of conclusion was discerned by the large stag. His antlers turned and his eyes steered themselves toward the valley. It all seemed normal. Fields lay empty, resting until the spring. Cabins sat with smoke pouring out of chimneys; people ran out to tend to animals, work a little bit on a fence here, and a corncrib there, check smokehouses to keep out critters trying to steal food, and then, finally, grabbing more logs and hurrying back inside for some warm stew and a heavy quilt over the knees to melt the chill in the bones.

By this time, Gatlin was well known to the justice system of this little corner of Tennessee—the judges and witnesses, jurors, and newspapermen who reported on such things all knew of him and his tendency to run to court over every imaginable issue. *Could he not get along with anyone at all? Why were his social skills so abhorrent? So strange, this personality of his. A very difficult person. Still, he was well-spoken, had manners when it suited him, helped his neighbors, always ran the store well, was respectable, was smart and savvy... why couldn't such a person make it in the world? Has everything going for him, except he can't get along with others. Fights with everyone. Can't apologize or even meet someone halfway. Fatal flaws. Yet, damn if he doesn't make sense when you talk to him man to man! Don't you hate that? When someone who may be wrong and who you hate makes so much sense?*

The newspapermen embraced the controversy here in Gatlinburg. Imagine a town named for a despised man! That alone made for good copy. But throw in arson charges, fights, women taking sticks to neighbor men, trials, lawsuits, and general stores and roads standing in the middle of all this tug-of-warring, why, the Gatlinburg news filled up half of their papers! And they knew that the folks over in Cades Cove, Maryville, Happy Valley and other nearby places hungered for the news coming out of this tumultuous area. They'd be sure to follow this story, increasing readership and ensuring jobs for the writers. And so, young reporters wrote the following words, with relish, and read the finished product over coffee, along with the rest of the smoky mountain communities who were following a real-life drama playing out in their very own backyards.

"Trial of these defendants, Thomas Ogle Senr, William Ogle known as the son of said Thomas Ogle Senr, Isaac Ogle Senr., Elisha Ogle and a certain Aaron Onsley, was before John T. Havis, justice of the peace on December 20, 1857. Witnesses for the defendants were Levi Ogle, Stephen Huskey, Nathaniel King, and Jesse Stafford. They testified they did not think the Gatlins were in danger from these men "On account of the trial just over about the burning of the barn," that they had not heard the defendants threaten the Gatlins, and that all of the defendants were "Respectable, quiet and truthful men." Justice Havis dismissed the case on the ground that the "prosecution was frivolous" and Gatlin was charged with the costs."

Radford Gatlin was many things, but one thing he wasn't was stupid. And he had deeper insights and reflections than he let on. Oh, he knew full well he didn't get along with hardly a soul, and had thought long and hard about leaving his namesake town. Lately, these thoughts had ramped up considerably. The trial did not go his way—none of them did. And this latest example cut deeper than all of them. *Am I wrong? If so, why? I am just trying to modernize, trying to make a living and bring this town some opportunity. No other town complained about opening stores, establishing a post office, making an access road. No other town complained when men with some money bought up more land. Those events are happening throughout Appalachia, and I never read about complaining in the newspapers by any other town. In fact, they are usually okay with it. Even welcomed the progress and jobs. I don't understand these people. They don't want to progress. Wasn't progress the key to success? Never received so much as a thank you! And yet, they come from near and far to buy sugar any day of the week, and cow bells, and anything else they need or want. I even stock pickles and candy for the children! And all they do is complain about progress. They say they don't want it. But they sure want it when they can buy sugar any day of the week!*

It was incredibly frustrating and Gatlin could not quite understand such deep controversy. He continued to extend what he thought of as olive branches. Inviting everyone over for a cookout in front of the store for New Year's Day, most all residents turned out for the event. Gatlin and his wife greeted everyone warmly, cooked up rabbit stew with dumplings and some salted ham and biscuits. Pies were passed around and preserves were eaten until the children's tongues were blue and black and red. Feelings were cozy that New Year's Day and the

Ogles returned to their homes with high hopes for the coming year. *Perhaps we've seen the biggest part of Gatlin's plans. Now, maybe things will be more of a compromise. More talk and more neighborly gestures. Seems he wants to include us more, tell us what's goin' on, and get our input. He just asked us what we think of a road that anyone can access. A road that can handle wagons, lots of horses. And he listened when we told him it may be a good idea, but the location will be the important thing. He says he won't do it without talkin' it out first. I tell ya, he just may be a changed man. Finally.*

Levi and Thomas Ogle, however, were not convinced as they walked home, and spoke out of earshot of the women, who were gushing over their newfound hope things would settle down.

"The Gospel of Matthew...you know..." Thomas spoke softly. "The wolf that has just softened here in Gatlinburg is false. He is simply disguised in sheep's wool at the moment."

"I believe so too," Levi replied, trudging through the sparse grasses and leaning against the quickening wind. "And not a heavy coat of wool at that. Can see right through that disguise."

"You know how the Cherokee have that wolf story? Something like two wolves are within everyone, one's good and one's bad. They fight within one's head. And the Cherokee—the wise one of 'em—always says, the one who wins is the one you feed. Meanin' you should always feed the good wolf—try to do good. Now, I don't have a fight goin' on inside my head—I know exactly how I feel and my God knows me to be righteous. But He is also practical—we got a fight goin' on *outside* ourselves that's worse. The fight with Gatlin. I say we take that story and turn it around to suit ourselves...let's feed the bad wolf for once so we run 'im outta town. Fight 'im with his own weapons, so to speak. For one, I can go to court just like he can."

Thomas thought a moment and continued, "Because no matter his nice, shiny new wool coat, it's false and strike three *will* occur, mark me on that." Pulling his hat down over his ears, he said the wind was increasing and urged them to hurry home.

"Strike three, indeed. Hope we can wrap up this game of folly once and for all."

Only a few weeks later, this game of folly had the Gatlinburg residents and Radford Gatlin returned to a state of conflict, and all warm feelings from the New Year's cookout had evaporated. Gatlin's side usually struck first and indeed, he wasted no time advancing, but this time, the townspeople used that very same tactic with extreme efficiency. All war is deception. And Gatlin never expected the Ogles to fight in court. But that's exactly what they did, choosing not to wait until Gatlin acquired another strike against him. No, this time, they would be the ones to take action, take control. Besides, there were rumors the Gatlins, despite their New Year's extension of an olive branch, were making inquiries about selling and moving out of the area. Why wait around for that to happen when they could speed up the process?

Thomas Ogle showed up at the courthouse a day or so later and, "Requested the County court, in January 1858, that he be allowed to remove the bars from across the road running through his field and close up said road, which request was granted on the ground that the "road *around* his (Ogle's) field had been opened and in good repair." Gatlin had stormed out of the courthouse in a storm of anger, noticed by everyone.

Thomas, Levi and the rest of the Ogles celebrated that evening. Though not yet Saturday, they had all had baths on account of going to court and were now eating together, and drinking a bit of the moonshine.

"That Gatlin tried to change the road, but I beat 'im to it! See, two can play at this game of folly, but right will always win. Now, the road will not be re-routed to please him and his business interests. We can have our say too!"

The women lamented, "We thought he may be changing. Just a bit. Just enough. Honestly, we thought he wanted to really try to get along with us. But did you see how he stormed off today? After the court hearing? He's madder than a tick on a hound. Sadly, though we all wanted to believe 'im; we was wrong. He hasn't changed at all."

Gatlin was furious, and though he had nothing new he could present at court, no new evidence or witnesses, no new suits, claims, or disputes he could fight, he remedied that quite quickly. Nothing new was no problem. He would simply revisit and reignite prior disputes.

"On March 17, 1858, in a petition filed before the Sevier County Circuit Court for a hearing before the latter (lower) court, Radford Gatlin objected to the procedure in Judge Havis' court." The reporters latched on to yet another feuding Gatlinburg story, but this one had a twist.

"Can you believe that? Havis was the judge who presided over the burnin' of the barn and fields...and now he's not only fightin' the Ogles, he's now fightin' the Judge!"

The newspapers had a field day with this news. The drama seemed ever to escalate here in Gatlinburg! And it always came attached to Mr. Radford Gatlin, the town's namesake. Readers from Maryville, Knoxville, from Cades Cove to Happy Valley, all the way to Charleston, read the news.

Gatlin said that when the peace warrant arrests were made by Constable C.A. Clementson he was "Quite sick and unwell so much so as to be confined to his bed in very bad weather," and that Clementson agreed to bring the defendants to his (Gatlin's) house for trial, but instead "Esq. Havis and defendants and all witnesses went to a small church or meeting house" for the trial, and the "cold and rainy" weather and his "feeble health" prevented him from attending some of the trial. Gatlin also complained that he had no witnesses and that the bill of costs, about thirty dollars, was exorbitant. Gatlin's petition was dismissed by Thomas W. Hurley, circuit judge, but his appeal to the Supreme Court was granted. Again the higher court affirmed the decision of the local court; thus, Gatlin lost again in his recourse to the courts to obtain a redress of his grievances against the White Oak Flats natives."

The reporters couldn't help putting in a bit of questioning conjecture at the end of the article. After all, they had to keep readers enticed with this human drama.

"Multiple reports have indicated Mr. Radford Gatlin is considering moving his businesses elsewhere. Will this be the last of the 'lawing between Gatlin and the Ogles?"

Hundreds read the report and wondered the same thing. The Ogles sat back, planted spring crops, watched spring births, noticed the large stag foraging and listening, and ate and drank a little bit more, all while planning the next move. One wolf was indeed emerging and they certainly would continue to feed it bitter and rancid food, to make it go away once and for all.

The next month, in early April of 1858, Gatlin tried his hand in the courts again, filing once more a petition to make a road.

His description changed just enough for persuasiveness: "Alteration in the road in the former White Oak Flats to commence at the mouth of Roaring Fork and running as near as practicable with the river to the upper end of Radford Gatlin's enclosed land thence with the enclosed land on the south side of the fence intersecting the old road at the fork leading to the Glades." This time, he did not mention Caleb Ogle or any of the Ogles. Nor did he mention the town of Gatlinburg, merely referring to it as the former White Oak Flats. Though the judge certainly knew the situation, Gatlin's strategy was to keep this most recent description in his petition focused on himself and his own land.

That made all the difference. The road was approved.

"He did it only for his own benefit! Not the benefit of the town! The road follows *his* fifty acres along the river and on the south side of his fields. He wants to bring more and more people here—people like him!—and change this whole town! We don't want no big city here or anything close to it! And that's what it's gonna be like soon..."

"It's time." the men told each other. "The wolf has now completely shed its wooly sheep coat. It's time to recognize this and feed it as much as possible." they all nodded their heads in unanimous agreement.

"We gonna run him out."

Just a couple of weeks later, in large part due to the new road now open, Daniel W. Reagan began as the first postmaster of Gatlin's General Store; thus far, Gatlin had been operating as his own, unofficial postmaster.

"On April 23, 1858, a mail route was established between Sevierville, and Casher's Valley, South Carolina by way of the new 'Gatlinburg' post office; the mail contractors were Daniel W. Reagan and J.S. Conner who received $309.00 per annum for the weekly roundtrip of 176 miles."

Gatlin was more than happy to embrace the Reagans and, in his eyes, this was but one more example of progress that benefitted the families. After all, now Daniel Reagan of that early and esteemed family, and a relative newcomer, Mr. Conner, would have good, steady incomes. And mail would be faster, more efficient, and overall better. What was the problem?

The newspapers ran the stories: *Gatlin finally won his road. The first postmaster comes to town. All victories for Gatlin. What will he do next in this growing smoky mountain town that bears his name?*

But something strange happened with this victory. Instead of Gatlin celebrating and gloating, he instead lamented how badly the situation in town had deteriorated. He was, of course, happy his hard fought war for his road and other such business interests were finally won, and were finally in place. And he still felt justified for all of his actions. *I feel I was right to do these things. After all, I am an American. And a civilized one at that. A free man in a free country. These men around here, they talk of rifles and staring men down with the barrels and such nonsensical noise, but I use our justice system and somehow, it works. Well, maybe not every time. Not most times, in fact, in my own experience. But in the end at least, it all works out if you try hard enough. And I'll be damned if I'm going to stop fighting for what I believe is right. But how can I live amongst those who think so differently? Wouldn't I be better off in a town that shares my fighting spirit? The good fight mind you...the fight for progress and business and making things better for everyone?*

Oftentimes, the fighter underestimates that other fighters also believe in their own cause and are just as entrenched to fight for their side. And when one realizes the deepness of that entrenchment, they usually stay stuck in place for a long time, striking offensively, and when necessary, waiting and defending. Then, they usually climb up and over, sometimes calling a cease-fire, but mostly spending the rest of the war shooting mad and planning the next move. Until they climb up and over and run so far that they run off the battlefield and into a place where no one is fighting anymore. Then, win or lose, the only thing to do is head back home.

Home to Gatlin was Strawberry Plains in Jefferson County, Tennessee, northwest of Gatlinburg. His old home. Oh, rumors were swirling at his leaving Gatlinburg to return to the Plains, despite his recent court wins and spoken desires for peace.

Some of the rumors were vicious. *His wife, Elizabeth, hated him! She was the one who burned the barn and stables and cattle. Hoping to kill him. He mistreated her.*

Yet others were more pragmatic. *For all he was, he never treated his wife too badly from what I saw. In fact, they always seemed like a team. Why, she seemed tougher than he! I think he was actually scared of her!*

And other rumors, with just as much possibility of truth: *He must've known he wasn't welcome here. We ran him outta town! Even the Cherokees—the few who are left and hiding around here—said a long time ago that they'd name the town after him if he'd just leave!*

Finally, there was wisdom nestled within such talk: *he's a wolf. Strong, powerful, yet cunning and ungracious at the same time. Like the Cherokee's wolf story...the one you feed is the one that'll grow. He just feeds the one who does things without thinking of others. That wolf is too much for us. The very weak good wolf inside him may grow his sheep-coat once or twice a year, but can never shed its natural disposition. He will always shed the wool disguise. Always. He will never fit in.*

For all the bombastic lawsuits and fights, Radford Gatlin finally came to the same conclusion: that he could never grow what he wanted to grow here in Gatlinburg. *Funny, it's my name on this town. Yet, all they did was fight me tooth and nail. And all I wanted to do was make the town better. Make my own way and my own living. A man should be able to do that. Just don't see the harm in it all.* He sighed, saddened that it had turned out like this. Oh, he didn't have to leave. Or even want to. But he was tired of fighting. Tired of being the outcast in a town that adopted his very name! *Oh, the irony. How sad it is that my idea of 'better', and everyone else's ideas were just too different. Thought I was being a strong wolf, just like the Cherokee story. I fed the one that was right—the one who grew and expanded and prospered. The one who could jump fences and bring two different packs together. But there could never be a compromise when the fence between us is too high. And too far away.*

By 1860, Radford Gatlin was gone from the town of Gatlinburg. He left in a hurry, saying goodbye to no one and quietly selling his land and store. The general store and the postmaster continued to run, under new ownership, but it had all been kept very secret. He simply disappeared.

"Guess he finally realized strike three...he's out."

"Good riddance! He was a will o'-the-wisp anyway."

"A what?"

"A will o'-the-wisp...an elusive and sly type. Evasive and undependable."

"Well, I agree 'cept that—say what you will—but he *was* dependable. Always had sugar in his store. Could buy it any day or even late into the night. One time he opened the store for me just so I could get some flour and sugar to make cakes for after Sunday church...remember that picnic where we had those little cakes? Yep, that previous evening, I went to the store and knocked. The door was closed and locked. But he came to the door, all polite-like, and let me buy some sugar. Even said some nice words to me. Wish he coulda been like that all the time ya know?"

"Yep, I agree. He wasn't really sly or elusive...it's just that he put it all out there. He told you what was on his mind. But then again, I can see how he could've been seen as sly and elusive because he went behind our backs and did what he wanted. Like with the road. Oh, we'd talked about it some, here and there perhaps. But in the end, he just did what he wanted."

"It *was* his land...we're always sayin' a man can do what he wants on his own land." They pondered that; yes, they said it all the time, but...this was different somehow...

"Bottom line. He just fought with everyone. And he didn't fit in. Can't put my finger on it 'cept to say he's a difficult sort."

"I think he tried..." They were silent at that, until Charity Ogle had the courage to state her mind.

"Yes. I think he tried too. I do. But in all the wrong ways."

"Funny how certain people rub others the wrong way. All the time. Like they can't help themselves. Or maybe they can and they do it all purpose-like."

"Who knows? Can't figure some folks out. All I can say is what I said before, good riddance."

They paused, taking it all in. Thinking it through. The breezes caressed their calloused farm hands and a large deer stood very close by, yet none of the humans noticed. *William's kinfolk. They are a wise bunch. Practical, yet kind.* The deer was watching the next generation navigate their tough mountain world. He was glad that fiery man and woman had left. *Those two had always tried, but could never find the social graces to allow them to assimilate to William's kind of people. Too bad. It could've been good for*

145

all. Alas, some bits of the nature of humans are too tough to crack open and rearrange. He walked slowly up the slope, the wondering eyes of the humans crowding the treed peaks and hazy sun. *Mountains have a way of peeling back human follies and faults. Some men tried to hide who they truly were, hiding behind a rock or drowning most of their spoken thoughts with the roar of the creek. But nature knows better. It softens the flow, edges the rock away, and always urges on the sprout of true nature, where it grows to the sunlight, visible to all. A gateway to the soul.* The deer walked higher, still listening to the spoken thoughts of these humans that could never be drowned out by a busy creek.

"It's like he came here, like a gateway to a new life. Instead, that gateway ran into an end just like a closed water chute. What do they call it? A dead end."

"Gatlin's Gateway will lead to something else now. Not to his new life, and not to any one man's new life either. It'll lead to something else...bigger than all of us."

"Why d'ya say that? That's almost like foretellin' the future...do ya think somethin' will happen to Gatlinburg?"

"Oh, I don't know. It's growing, that's for sure. Gatlin's store and road and such certainly made us known."

"And we do have beautiful surroundings. I wonder if someone will come along one day and snatch up our land. Make it so they want to "share" it with everyone. I kinda think that was Gatlin's vision all along. Building a town, getting people to come and know it and sharing it with others."

"As long as he controlled it of course!"

"True!"

"Well, now playin' his advocate for a moment...wouldn't we all do what he did?"

"Not sure we'd do exactly what he did. Would sure be more neighborly about it. But I catch what you're sayin'. Heck, if we could open a general store, get a postmaster in here, buy up land and build roads, wouldn't we do it too?"

They had to admit they would.

Radford Gatlin was never seen in Gatlinburg again. But from time to time, the healthy and hearty community heard about the difficult man and his wife.

"Gossip somehow travels along these ridges! Amazin'! It's like that new machine built by Samuel Morse way back in 1835—the telegraph they call it."

"But ya know it wasn't 'til 1844 until they transmitted anythin'."

"Ah. A long time ago now. But d'ya know what that first transmission said? I read it in the papers…"

"What? Come get some of the best 'shine up yonder in them Smoky Mountains?" They laughed at that.

"Don't let Mama hear ya! She and Pa have some ever so often, but they'd take a switch to us if they hear us talkin' about it!"

"Chestnut Flats people…you know them. Over by Cades Cove. They're all 'shiners. All of 'em! Well, most of 'em anyway. Oh, there's some fine folks there. Some. Not too many though. Hear they have other stuff goin' on there too."

"Like what?"

"Well, girls who…don't quite stay close to their mamas….ya know what I mean?"

"Hmmm…Maybe a trip up there would do us good."

The girls threatened to tell the boys' mamas. "Oh, we was just jokin'!"

"But imagine if the Gatlins wound up there! Oh, what a hoot!"

"Now that would be funny. He'd either whip 'em all into shape or increase their 'shine production a hundred fold! Imagine the newspaper stories if Gatlin and the Chestnut Flats folk mixed up…" They laughed at the thought of such people trying to exist together in the same tiny mountain town. "What a disaster that'd be! Rifles would be pointed day and night. Doubt they would last even five days and nights…"

"Oh now, hush up! I want to know, what did they transmit on that tele-machine?"

"Oh, yes. The telegraph. The first message was: *What Hath God Wrought.*

"My goodness, our world is changing. Sendin' messages all over!"

"Well, God hath wrought Radford Gatlin for a few years. But he sure placed him somewhere else—yessir. I agree it's like he used this place as his gateway and, even though he tried to tear this place apart, I thank the Lord for his coming here. There's some good stuff we got out of it. Store open all the time. Sure made life easier. Sugar anytime we want it. Them cowbells and pickles. Can post a letter every few days. Or at least once a week. Receive more newspapers and such so we know what's goin' on. And now, God hath wrought Gatlin somewhere else. Lord knows, wherever he winds up, and whatever good he manages to bring, people will need more than the 'shine to get 'em through his wrath." Laughing, they walked along the dusty road toward the Ogle porch.

"Aw, c'mon now, was he really that bad?"

The deer listened for any response. There was none. And as the hearty humans walked away, even the busy creek could not compete with the deafening silence.

CHAPTER TEN

1860s
The Civil War

W HEN STARTING CROPS, seeds are the first things in the ground. They must be planted, watered, and patiently waited on to break through ground toward the sun and growth. Likewise, seeds are needed for conflict and war; ideas must be planted, watered, waited on, and then all that patience pays off when one day too many people think the same way. It is this single-mindedness, unencumbered by winds and thunder that grows hardened by droughts lacking the light of human empathy. Want of sensibility's illumination equals the perfect conditions for these particularly dangerous but hearty seeds to flourish.

With Radford Gatlin now gone, the town of Gatlinburg was peaceful once again. The Ogle family still dominated the landscape, and the other families were prosperous, well-fed, and happy. But America was anything but peaceful. Farmers and mountain folk kept up with the news of the day, but it did not run their everyday lives. They were too busy. Tending fields, tending children, tending animals. Cutting, weeding, repairing fences, cabin walls and roofs, chimneys, and fetching water from the creek to wash clothes, cook food, and wash bodies on Saturdays before meeting on the Ogle porch and picking up a banjo and a slice of pie and a little 'shine. Attendance at church and other gatherings—mostly centered around harvests—rounded out the social lives of the people of Gatlinburg. But the larger problems of America did creep in, and when the seeds of civil war took flight on a warm breeze and settled on their mountain land, it left an indelible mark on their way of life. Forever.

It was known that Radford Gatlin was a Confederate sympathizer, which amongst "a million other reasons" was just one more to run him out of town. Even before the war began, his southern leanings put him at odds with the rest of the community who generally sympathized more with the Union side of things. The families of Gatlinburg may not have understood every single nuance to the issues swirling around the country, but they did understand the basics of the power of industrial jobs and interests in the north, and the sustaining crops and need for labor in the south. They certainly understood the slave uprising way back in 1831, led by Nat Turner, frightening many slave owners who stepped up patrols for runaways and tightened the rules of assembly and movement of slaves. And they understood that Tennesseans had an honored tradition of serving their nation, which they were very proud of. Yet at the same time, they understood that the south was very different from the north, that they had very different needs and lifestyles, values and traditions. A very balanced and practical people, they wished there could be a compromise. But the desire of the north for control and bigger government, and the desire of the south to oppose government interference of the agrarian way of life, had stoked the fires of the people to the point where no compromise of economics and political control could be had.

As the Gatlinburg residents read their newspapers, the list got longer: "And so one after one, here are the states that have seceded: South Carolina, Mississippi, Florida, Alabama, Georgia, Louisiana and Texas. And four more threatened secession: Virginia, Arkansas, Tennessee, and North Carolina."

"My word. We're goin' to war against our own people!"

"Well, we supposed to be one country but really, we're two."

"We're even more than two. Lots of ways to do things. Maybe too many. I much prefer to think we're part of America, but then we sort of also have our own little country goin' on right here in the mountains. You can think of it that way, our own little country. Got our own way of living. And we sure don't want those factory men tellin' us how to farm any more than they want us tellin' them how to make their steel and railroads."

"Why can't they let us be?"

"Because they just can't."

"No they *can*. They just won't."

"Man, Ogle. No truer words were spoken."

On April 12, 1861, the war between the states began with shots fired at Fort Sumter, South Carolina. This was after a decade or more of John Calhoun's planting the seeds of secession. After a Confederate Constitution was created in February, 1861. After Jefferson Davis was named President of the Confederacy. After March 4th, when Abraham Lincoln was inaugurated, stating he had no plans to end slavery where it already existed, but he would also not accept secession of any states.

"But they already seceded. Whether he accepts it or not."

The seeds of war broke through and grew with amazing speed; day after day the bruised clouds and dim sun witnessed the roots growing deeper and deeper. Despite its sentiments landing on the Union side, Gatlinburg like most mountain communities, tried to remain neutral. They busily went on with the routines of their lives. But then, something happened to change that.

The corn was in its earliest infancy for the season of 1861. April saw the farmers planting and filling their rows and rows of cropland. The weather was a bit colder than usual, and they just had a late snowfall of nine inches.

"That almanac says we're in for a warmer season and cloudier than normal. Rainy."

They were so busy checking the weather—the biggest factor for those who relied on the land—that they didn't have much time to think about politics and such. Children ran around, busy with chores and play, and women sat at their looms on the breezy front porches, stirring the stew in the pot every so often, and chatting with visitors about gossip, how tall this child was growing, how that one fared with his cough, how fair this young girl was, how skilled that other girl was with the gun. And then when their small world's issues were hashed out, when these men would stop this newest war against our very own.

It was during one of the finer days, deep in the springtime when the warmth was welcomed and the valley was in early bloom that the war that had thus far stayed beyond the protection of the mountains, showed up firmly on their doorstep.

"Who is that comin' up the road?" Charity Ogle put down her sewing and stood up. Squinting to see, she saw the man wasn't alone. There were a lot of men. "Why, those are soldiers!"

"And look. They ain't in blue."

"Jesus..."

The women scrambled inside the closest cabins and barns to grab rifles and long needles, knives and scissors, axes and such, all while frantically yelling at the fields for their men. Of course, the men, while working their fields had also seen this warring group walking toward them on the road, and were now running at full speed toward their respective homesteads, rifles at the ready. They managed to congregate in record time at the edge of the road; even children watched from behind trees and brush, directed by their parents to stay back and run up the slopes to hidden hollers if needed.

"We're here to hunker down a bit!" A company of Confederates arrived within feet of the Gatlinburg residents who were, by now, as heavily armed as they could be.

For their part, the soldiers did not even touch their arms, entering as non-threateningly as possible.

Tipping his hat, the soldier in front spoke. "Colonel William Holland of Thomas' Legion here."

To their surprise, some Cherokee Indians were also part of the group. And the women noticed many soldiers looked very young. And hungry. And barefoot.

"Folks. We need to stay put here to protect the saltpeter mines at Alum Cave. Need it for gunpowder."

"Alum Cave? That's near the Tennessee and North Carolina border! Why'nt you just go there?"

"Cause ya'll got a nice town goin' here. There ain't nothin' over at the caves. We need to eat. Sleep. It's near enough."

"Well now, don't know how much hospitality we could offer. We really stay outta this war. Tend our own land. No industry here. No slaves here. No need for government; we run our own lives."

"That's alright with us. Stay outta the war if you want. Take sides. Whatever it is you want to do. We are going to be here for a long time, so we may as well get along. We will be as respectful as possible toward you folks. But we are going to stay."

Residents sent word out through the postmaster, who alerted federal forces, asking them to intervene and force the Confederate Army to leave. As soon as possible.

But despite repeated efforts, two years passed before the armies finally met; Union soldiers taking that much time to travel to the rural area. They had run into skirmishes along the way, greatly slowing them down, dwindling their ranks, forcing rearranging and reinforcing. In the meantime, Colonel Holland and his Confederate soldiers kept busy mining at Alum Cave, all the while keeping watch for any hint of interference. Of which there was none, for what seemed like a very long time. Residents grudgingly fed, housed and tolerated the soldiers through the cycles of the seasons, hoping the Union army could arrive. As the days marched on though, it all appeared as if this war of brothers would never end, that the young country would be left bleeding and lifeless, under blackened, unblinking skies, one lone stag simply watching and recording yet another dark chapter of the history of these human creatures.

But the time of peace for the Confederate Army that had settled into the Gatlinburg area to mine saltpeter did run out on one snowy day, December 10, 1863, when federal troops, wrapped in warm blue coats, finally showed up. Soldiers in blue had "marched south from Knoxville and Sevierville to drive out Thomas' men, who had built a small fort on Burg Hill."

The Ogles, of course, were witness to it all:

Here I am, a sixteen-year-old boy during the Civil War and hiding under a big cliff on Turkey Nest Ridge and watching the Blue Coats ride their horses around the graveyard hill, shooting their cannon toward Burg Hill where the Grey Coats had a fort and would ride their horses around the Burg Hill...

The Union forces converged on the small smoky mountain town daring the ragged band of southern soldiers to fight against their large numbers. Though spirited, the obviously outnumbered Confederates were forced to retreat across the Smokies to North Carolina. After all, they didn't have enough ammunition for the number of men running them down on horseback, nor did they have enough food or even shoes. No men were killed, but shots were exchanged and several men were wounded. The Confederate soldiers did not return to the area after that, although "sporadic small raids continued until the end of the war, harassing residents and animals alike." Many a night when cows and horses clanged around the barn, restless from sneaky human activities, and quite a few chickens seemingly disappeared overnight.

As the war continued, most residents still sympathized with the Union, but not all. Confederate leanings were few but were more fervent. And when one of their own was involved, it was all they could talk about.

"John Reagan. Remember him? Born right here in Gatlinburg in 1818. Well, it was White Oak Flats then. Reagans came in shortly after Martha settled here in 1807. Well, remember John moved to Texas when he reached adulthood? Always had that wanderlust about him. Always sayin' he'd get away from these mountains and have some adventure. Find some adventure to life."

"*Find* adventure? Find adventure indeed! Why go find it...we live it every day. It lives around these parts like wildfire."

"Right so. Bears give us enough adventure. That and the Ogle girls. They make us spend our lives like we had another in the bank." Chuckling, the boys winked at that.

"Anyways, Reagan's been in the Texas House of Representatives, the U.S. House and Senate and now, he's up for the Postmaster General and Secretary of Treasury for the Confederate States of America. The one led by Jeff Davis."

"Well, he always was a leader. Led us all over these hills when we was young. And I don't think it's fair to say he's *on the other side* like a lot of folks are sayin'. This war has a lot of sides, lots of hoppin' the fence. I mean, we don't use slaves. We work our own land. But the south, they got such land to work! How're they gonna do it all without labor? And why should the north run everythin' in America? Don't the south have a say so?"

"Yeah, I see that. Though I still would like to till my own soil with my own hands. But now, here's another side: they're all factory owners and businessmen up north. Will they themselves fight? No. Also, they're all elite landowners there in the south. If they start a war, will they themselves fight? Also, no! It'll be a rich man's war but a poor man's fight. On both sides."

"Ah, I see that. We'll have to actually fight and eat hardtack all day and night. But they'll sit in their comfortable offices and plantations, readin' all about it in the papers, never even shootin' a rifle!"

"Or even loading one. And the north, who we're aligned with mind you, well, they ain't no saints neither. Lincoln wants to send all the Negroes to Liberia! Doesn't necessarily want 'em mixin' with everyone."

"Guess it ain't so black and white, so to speak, as everyone thinks it is."

Mmm hmm. Boys nodded their heads.

"Lots of hoppin' back and forth over the fence."

Union forces roamed all through the Smoky Mountains during those years. Late at night, at a place not too far away, some fifty federal soldiers were resting from their wounds on the upper floor of the Old Mill, a place over in Pigeon Forge, the site of an old iron forge built long ago in 1820. The other half of the name *Pigeon Forge* came from passenger pigeons that frequented the banks of the Little Pigeon River.

"Those birds were in such numbers that they darkened the sky as they flew into the valley and the beech trees along the river were stripped of limbs by the weight of their great numbers."

"I heard about them pigeons. There's an Indian story about them. Let's see if I can recall... In about May of 1850, a young tribal leader named Simon—he may've been about twenty years old—was camping when a loud sound startled him. He said, "It seemed as if an army of horses laden with sleigh bells was advancing through the deep forests toward me. As I listened, I concluded the horses may have just been thunder. Yet, the morning was clear, calm and beautiful. But the sound came nearer and nearer until I saw it. While I gazed in wonder and astonishment, I beheld moving toward me in an unbroken front, millions of pigeons."

"Pigeon Forge." the Ogle boys chuckled. "I hear the pigeons on the river banks are so many you can't even walk by the Old Mill without wading through 'em all. It's like they've got two rivers—one is water and the other is pigeons."

"Well, the owner of the Old Mill, John Sevier Trotter, supports the Union. He's a big supporter. And he put looms in the mill and has been makin' Union-blue uniforms for the soldiers. Fine material, from what I hear. And, on the third floor where the air is clearer, he uses it as a hospital to tend to the wounded soldiers."

"I even hear he tended a few Confederate soldiers there. Just a few, mind. But John does have a heart even if his sympathies lay firmly with our nation." One of the Reagan boys offered.

"I hear the two sides—a few Union soldiers and 'bout two Confederate boys—were all healin' from gunshot wounds. Well, the postmaster reported they all formed up a group one late night and sang, "O Susannah!"

"Oh yes! That famous song! We play it on the front porch of the Ogles on Saturday nights. Least, we used to before the war. Less so nowadays. And folks played it while travelin' to the gold rush in California. I've been tryin' to play it on my banjo...been a while since I tried though."

"Well, both sides know the song. Our two halves of our country never felt further apart, but somehow one song brings us together."

"Well now, it's funny. See here. The Union sang the song, yet it has some southern pride in it: *I come from Alabama with a banjo on my knee....I says, I'se coming from de souf.* But Confederates also sang the song...some say some of the words are really cheerin' on a runaway slave as he fought and died for the right to preserve the south's plantations. *It rained all night the day I left, the weather it was dry. The sun so hot I froze to death...* Both sides layin' there in the Old Mill in Pigeon Forge seemed to be reassuring themselves that in the end, all would be alright and there could be good found from either side you're on: *Susannah, don't you cry...* Somehow, this song is liked by everyone."

One song, sung by both sides. The war raged on.

It was the morning of April 9, 1865 and the deer was foraging for early spring shoots. A beautiful and cool spring day emerged as former West Point student, General Ulysses S. Grant accepted former West Point superintendent, General Robert E. Lee's surrender. Far away, at Wilmer McLean's house in the village of Virginia's Appomattox Courthouse, the two men exchanged a few respected shared remembrances, treated one another with deference and the victor said that he, "Felt like anything rather than rejoicing at the downfall of a foe who had fought so long and valiantly and had suffered so much for a cause though that cause was, I believe, one of the worst for which a people ever fought, and one for which there was the least excuse. I do not question, however, the sincerity of the great mass of those who were opposed to us."

Lee ordered his Confederate army soldiers not to take up arms against the U.S. government, and informed them they would be allowed to return to their homes immediately, with their horses and their guns. Just in time for planting season back home on the plantations and farms.

The deer stopped just then, listening. Tilted his head with the budding crown of new antlers. Yes, there it was, rising from still sharp breezes. Notes sung from the depths of human souls—all of the men in gray and in blue saying the same words in imperfect harmony:

Appomattox, here the officers of both armies came in great numbers, and seemed to enjoy the meeting as much as though they had been friends separated for a long time while fighting battles under the same flag. For the time being it looked very much as if all thought of the war had escaped their minds.

The voices floated up from the grove of trees. Not too thickly planted, the cool shade beneath the spreading branches were of a good height and afforded refuge from the burning heat of war. The men's musical talk spread over all of America, arriving to envelop his own dark brown body as he lay down in his bed, listening to the gentle sounds as it aided the whisperings of woods and winds with ever-sweeter melodies. He slept, sporadically at first, as deer tend to do. Always on watch. But tonight, after four long years, knowing that no protection from rifles and barefooted men in gray clothes was needed, he slipped into a dream.

CHAPTER ELEVEN

Aftermath

THE DEER AWAKENED, stood for a moment and began walking; sniffing the air, carefully heading down a slope toward the town. The valleys were now cleared of most of the dead smoke, yet wisps of divisive hardship still lingered. Reconstruction had begun.

The Civil War in America touched everyone, even in the most remote places of the young country. Certainly the Ogle family and Gatlinburg community felt the sadness, anger and uncertainty of the greater nation. Yet, they largely continued the way they always did; farming their land, raising their families, and making their unique mark on Appalachian history with their fierce family loyalties, self-reliance skills, and the desire to live on their own terms. They were, almost all of them, descendants of England, Scotland, Ireland and Germany, having come to America just like William Ogle's parents. Many had been supporters of William of Orange, the Protestant King of Scotland, England, and Ireland, whom the Scots still called "King Billy" when telling folklore.

"You know, that's where the word "hillbilly" came from." Levi Ogle told the story on a day when the fields were ripening under a smiling sun. A group of children was also listening.

"When James II invaded Ireland way, way back in 1689, William of Orange's followers 'came known as "Billyboys." They hid out in the forests and hills and attacked in sneak attacks. When our ancestors came here to America, British set-tlers were already all over the place and so us "Billyboys" came a bit south and settled here into the hills of Appalachia. Billyboys and hills. Hillbillies."

"Is that right?"

"Interesting...I never knew where that sayin' come from."

"Yessir. Think on it. Bill is short for William. So, Billy, and his followers were boys...Billyboys. Hills and Billyboys don't go together very well. Can you imagine hillsbillyboys? Or billhill-boys? Billyhillboys? Too hard to say. But hillbillies...now that rolls right off the tongue."

"To think—William of Orange made his mark all the way over here in the deep hills of America. Goes to show how small the world really is...when somethin' directly connects us all the way from the stone castles of England to our wood cabins here in Gatlinburg. Kings and Hillbillies. It's all one world."

"Kings and hillbillies!" The children chanted it all the way home.

One of William and Martha Ogle's descendants, Mary Ogle Maples, was married to David C. "Crockett" Maples. Born in 1840, Crockett, as they called him, served as Private and Corporal in Company H, Ninth Tennessee Cavalry, from October 1, 1863, through June 8, 1865. Led by Colonel Joseph H. Parsons, the Ninth Tennessee Cavalry was "assigned to small towns and communities across southwest Virginia, eastern Kentucky and east Tennessee." These soldiers were not equipped very well at all—hungry, cold, and even barefoot sometimes. Crockett was honorably discharged when the company mustered out of service on September 11, 1865, in Knoxville, Tennessee.

When his service was completed, Crockett returned to his wife, Mary, in their home just north of Gatlinburg, with strong confidence and belief that he could face any adversity.

"Now that I'm home, I figure on a small supply store at the base of Mount LeConte. I reckon a good many travelers and even locals would need supplies and this is the perfect place for it. In fact, I want to make them my world famous pancakes. My breakfasts will be the best in the country. Maybe even the world!"

"Oh, Dave...that's a great idea!" The rest of the Ogle and Maples family agreed. "Especially your pancakes. I don't know how you do it. But they are the best around."

Soon Mary and David Maples were known for "Serving hungry travelers the best home-cooked breakfast in the Smoky Mountains."

"Grits, eggs, bacon, my special thick pancakes...heck, we can start a breakfast tradition here in Gatlinburg!" David chuckled, proud of his growing reputation.

Mary laughed. "Surely, we can."

The couple proved very self-sufficient. Mary, from Ogle stock, was particularly resilient, raising seven children—her eighth currently on the way—while her husband was frequently away. But one night in the winter of 1875, proved almost too much for even Mary to take.

Sitting by the fire, she has just said goodnight to their guest—a traveling salesman—who spoke of traveling to the town of Cherokee. "But I am not sure the exact way, and I would like a guide to lead the way."

"I'll do it." David jumped at the chance for adventure. "We can take the horse and load up your supplies. Can take turns ridin', walkin'..."

David Maples was born on October 20, 1840, and had grown up about two miles from the Gatlinburg Post Office. "As a boy, he learned to trap, hunt, and fish throughout the Smokies, and to tame the rugged terrain into productive farmland. He was a skilled outdoorsman and confident in his ability to survive in the harsh, uncertain times in which he lived." He even "conducted the postal service and delivered mail from Sevierville on horseback." In other words, he knew these mountains as well as anyone ever could.

Which is why it bothered Mary that, despite knowing her husband's formidable wilderness skills, she had such an ominous feeling about him guiding the traveling salesman over to Cherokee. Polly, as Mary Ogle Maples was called, "had observed the rhododendron leaves curling into tight pencil-shaped rolls, unusual squirrel and bird activity, or one of numerous other folk signs pioneers relied on to predict the weather." And she just knew that particularly bad weather was coming. "She had an unexplainable gut feeling she could not shake."

A man's word being his bond, her husband left early the next morning with the salesman. Sitting by the fire that very night, the snow clouds began forming. Known as "Crockett", her six-foot-three-inch blue-eyed and blond-haired husband had caught her eye from the start. Growing up in the same area, they knew each other's families and of course, a girl from the Ogle family was deemed a catch. She was twenty-five, and he was only twenty-one when they married on March 17, 1860. A nice wedding in the church, family and friends gathering afterward at the Ogle front porch to share food, good wishes and a bit of 'shine to toast to the future.

The weather was certainly noticed by Crockett, but he was confident in his survival skills to make it back home. "Heck," he told the salesman as they watched the clouds roll over the hills, "I earned my survival skills barefoot in snow, never enough to eat. Ate bark right off the trees some nights. But I always make it back home." With that, he led the horse south through Gatlinburg and the neighboring Sugarlands community and headed up the crest of the Smokies. Riding into the valley, switching back and forth across the slopes so the horse would retain its footing, the weather closed in on them.

Polly, by the fire, sat rubbing her belly, pregnant with their eighth child, while keeping an eye on the seven others, aged one through fifteen. She saw the snow and visibility decreasing with each minute. Snow began to fall steadily and heavy winds soon created massive snowdrifts. It was now well below freezing, and she worried more about David right now than when he was at war. At least, in war, they had help. Other soldiers. Supplies, even if they were nothing more than hardtack. Or bark from trees. Someone always knew where they were. Someone would always look for missing soldiers. She wondered how they all kept track of one another in the woods, hills, valleys, caves and everywhere else a man could find himself in the rugged wilderness of these mountains. She sat in front of the fire and fretted.

Crockett guided his client all the way to the path toward the town of Cherokee. Pointing the way to his companion, Crockett helped him gather his goods that were hauled by his horse, told the man to continue straight until he'd reached an even lower valley, and then he would see the town of Cherokee. "You will know it because you'll see Indians out and about. They may hide a bit, but you'll still see 'em."

"I thought most of the Indians went west? Thought I'd be sellin' mainly to white men." the traveling salesman questioned.

"Most did. But some stayed and hid in these mountains after the Indian removal. They hid so well, they were never found. And some even walked back from Oklahoma! Imagine that! Removed, walked to Oklahoma then became resolved to walk back home, hidin' all along the way. And now, they stay around this town they named for themselves, and most of 'em even show their faces. No more paint or feathers or disguises. 'Cause nobody bothers them now. They're here to stay. There's some whites around. But you'll see lots of Indians."

Crockett bid goodbye; the traveling salesman confident he could reach Cherokee and sell his wares to the Indians, who, he was assured, were more and more eager to continue and increase trade. Crockett looked up at the sky, closed his jacket a bit tighter, and started his horse back up the mountain. *I'll have to hurry to outrun this storm. But if I don't, I will hunker down 'til it passes.* He knew these mountains like nobody else and knew caves, hollers, and sheltered outcrops. There was no worry whatsoever, just a bit of inconvenience may lie ahead. His horse was hearty and had been through many smoky mountain winters.

But the storm had other plans. Soon, it had David "Crockett" Maples firmly in its grip, relentlessly pouring snow upon him and his horse. *I can't see the trail anymore.* He squinted, trying to keep the snow out of his eyes and get his bearings. But it was to no avail. The blizzard had enveloped every direction and there was nothing left to see. Survival skills set in. *When in doubt, stop. Just stop and stay. Have to let this storm pass. Surely it was furious, but it likely will be over just as quickly.* He dismounted from his horse, who was still very calm and sturdy, was fortunate enough to find a large hollow log, crawled inside and looked out at his world. Food, he had, but as the violent hours raged forward, he had no more clothes to put on, and nothing to shelter him save for a crumbly hollow log. Distrusting thoughts crept in no matter how he tried to stop them and no matter how against his very nature they were. *This is bad. Never seen a storm like this.* And, as the snow piled up, the icy fall stinging his limbs, his mind told him the truth: *I doubt I will see the light of another day.*

Back at home by the fire, with the swirling snow beating at the tightly latched door, Polly did not allow any of the children to fetch as much as a pint of milk from the cows in the barn. No, they'd make do with the leftover stew in the pot, constantly kept warm in the kettle hanging in the hearth, and the small cakes she had baked a couple of days ago. Thank goodness their supply of logs was adequate. If not, during a break, she may walk outside to the pile right outside the porch. But so far, she had only placed her chair close to the door, listening for any indication of her husband. The children kept busy reading their primers from the schooling she gave them in the afternoons, and in between, the girls sewed and the boys whittled wood and cleaned their rifles.

Looking around, she saw her children silent, absorbed in what they were doing, yet distracted and worried. *Have to be strong for them. For myself. How to pass these hours that never moved forward?*

"This will not do!" she said suddenly and walked to the shelves, unwrapped a loaf of bread from a cloth and told them all to sit around, spread some butter on the bread, and listen. She opened up the family Bible and began: "Be strong and bold; have no fear or dread of them because it is the Lord your God who goes before you. He will be with you, He will not fail you or forsake you. Do not fear or be dismayed." As she read to her children, the words provided some comfort, but as she listened to the unrelenting storm and snow piling up in drifts as she peeked out the door, and with no means of communication with her husband or even with neighbors, she "prayed and worried, hoping for the best and fearing the worst." Putting the children to bed after wiping buttery crumbs off their faces, she sat and listened to the wind that reported absolutely nothing to the lonely, scared, pregnant wife.

Crockett awakened and was immediately amazed he had not frozen to death in the night. And there was his horse! He could see his surroundings now, snow softly falling, but no longer whipping the landscape into a complete whiteout. Stomping around and in constant motion, the hearty horse had survived. Giving a little laugh, he saw that his horse had as many survival skills and will to live as he. But as he stretched and tried to stand, he found his legs wouldn't work. Numb. So numb he felt like he was dragging around two weighty logs. It took all his will and strength, and at least an hour, to mount his horse, and, breathing heavily with equal parts pain and grit, rode several miles down the mountain until he found the nearest house. Of course, he knew who would be inside—knew every inch of these mountains and every family—and he knew if he could just make it there, make it to a fire, and make it to some hot food....

David Brackins was holed up with his family just like all other families during this terrible storm. He kept busy, as mountain folk do, whittling a small bear for one of his children and cleaning his many rifles. He had just put another log on the fire and stirred the pot of stew while his wife's fingers were busy with her embroidery. "Makin' another pillow?" he asked his wife. And she smiled and nodded. Their beds were piled high with embroidered pillows, her specialty.

"Hello?!" A voice from outside the cabin. "Need help...."

"What the..." Brackins grabbed his rifle and listened at the door. Horse hoofs. Who was traveling now, after the worst storm he'd ever seen? Cracked open the door just enough to hear the thud on the porch. Gripping his rifle, he steadily opened the door, only to find David "Crockett" Maples collapsed on the porch.

"Crockett! What…?" He quickly lifted the man to a sitting position and looked into his face. Gaunt, sickly and pale.

"Caught in the storm…" was all he could manage.

"How did you make it…" he whispered to his friend, as he hooked two arms under him and tried to drag him as gently as possible.

"Come quick!" he yelled to his wife, who threw down her embroidery and came running, as Brackins reached the door-way. The children also came scurrying from the upstairs loft.

Warmth embraced Crockett for the first time in days as they carried him inside the cozy cabin and laid him on a bed, covering him with every quilt they had.

"Go." He told two of his oldest sons. "Take the horses. The storm has let up. Send word to Polly Maples…she must be worried sick." The two teenage Brackins sons dressed as quickly as they could, took some biscuits and dried deer meat, and hurried over the mountain. The snow crunched under the horses' hooves and though it was still incredibly cold, visibility was excellent.

⌒⊙⊙⌒

Banging on the door of the Maples home, it was immediately opened by Polly, who heard the horses coming up to their homestead. She braced herself for bad news, hoping it wouldn't send her into early labor. Her belly was awfully big and the baby had seemed to drop just yesterday. Her time was quickly approaching, but she knew there was about another month to go. Eight month babies were usually fine, but it was always best to keep them developing for the entire time allotted by nature.

"Mrs. Maples! We got your husband!"

"He's alive. We're nursin' him. But his legs don't work. Come quick."

Legs don't work? But he's alive! She caught her breath, couldn't breathe quite right, didn't know what her husband's condition would truly be. *Legs don't work.* But she knew, with those three words, that their lives had just changed. *I hope he's still the same man. Hope he's not all still-like, like a tree. Oh my goodness, what if....* Oh, she could not think of it now. *One thing at a time. Don't go into labor. Take deep breaths. Send the boys. Stay here with the younger ones. Once they bring him home and I see him for myself, I can tell what to do. How it will be. Still, he's alive! Amazing. He really can survive anything. Damn that man.*

Mary Ogle Maples sent her oldest boys back with the Brackins sons', along with some other relatives they rounded up thanks to the quick thoughts and even quicker little feet of children.

"Pa's alive! He's down at Brackins'. We gotta go get him!" Excitedly, they ran around to all the closest log cabins and within minutes amassed a party to retrieve their fellow Ogle family member.

The Ogles always, always stuck together, pulled together whenever a crisis occurred, and were a very resourceful and industrious bunch. Within half an hour, a homemade litter of strong logs and crisscrossed smaller branches was made, lashed together with sinew and some rope, cloth and quilts piled high upon the lattice-like structure.

"Here," Mary said, pushing two loaves of fresh bread onto the litter, "Take this to your parents and express our deepest thanks and gratitude," she told the two sons of their neighbors.

"Yes, ma'am."

Carrying the litter, the party made its way to the Brackins' homestead. Smoke was rising out of the chimney as they approached and some of the younger children were waiting outside. Upon seeing the small crowd, they alerted their parents, who helped carry David "Crockett" Maples, husband of Mary Ogle, to the litter. As they placed him as gently as they could, and covered him with quilts, he bid his goodbyes with gratitude. "Thank you, Brackins, Mrs. Brackins. I'll be alright. Don't know about my legs though. But I will be fine. You saved me. I can't thank you enough." There were tears in his eyes, shocking for such a formidable man. Mr. and Mrs. Brackins bid their good-byes: "Happy to help, just get better now ya hear? Send word about how you're gettin' along."

Each of the sturdy boys took turns gripping the ends of the thick parallel logs that made up the frame of the litter. Lashing it to the horse would've made it too bumpy and may cause his deteriorated body more damage. Luckily, the snowy track they had made on the way was still present, making the return trip much easier and quicker.

Groaning at times, and sometimes falling into a groggy sleep, Crockett was carried home to a crowd of relatives who were already cooking, cleaning, preparing a fresh bed with piles of quilts, gathering more firewood, making sure the animals were tended to, and providing moonshine to ease the shock. "And to provide anesthesia", they secretly whispered, if past experience proved a grim prediction of what may come. *Frostbite, I imagine. Can't walk, they said. If he was injured, then he surely has frostbite. Even if he wasn't injured, he probably still has the frostbite. The foot and leg die. Turn white. Then black. Then, it's gotta come off. Or he will surely die. Better to lose legs than to die.*

The women whispered and tried to remember if they had rosehip from their pink and orange summer flowers. Dried, the blooms kept nicely in jars for a long time. *Good for healin' frostbite. At least a bit. Some kind of vitamin in it. Put it in hot water and make a tea. You know, my Luke was out one day, too long in an icy storm, and his feet turned white. Couldn't feel 'em. Well, he drank rose hip and sage and he's fine now. Gets a bit stiff when the wind blows too hard, but he has his foot and all his toes. Thank the good Lord. Do we have any sage? No? How about an onion poultice? I've got a few onions stored...I'll run and get them...grind them up so we can rub it on the skin. That works real well, so long as it's before the black settles in the skin. Better get that jug of whiskey too. Yes, two jugs would be better. All that you can spare.*

The mountains possess multiple personalities. Some peaks have rough, ragged and heavily bearded slopes, others have agreeable lines etched into their faces, soft trees standing tall in their proud solitude. Romantic and mysterious, they are great listeners but demand the same in return. All mountains show their adventurous side, wild-haired and free, and keep their residents embraced in their special brand of peace and treachery. Mountains show their love in meaningful ways, yet can also challenge that love. *We are what we are,* they say. *Respect us and life is closest to God you will*

ever be, the soul recognizing its home. Test us and our very nature prevents us from intervening in disaster.

Upon seeing her husband, Mary burst into tears. He couldn't walk. Her big, strapping husband couldn't walk! They had told her, but it was another thing entirely to see it with her own eyes. And he was barely conscious. *My God, what am I going to do? And another baby coming so soon...David! Tell me what happened!* she wanted to scream. But there would be time for that. And it didn't matter what happened or how it happened. She simply had to deal with what had *actually* happened. Damn.

Lifting the quilt, fear forced her stomach to drop to her knees. *Oh no.* And then, *do not go into labor. I need this time with David before this next baby comes.* Placing her hand underneath her belly, she took a breath, held it until the knot loosened, and forced herself to get busy.

"Get the doctor, please. Tell him it's...the feet...they are rotten." She took another deep breath, held it, sat in a small chair by the bedside, and slathered onion poultice on the wounds, knowing it wouldn't matter. But she needed to do something. Packing onion paste onto the black flesh, urging rosehip tea, praying to God, more onions, her eyes tearing at the fumes. She couldn't stop herself from patting more and more onion onto her husband's charred feet. *Charred*...she almost laughed. *They look burnt, but heat had nothing to do with this. If only he had had heat... didn't he have a match? Couldn't he have started a fire?* But of course, he couldn't. She knew her husband. Anything he could've done, he would've. He knew how to listen to the mountains and knew when they had turned their backs to the wishes of humans. He had done everything he could. *I need more onions.*

Someone took her arm, gently, and lifted her to her feet. "Stop, Mary. Onions won't help. Come, come outside for some air." Sighing, she stood and then felt a familiar hand reach out to her.

And then, a weak voice. "Polly dear, you've already seasoned me quite well. Please don't smear any more onion on me. It won't work. And it stinks to high heaven. Why I smell like a vinegary garlicky squirrel and I'm about to scoop up all that onion paste sittin' on my feet and throw it all in the pot..." he managed a pained chuckle. "God I'm hungry."

"David!" She laughed softly, but then put her hands to her face and burst into tears because she knew then, in hearing the familiar humor in her husband's voice, that no matter what happened, he would live. He would be okay.

She was on the front porch, two quilts wrapped around her, holding her belly, waiting for the doctor, when he appeared on the far side of the dry and still-snowy fields on horseback. The wind had died down and it was still. The nearby creek was flowing softly and a large lone stag deer watched from a higher ridge. She blinked, watching the deer's eyes match hers, asking why nature cares not a wink for those who are good. Those who deserve life. How did nature simply turn a blind eye? The deer kept its lock on her eyes, and then lowered his head and walked a little higher.

"Gangrene." the doctor said grimly, feeling the dead feet in his hands, feeling for any pulse, any sign of life. He sighed. There was none. "There's no other choice, ma'am."

"No other choice at all? No more onions? No chance of it at all?"

"None. It's either take them off or let it be and he will be gone within a week. Probably days." She gasped. Shook her head and looked up to find her God. She believed of course, but right now, she could feel nothing. Find nothing.

"It's the only thing we can do." She was told. By whom, she couldn't tell you, because the doctor was now talking outside and most everyone else was with him, whispering, wondering, scared. *I need him. Want him to live. Even if he can't walk. Even if…* she couldn't think just then of all the things that could be, would be, different. Rubbing her belly, trying to stave off the knot and the pressure, she looked at the ceiling of the humble wood cabin. Looked at the fire licking the hearth. Looked at her youngest children up in the loft, ordered not to look, but of course, they watched and listened. Worried little eyes were wide wondering what would happen. *Have to be strong. Do what's best. Face what is.*

Finally, she looked at her husband, laying there. He smiled at her, even a dim twinkle in his eye. "I've still got a lot of flavor left. You'll see. Thanks to you and your onions."

She laughed, smiled back at him, nodding her head in agreement. And then, sat down and wept.

"Take him out to the woodshed. We'll do it there. And bring all the whiskey you can find."

Shaking, Mary took his hand, warm. The small structure smelled of wood chips which would soak up the blood. She couldn't keep track of everything going on and everything that the doctor was saying. *Infection...must wash it, watch for it...bandages, every day, sometimes twice a day, watch for green ooze, onion poultice won't help....yes, as much moonshine as he wants for at least a week. Maybe more. No, there's never too much moonshine at a time like this.*

"Sip this. More. Yes, more. Until you pass out." The doctor kept urging him to drink, drink. Satisfied his patient wouldn't wake, he ordered Mary out of the woodshed. And then, with a firm grip, the doctor held the crude hand saw and sawed off the bottom third of both of David "Crockett" Maples' legs.

Spring arrived, flinging off her heavy winter covers; she relished the sensual warming breezes on her skin. The trees tilted their leaves upward toward the sun, and the bear cubs, fawns, eaglets, and the eighth Maples baby, found themselves the newest members of the land of the blue smoke, slivers of lowland valleys slicing through spired peaks, scalloped shapes against the bluest of skies. Mary Ogle Maples closed her eyes as she pulled weeds from the kitchen garden, laid out on a warm south slope convenient to the house. Tilling the soil, she imagined the rows of field greens, peas, cabbages, potatoes and onions that would grow in their own due time. A noise over by the barn raised Mary's attention. She stood and walked closer, catching sight of her husband with his canes. Hobbling on his stumps, he was surprisingly strong this spring. If not for his three-quarter legs, he acted like he had turned back the clock ten years. She'd never seen him so determined, so full of life, as she watched him.

Sitting on a stool, he was handling some wooden planks. Turning them over and over in his hands, trying them on, shaving them here and whittling them there, a crude, but smooth foot form emerged; he'd been working on his project for days. Seeing Mary, he called to her.

"Polly—can you get me that leather strap? The one hangin' on the peg?" She took the strap and handed it to him. He grunted as he placed rags on his stumps for cushion and placed the wooden feet inside his boots. Then, he strapped the boots with the wooden feet inside to his stumps and legs and stood up. Grabbing his two canes, he took a few tentative steps. Smiling, he winked at Polly.

"Ya know, Polly. I heard about these walkin' onions. They don't grow here. Somewhere in Africa. Egypt, I heard. Anyways, it blooms bulbs that become so heavy they flop over and replant themselves. This starts their walk across the garden—that's why they call 'em walkin' onions. See?" He motioned toward the ground in a sweeping gesture. "Those newly replanted onions grow, sprout, grow heavy and replant themselves about one more step from the original. And so on and so on. Well, I got my new feet and I'm gonna call 'em my walkin' onions."

"Oh, Dave." Polly sighed but smiled at her strong husband. "I still can't believe you survived. But oh, how I wanted to save your feet. Took all the onions in Gatlinburg to try to save 'em. But I couldn't. And now...now look." She closed her eyes, finding the right words. "Now, you have wooden legs. I so didn't want…"

"Don't be sad. These are better than any legs saved by onions. I got walkin' onions now!" He hobbled over, gained a tentative balance, threw down his canes and took her in his arms. A rare show of affection for such a rugged mountain man. He kissed her, patted her on the backside, and, then, with the canes back in his hands, turned his attention to his crops.

"Within a short time, he was attending to many of the tasks he had done before the incident. And for the next ten years, Crockett and Polly raised their family together and even continued operating their store and then, a boarding house. Travelers listened to the story of the amazing David "Crockett" Maples and were "duly impressed with his dogged determination.""

The deer liked to watch the man tell his stories. He walked surprisingly fast, with the help of two canes and wooden feet and he told the tale every time there was a traveler. One and all were awestruck at this legend who survived the worst storm they'd ever known, lost his feet, and crafted new ones. *Thank the Lord for whiskey. I don't know if I woulda made it. How do the feet work? How'd ya make 'em? Wood and leather straps? Genius! Cushioning the stumps...yes, I can see how that hurts a bit, but you manage pretty well I see. Indeed, I am sure you get used to it all. Becomes almost normal. Yes, yes...I agree David—it's amazing how humans can adapt when they have to. Thank goodness for the 'shine. God knew what he was doin'. Given' us some help here on heavenly earth. Not too much on Saturdays because of church on Sundays, mind, but when losing limbs, and healin' cut-off stumps, drink all that you can. I'm glad you survived. Your wife is one tough woman. Nursed you back for months, I hear. A good woman. An Ogle you say she is? Oh yes, anyone associated with that family has true character and grit. Been around these parts forever. Good people.*

As the deer bedded down for the evening and the moon took its time rising, the mountains continued to listen, and, true to their nature, did not disrupt the immense durability of the man with no feet.

Reconstruction was ongoing, as America entered the 1870s; the effects of the civil war and its aftermath were still felt throughout the young, fragile nation. Union troops continued to occupy large swaths of the southern states, and promises of restoration, transformation, and equal rights were made on both sides that would never happen. The southern states that fled the nation, and that were now returned to their mother's arms, had not quite integrated nor did they ingratiate themselves back into the larger unit, never having flung off their unique social fabric. Even in the north, slaves were not simply merged into free society and lack of unity with laws and states' enforcement plagued the path forward. True civil and equal rights stumbled under the agonizingly slow weight of societal change.

But the United States did move ahead and so did the town of Gatlinburg. So much so their first school had opened in 1867, just two years after the war ended, and when everyone—slaves, white men, Indians forced west, Spaniards, Irish fleeing to America back in the 1840s—their potatoes all rotting in the fields—were all still adjusting to a new way of life. Nobody, no group, race, or culture is immune from an altered life. And oh, how the residents of Gatlinburg longed for the "Golden Age" of Tennessee agriculture! But that time lay way back in their memories—a lifetime ago in the 1840s and 1850s—and thank goodness they had those good times to remember. How comforting it is to travel back in time when the cherished rights of each state and a strong Unionism lived together in peace. Was there ever to be another time when the two sides of America would hold each other at night? When the sighs of the mountains traveled lightly into the inky blackness and when the deer listened to the hopeful dreams of freedom?

Between harvests and such, the first school in Gatlinburg was known as a subscription school and was in session three months out of the year. Subscription schools were not public schools. Instead they were paid for by parents of the children and were found in rural areas, and Oklahoma and Indian territories. One dollar per pupil, per month, was the going rate for teachers, who were almost always women.

The teacher that came to Gatlinburg was greeted warmly and had wonderful stories to tell the children of her travels and adventures. In between reading, writing, and arithmetic lessons, as well as lessons in sewing, forestry and other practical skills, she would gather them outside at lunchtime, each student having their own pail of biscuits, ham, bacon, or deer meat wrapped in cloth, and perhaps a bit of cheese, nuts, berries, or cake.

"I met a fellow teacher in Oklahoma near Hogshooter Creek, where I grew up." The teacher began one day, while resting outside with her class, in between lessons.

"Hogshooter Creek! That's a funny name…" a young Ogle boy exclaimed.

"Well now," the teacher continued, her eyes sparkling as they always did when the time had come to relax, take a break from arithmetic or writing and reading, and tell her tales. "His pupils were Indian girls and boys who were…" she lowered her voice, "… fugitives of the law."

"They had Indians in their school?" Incredulous, the girls and boys sat under an old oak tree, shaded from the smiling sun, listening to their teacher who seemed to know everything.

"Oh yes, He had Cherokee, as well as Delaware and Quapaw boys and girls. And one Negro girl too, who used to work on a plantation." The children were silent, thinking how different things were in different areas of America. They looked at one another; they had like minds having grown up in the same environment, with the same values. *We never knew this. Golly, everyone thinks their lives are exactly how everyone else lives…until they climb over these mountains and see there are other worlds out there. Cities, farmland, places with no mountains at all…and perhaps they do things differently.* And then…the thought that most everyone has upon this realization and that the teacher now posed to her students: "Is that difference good or bad? Or a little of both? Or neither? What do you think?" Her students were intrigued. "Never thought about it, Miss."

"Well, she said, "start thinking."

As the students pondered the greater world, the spirited teacher continued. "Well, the Indians didn't have any money, so the teacher accepted produce—corn and radishes, carrots and such as payment." She smiled; it was great storytelling, a tried and true technique for engaging young pupils. "Students sat on planks made of pine and a large board painted with lampblack was our blackboard. Chalk was scarce, but he managed to write with it 'til it was down to nary a nub. Anyway, the boys were very mischievous! Just like here, breaks were taken at school to tend the harvests and such. When the boys came back from working in the ripened fields and school began again, they needed a week or two to re-learn their manners and get back into the routine. Well, listen close, now. That very first day back to school, and the second and third too, they hung dead 'possums on the school walls!" The children laughed and slapped each other's backs. Some stood up and doubled over in laughter.

"That teacher almost ran back north! You should've seen him, entering through the door, only to be met with the fixed face of a dead 'possum swinging from the beam. He almost had an attack of the heart, the poor soul!" The children were rolling now, howling with humor. Oh how she loved that sound! And then, she winked and told them to listen closely to the Cherokee legend about how the 'possum got its hairless tail.

It was a vain animal—so proud of its glossy, bushy tail. One day, a jealous rabbit decided to play a trick on the 'possum. Rabbit asked him to a dance but secretly told Cricket, a barber, to trick him into thinking he would clip his tail to enhance its grandeur. 'Possum was so confident that he fell asleep, not knowing what Cricket was doing to his tail. Well, when they got to the dance, all the animals were laughing. 'Possum couldn't figure out why until he realized they were all laughing at him. He then looked at his tail and, to his shock, there was not a hair left on it! It was bare as the tail of a lizard! 'Possum was so embarrassed and surprised he could not say one word. Instead, he dropped to the ground, rolled over, and played dead. That's why the tail is bare and that's also why he plays dead.

She loved telling Indian stories; felt it flavored the children's lessons, basting their knowledge of the larger world. But then, she caught the prankish gleam in their eyes as she told the story and abruptly rose to her feet, wiping down and straightening her skirts. *Oh boy, I may have planted a seed I don't want to grow. Better get them back in and learn their letters before they decide to try this themselves.* Walking away now, the teacher wiped the smile off her face and motioned for them to come back inside of the cool, wooden schoolhouse. The boys were whispering; she couldn't make out their words, but if she did, she'd hear how they had a mind to clip her hair when she wasn't looking, or pretend to play dead during arithmetic lessons...or hang a dead possum....

Oh, now, we wouldn't actually do this...we like our teacher! And our pas would be so angry! Our mamas though, they would threaten to lock us out 'cause we done went to live at the Devil's house...and they'd scream that they'd hit us 'til we're cured and come back home. But when a seed is planted and watered...

"Students. Don't ever do this to me. Ever." She took the hand of a little McCarter girl and clipped their planned antics off in mid-contemplation. All teachers were skilled in pranks and young jokes. And all teachers knew the key was to keep them busy. Don't give them time to plan. Take their minds off of their scheming.

"Come on....let's get back inside. They're just stories. Legends and tales. That was our fun lesson of the day. But we've got lots more to do..."

CHAPTER TWELVE

Noah "Bud" Ogle
1870s-1880s

N O DEAD 'POSSUMS ever hung from the school-house doorway, to the great relief of the teacher, although the students insisted 'possums tasted just like pig. "Bacon and ham...the 'possums taste just like 'em! They're a good substitute when the pork is runnin' low."

"Hmm...I'll take your word for it." the teacher replied, secretly thinking she'd never eat 'possum if she didn't have to. *I will never get that image of a hairless tail out of my head!*

The schoolhouse grew to be an important hub of the community; children and their parents and grandparents frequently assembled for spelling bees, readings of student work, and other such events. But the church and religion remained at the very core of mountain life, the major place to gather, worship, marry, grieve, and exchange news and gossip.

White Oaks Baptist Church had endured for nearly forty years, since 1837. It had seen much progress and now, parishioners could hardly believe what the greater world was inventing: the 1870s brought the patent of the electric dental drill and Congress passed an important Civil Rights Act. The twenty-cent coin was introduced, but the people of Gatlinburg rarely saw one, still farming their land, sustaining their family and maintaining their homesteads and culture that had deepened over the decades. Fields still swayed in the wind, young children still sniffed the soil for minerals and the general health of the dirt, and porch parties dominated their Saturday nights, with churchgoing on Sundays and barely a rest in between. One lone deer still made its appearance, watching over all of the activities of these busy people.

Things do change, however, even in an area that crawls through progress. Families grew and the population was increasing; they needed a larger church building, new pews, and a general overhaul of their sacred space. And so, as mountain folk do, they assembled, planned, and collectively and quickly, pooled resources to construct a frame church building at a well-traveled corner of Gatlinburg. In between nailing boards and painting, constructing pews and laying floorboards, talk turned to wondering about what had happened to the man who began their town that was now growing so rapidly. It had been years since anyone had heard of Radford Gatlin and his wife, Elizabeth, other than the occasional rumor that he had softened.

"He's old now. Diminished a bit and more like to listen, they say over in Strawberry Plains. Yet even in his old age—I hear now and then from the postmaster and a few other visitors— he's still a firecracker when it comes to his views, exploding in passionate defense of what he deemed right, and ever-ambitious in his goals."

"Sounds 'bout right." they laughed; time tempering some of the bitter memories of the enigma that was Radford Gatlin. His legend had actually grown lately. A mysterious, complicated and tangled personality, he still left his mark on the area; after all, his name was still used for the town. And though they could've changed it at any time, they never did. Gatlinburg still remained a gateway to a successful and productive life for many families, including the everlasting Ogle family. *We've been here since day one,* they liked to remind themselves, *and it's forever a gateway to our ancestors, our history, our present lives, and our futures.* Indeed, Radford Gatlin had left this slice of the Smoky Mountains with a legacy of increased opportunity; a man ahead of his time, perhaps too ambitious for the era, but seeing clearly the chance for a gateway to bigger and better things. *I am sure that people will come from far and wide to the place of the white oaks,* Gatlin had often thought. *I may not see it in my lifetime. It may not be appreciated anytime soon. But I know it will happen. One day. I know it.*

Indeed, the 1870s dawned bright in America, and with it came the Second Industrial Revolution and new inventions including the cable car railway, loudspeakers and microphones, the stapler, and the cash register. The fifteenth Amendment was passed giving any man, regardless of race, the right to vote, and millions of immigrants descended on the young country that beckoned all who sought freedom. Women continued to exclaim that this amendment was a step forward but still didn't include them. Over thirty-eight million people were included in the 1870 U.S. Census; cities were booming. John D. Rockefeller formed the Standard Oil of Ohio Company, and Andrew Carnegie was well on his way to founding the Carnegie Steel Company near Pittsburgh, Pennsylvania, and expanding his wealth. Elsewhere in the world, the Franco-Prussian War resulted in the defeat of France, Wilhelm I was made emperor of Germany, and Charles Dickens, the author of *A Tale of Two Cities, Oliver Twist,* and *A Christmas Carol,* died at fifty-eight years of age, a ripe old age when compared to the average life expectancy of around forty-three years old.

While America's titans of industry were building, laying rail, investing and expanding their empires, things were a bit different in Gatlinburg. In the crisp mountain air of the country's Appalachian region, each day, as the country continued its march through the 1870s and beyond, descendants of the original William and Martha Ogle continued the tradition of living as mountain folk had always lived—self-sufficient, rustic, farming, and free.

The well-established Ogles flourished in the Gatlinburg community. Though a few moved away to other areas, most members of this preeminent Appalachian family stayed and lived their lives, tending their land, helping one another, and remaining very close-knit. The large original family was well loved and respected throughout the area. Growing up quickly in the mountains, most were married by their early twenties and became parents by twenty-five or so, and the generations kept progressing forward with the rising suns.

True to tradition, this next generation of the Ogle family continued their ever-deepening legacy in the former White Oak Flats area, and one in particular, great-grandson, Noah "Bud" Ogle, born to Caleb and Lydia Ogle, in 1863, would leave a permanent mark on his great-grandparents' heritage.

Bud Ogle grew up in the bosom of the Smoky Mountains, where the crowns of the white oaks lay gilded in the sun. Mirror-like sheets of water lay silent in the pools of the creek, before, around the bend, rapids swept it all away. A lone deer, a huge stag, roamed around his childhood, an ever-present comforting presence. He'd heard the stories—there was a deer that saw and protected his great-grandmother, Martha when she came to this area. And though that original deer was long gone—he liked to think the first deer had joined his great-grandfather, William, for eternity—its offspring instinctively hung around the Ogle family, observing, and somehow protecting. *But what was he protecting? I have a gun. Many in fact. And, we know these lands like the back of our hands. We are such self-sufficient people we can survive just like any animal. Maybe even better. We don't need protection. Haven't for a long time, or even ever. Our lives wax and wane, ebb and flow, and follow the cycles of nature. Every stage is like a gateway: birth, growth and maturity, and death, back to God. No, it's not our bodies that need protection. Nor our souls. What is it, then, that this deer was still looking out for? What exactly is he protecting?*

The deer walked into view just then and held in his heart the answer. *It is your heritage and way of life that needs protecting.* But that very real need was still far enough away. For now, the deer simply watched the newest young and strong Ogle member make his way in the equally ancient and harsh cycles of the mountain world.

Bud Ogle could usually be found hard at work on his 400-acre homestead and farm. Born in 1863, Bud was a lean, strapping young man who built his cabin in a slightly different way than most. As was usual in these parts, he mostly farmed corn but also had an impressive apple orchard that grew multiple types of apples. Rocky and unfertile, the land was pretty poor for any type of farming, but he still "managed to grow his corn crops to much success." So much so that he sold his excess to the Knoxville markets and managed to make a decent income. He even had a tub mill that he allowed his family and friends to use either for free or he took a small percentage of the meal produced. As is the case with younger generations, they improved and built upon things their parents and grandparents had done such as design of cabins, homesteading, modern building methods and trying new ventures. Bud Ogle was the next generation of Ogles who embraced all of these ideas with relish.

Bud had married Lucinda Bradley Ogle who was a local midwife and was as hearty a woman as they come. Together, they built a sturdy and effective homestead.

After getting their bearings as a young married couple, Bud eventually built a "saddle-bag" log cabin home, which consisted of two houses, eighteen by twenty feet, joined by a common chimney; each side having their own hearth. One side was built, then the other side was built about five years later. They were identical on both sides—both having a sleeping loft and both well-built. Rare to see this type of cabin, this saddle-bag design served Bud and his family very well. Walking in from the fields, the kitchen garden was on the right side, where it received the best sun for the peas, beans, carrots, potatoes, and onions that grew healthy and hearty.

Stepping onto the front porch that spanned the entire length of the structure, the large family was met with three doors, one for each side, and one for the middle area. When they walked through the middle door, the chimney stack was directly in front, and either side they went to had their own open hearth in which to cook, dry clothes, and warm themselves. Each side had their hearth area, and each had a loft in which to sleep and store items. Back doors led to the other side of the cabin and wooden shutters could be opened to air out the smoky aromas that settled so well into the hewn logs of the walls. At night, lanterns and hearth fires lit the humble home; while Ma and the girls sewed, the younger ones played with corn husk dolls and the boys played marbles. The saddlebag design was perfect for this branch of the Ogle family; they truly needed the room. There was Noah, his wife Lucinda, and their children: Frances, Lead, Materson, Becca, Isaac, Robert and Winey, aged seventeen all the way down to two years old.

"Kind of a weaner house, but attached." Lead always explained when talking about his father's saddle-bag cabin. He was referring to the weaner house concept where young newlyweds would build or move into a small home on the parents' property so they could get a head start in their own homesteads. Oh, they had worked on the farms and tended animals their whole lives, but there was still nothing like the experience of doing it all on your own. It was one thing to take care of animals in the barns, weed the garden, or repair a fence, but doing all of that on your own, all the while repairing shingles, cooking food, planning out a large crop and sewing clothes was another. Not to mention usually adding a little one very shortly after the wedding.

"Weaner houses. They're so good 'cause you get to share resources, food, and such, but still have that privacy."

"Yeah, we have a weaner house...a real one, right down there." A newly married Reagan young man pointed past huge rocky land toward the creek. "We need to be a little further away than an attached house," he winked.

"Yeah, the saddlebag is good for growin' up, and it gives our parents a bit of space of their own, but once we all marry, we definitely want to put some distance between our parents and us!" Lead said to his older sister. He was fourteen years old now and Frances was seventeen. Both had their future lives spinning around their heads; marriage, weaner house for a year or so, then building their own cabins on the land or purchasing their own tracts. Children, animals to raise, their own hearths to fill, and front porch parties with their own banjos and a just touch of the 'shine every so often.

"Or *every* Saturday night, depending on the weather." Lead winked and laughed.

"What does the weather have to do with it?"

"Well now, if it's hot, the water escapes...evaporates much faster. And that'll make the alcohol much stronger. Helps you through the long, hot days. Somethin' to take that edge off. But then, you also gotta keep some of that strong summer drink for the winter. In the cold weather, it warms you up faster. Gets a bit spicier too. Nice and warm goin' down your throat and settlin' into your stomach when the snows outside are swirling." He smiled.

Frances narrowed her eyes at her younger brother. "How do *you* know? You're only fourteen! If mama ever found out..."

"Oh no." Levi recovered himself quickly. "I don't *know*. Not from personal experience anyways. It's just what I hear."

"So dependin' on the weather, eh? Seems that every Saturday toward evening, any type of weather is fine..."

"Exactly." And with that, Levi winked and walked down the gravel path to the barn. It was time to milk the cows and fetch more water for Ma's kettle.

The apple orchard and a tub mill were indeed unusual and rounded out the expansive homestead. Bud Ogle also had a four-pen barn, which was also rare. Four pens of around eleven square feet each, the barn was a one-story with a loft, covered with a split-shingled roof. Very well constructed of rough-hewn logs connected by half-dovetail notches, it housed cows and a few horses. Earthy scents wafted out toward the creek, the barn being situated so that the winds kept the animal's musty smells from invading the saddle-bag cabin.

∾⊚⊚∾

The tub mill was constructed along LeConte Creek. Another rarity among mountain architecture, this type of mill was used to harness the power of water. "It rested on mudsills and round log supports above the creek. It sat about half a mile from the cabin and barn. The walls were made of thick logs connected with saddle notches, and the floor was hewn puncheon logs." "A vertical shaft beneath the millhouse connects the grindstones with a "tub wheel" turbine. An eighty foot (24 m) hollowed-log flume diverts water from the creek to the turbine." "Handling about a bushel or two of corn per day into flour. Ten hours could produce a half a bushel."

Despite its importance, tub mills were not found very often because first, it took the right terrain and natural resources to create one. First, does the stream have an abrupt descent, rapids, or succession of falls? If so, put the mill there because it will only help the power. Needing hilly terrain, the rocky, hilly slopes of the Ogle homestead were ideal and made it easier to build the mill. Once the site was decided upon, hollowed logs served as a flume. Specialists were brought in to make the actual millstones made from granite or sandstone. Around three to six feet in diameter, and averaging ten to fifteen inches in thickness, water flowed down the chute and caused the wheel to turn. It's all about the weight of the water. Smooth and making sure the millstones never touch—you don't want to eat small rocks in your flour, do you?—the flour came out finely ground. As long as the faces of the stones are sharpened, along with the grooves and strips between the grooves. Smooth milling was desired. And from there, cornbread, bread, and biscuits could be made.

Bud Ogle was fascinated with different building methods and he left an indelible mark on Gatlinburg's architecture and way of life. He was as resourceful a man as they come. But even he knew when to leave a job to men who specialized in certain skills. Every year, a trusted craftsman was summoned to the Ogle homestead and stayed for up to three days to "dress a set of millstones." If the mill was well used, as his was, the job had to be done annually. After turning the heavy stones, the craftsman had to 'true' the faces, then sharpen the grooves and lands—strips between grooves—with picks to ensure smooth milling." And then, once the stones were readied again, it was back to milling, the "thumping of water against the wheel, the rhythmic click of gears and whir of millstones" creating the finest meal to make the softest bread in Gatlinburg.

cᔆᓌᔆᓑ

Songs were sung during milling times and the connection between machine and man, the ability of water and stone to make meal and flour and then, freshly baked foods, was highly respected.

"You know that teacher who came through here a few years back? She said back in the day of Chaucer, the one who wrote *The Canterbury Tales*, there was a story about some miller, and she said that the rapping sound that a shoe makes against the turning shaft when milling is like a damsel singin' her song. And the mill was never idle or silent as long as she sang her song. So, as long as the damsel constantly sang her song, the mill went on working."

"I heard that story too. Pro'lly in school. From that teacher who was always talkin' about those *Canterbury Tales* or that Shakespeare fella Hamlet—that brooding, ticked off the prince. Kinda liked that story." They paused, recalling their collective history with mountain education. They received quite a bit of schooling despite being far away from towns with larger and more organized systems. In fact, their subscription schooling could arguably be *better*—it was more practical. Basic math for adding up the price of corn, or staking out acreage. Reading and writing for understanding deeds, lawsuits, or penning letters to relatives and friends. History and the classics for pride and heritage, and for the lessons that came with having a ready-made guide for navigating human events and types of people. Their parents were always saying: *I may not have seen many places, but I've met all types. Believe me, I can spot a tick on a hound a mile away.* The older family members always said: *I've met that type before. They're all in the Bible. Already know what he's gonna do. Trouble. Stay away...you'll understand as you get older.*

"Well, Canterbury may've had the damsel. But we have our own classy lady of the corn, tellin' us to come home after the harvest. And you know what that means!" one of the boys said, winking and ribbing the others. "Let's sing our own corn milling song ...they say the classy lady is from the Old World just like Canterbury...everybody join in! Here we go..."

Your Hay it is Mow'd, and your Corn is Reap'd;
Your Barns will be full, and your Hovels heap'd:
Come, my Boys, come;

Come, my Boys, come;
And merrily roar out Harvest Home.

"How does someone always have a banjo?" One seemed to always appear as the tunes began. All someone had to do was slip away, take the shortcut through the creek, grab the banjo sitting by the hearth, and bring it out for the boot-stomping to start. Many others used spoons to make music. Sounding like rubber bands or clicking rain on a tin roof or even a twangy old grandfather's voice, the pulse of the youth of Gatlinburg throbbed with spirit:

The corn, oh the corn, 'tis the ripening of the corn!
Go unto the door, my lad, and look beneath the moon,
Thou canst see, beyond the wood rick, how it is yellowin'
'Tis the harvesting of wheat, and the barley must be shorn.
The corn, oh the corn, and the yellow, mellow corn!
Here's to the corn, with the cups upon the board!
We've been reaping all the day, and we'll reap again the morn
And fetch it home to mow-yard, and then we'll thank the Lord.
(Richard Blackmore)

Between building, maintaining, farming, running a mill, and hunting, Bud Ogle was one busy man living in the shadows of the Smoky Mountains. Perhaps the only one busier was his wife and the women and girls. The huge stag deer liked to peer at them from a high slope and marveled all day long—hours upon hours—at their constant motion, a world in which the players never stop.

"Long before the pallid dawn came sifting in through chink and window, they were up and about. As there were no matches in those days, the housewife 'unkivered' [uncovered] the coals which had been smothered in ashes the night before to be kept 'alive' till morning, and with 'kindling' in one hand and a live coal held on the tines of a steel fork or between iron tongs in the other, she blew and blew and blew till the splinters caught fire. Then the fire was started and the water brought from the spring, poured into the 'kittle' and while it was heating the chickens were fed, and cows milked, the children dressed, the bread made, the bacon fried and then coffee was made and breakfast was ready. That over and the dishes washed and put away, the spinning wheel, the loom or the reel were next to have attention, meanwhile keeping a sharp lookout for the children, hawks, keeping the chickens out of the garden, sweeping the floor, making the beds, churning, sewing, darning, washing, ironing, taking up the ashes, and making lye, watching for the bees to swarm, keeping the cat out of the milk pans, dosing the sick children, tying up hurt fingers and toes, kissing sore places well again. Then on to making the soap, robbing the beehives, stringing beans for winter use, working the garden, planting and tending a few hardy flowers in the front yard such as princess feather, pansies, sweet williams, dahlias, morning glories, getting dinner, darning, patching, mending milking again, reading the Bible, prayers and so on from morning till night, and then all over again the next day."

Antlers brushed against the white oak trees as the stag walked to his bed at twilight. As he circled, tamping down the grass and pine needles, under thick, low-hanging branches, he tucked his legs under him and tilted his head down. It had been a long day of walking, foraging, and rutting. Yet, as he closed his eyes, he pictured the women puttering around the cabins, tucking children in, checking on everything and everybody, sitting down to read the Bible, fingers darning holes in pants and socks. Their work, the deer knew as he lay in the peace of the mountain moonlight, had only just begun.

CHAPTER THIRTEEN

1879-1880

"Hey! News on the Gatlins!" The newsboy waited until the children could round up as many neighbors, friends, and family members as possible. When they returned, panting in the summer heat, a string of Ogles, Huskeys, Reagans, Ownbys, Whaleys, Tranthams, and Bohanans were rushing up the pathway to the general store which still housed the post office. And then, after exchanging pleasantries and making sure the thirsty children drank water, he began to share his news to an eager crowd. No matter that Gatlinburg was growing and well-established, it was still isolated in many ways, and news provided them with new and fresh fodder for months.

"Miss Laura Luttrell, she's a lady who is a former McClung Room custodian of the Lawson-McGhee Library over there in Knoxville. Well, her old home was in Strawberry Plains 'fore she went to Knoxville. She been talkin' to some old residents who knew Gatlin and they told her what's been happenin' with them."

The crowd gathered closer. Especially the Ogle family members—the largest group; they'd had the most trouble with the Gatlins.

"Some of those older men told Miss Luttrell of being students in Gatlin's school on Lyon's Creek near Trentville and Strawberry Plains, about the time of the beginning of the Civil War. They recalled that Gatlin, in addition to being a "real character", as they called him, was a good teacher, wrote a beautiful hand and carried a pistol to his school."

"Well now, that's not unusual. Need to protect the children. What if a bear comes sniffing around the school?" One of the adults stated.

"True" the newsboy agreed. "But I don't know if you folks know this...don't know if it made it into your papers or not. I deliver the papers...don't get to read all of 'em. Anyway, a pistol is fine, mind...we all use a rifle or a pistol. Never go anywhere without it. But what happened is, in 1853 at a school in Louisville, Kentucky, a Mr. Butler was a twenty-eight-year-old teacher and his pupil, William Ward, was the son of a cotton merchant. Very wealthy, mind, and raised him to know it. Well, young William was eatin' chestnuts in class one day—sneaking 'em when the teacher's back was turned. Well, Mr. Butler caught 'im and asked 'are you eatin' in the classroom?' Young William denied it, but Mr. Butler gave him a whippin' anyways. Was makin' a mess in the classroom and was surely disrespecting."

The adults nodded their heads. They knew teachers had that authority and would be very ashamed if their child misbehaved in such a way that the teacher had to take such action.

"Anyways, William goes home and tells what happened and the older brothers, Matthews and Bob, go to school the next day and call Mr. Butler a damned scoundrel and coward!" The women glanced at each other and then at the children. Frowning, they didn't like such language, especially in front of young ears.

"They mixed and scuffled and Matthews pulled out his pistol and fired at Mr. Butler, straight in the chest. Bullet didn't kill him right away, but he did die a few days later. Matthews was picked up for murder."

"So, there was a trial, but Matthews was acquitted. Said he used it in self-defense. There was a scuffle after all. But a lot of people didn't like that verdict. Said the south runs itself by the pistol and the lash. This was back in 1853, mind you. 'Fore the war between the states, but after tensions were already boilin' over between the north and the south."

"What a story! Terrible!" the women exclaimed. And then, "What is the world comin' to where we have to worry about shootin' in our schools..."

They couldn't imagine it, they all thought, reflecting on their lives here in Gatlinburg. Thankful that they were away from the larger cities where one may not know who their neighbor was, and the irony that there was less room for everyone, yet more than enough room for disputes. They read it in the papers every week and the postmaster came with more and more stories of such conflicts with each passing month. Too many minds in one place led to clashes. Here in their little mountain town, there may be more minds than back in the 1850s when Gatlin was here, but those many minds made up one mindset—farm the fields, raise the children, take care of families and animals and homesteads, and keep the peace. Mind your own business, help when needed, and stay close to the land and God. It's so simple, really. And, isn't that the solution? Respecting and even wondering about differing views and wanting to try new things, but keeping your area of the world true to one, basic, world-view? Seek out people who feel the same. *Stick to your own kind,* the English and Irish and Italians and Jews and Christians and Indian tribes and practically every other human group always say. *Let them over there do what they want. But let us do the same. Don't tell me what to do and I won't tell you how to run your life. It's easier that way. Iron doesn't mix with clay.*

They snapped back to the newsboy's voice, who continued to share the news, after drinking a long gulp of water mixed with a little whiskey. A treat for a long ride into the town to bring mail and news. Gatlinburg's wonderful folk never disappointed.

"Now, back to more news about Gatlin," he said, still standing in front of an even larger crowd now. "So, folks were tellin' another story about how he was at Strawberry Plains. Back on the night of November 8, 1861—some years after he left Gatlinburg, eight or ten Sevier County Unionists attempted to burn the railroad bridge across the Holston River in that town and were prevented from doing so by a lone Confederate guard, James Keelan. Recall that our Gatlin was a Confederate sympathizer. Sided with the south. So this ticked him off that Union soldiers wanted to burn that bridge. Gatlin wrote what they called 'a very exaggerated and bombastic account of this affair, making the lone Confederate guard, Keelan, a great hero and claiming that forty "Lincolnites" attacked the bridge and that Keelan killed three of them with his dagger...all of which was untrue."

"But that didn't stop the story from runnin'. In 1862, Gatlin's bridge-burning story was published in the form of a pamphlet entitled, *The Immortal Hero—James Keelan*, by the Atlanta newspaper, *Daily Intelligencer* and was doubtless used as Confederate propaganda and a morale builder among Confederate troops during the Civil War."

The crowd murmured and one Ogle boy spit out: "Seem to recall another burnin' story of Gatlin's that was untrue...." Mountain folk's memories ran forever and were passed on to generation after generation. The Ogles never forgave Gatlin for accusing their kin of burning barns and fields, and Gatlin's hauling them into court to face those accusations.

"Miss Luttrell also learned that Gatlin left Strawberry Plains about the year 1863 when federal troops occupied East Tennessee. She was told he went to Georgia, and was associated with the Confederate Provost Marshal in Atlanta until the end of the war. And one Mr. A. C. Parrott, told Miss Luttrell that both Radford and Elizabeth Gatlin—yep, they're still together—were living in Union, South Carolina, as late as last year in 1879, and that both were quite old and feeble. Probably gone by now. Or at least closer to God than he ever was."

In the 1880s, Gatlinburg was home to hundreds of people. They were still largely farmers, planting crops in the spring, and harvesting in the fall. Though many other crops were grown, including cereals, wheat, oats and field greens, corn remained the major crop. Harvest time was hard work, but like all chores large and small, it was made into a social event. Everyone pitched in from sun-up to sun-down and gave thanks for a bountiful crop which usually occurred. Gatlinburg was not plagued by much drought or crop failure and was a major reason why the population was largely healthy and hearty.

Corn harvesting occurred about twenty days after the first silk appeared when it turns brown and the husks are still green. Grab the tops of the stalk...the lower ones can ripen a few more days. Cut a kernel to make sure it's still in the milk stage. If it spills milky liquid, go on and harvest. If it's clear liquid, it's not quite ready; you should give it another day or so. But if it's dry, you've waited too long. Once you've harvested all ears of corn, pull up the corn stalks and use them for fire-starting, animal feed, baskets, brooms, and the backs of chairs. So many items and foodstuffs were made with their king of crops. Bread, corn on the cob, hominy, grits, popcorn, corn pudding, cornbread, and...the adults used to whisper on the porch on Saturday nights...scorpion juice.

How did you get to call moonshine 'scorpion juice'? We used to call it the 'shine. Well, now scorpions pack quite a sting. And our juice around here does the same. Can sting you if you're not careful. Makes you dribble and drool and swell and vomit. Sweat and keel over too. Yep, sounds about right. Indeed, why are you tellin' our youngins about the juice? Children, don't listen to your Pa...Stay away from it all. No matter what they call it. 'Cause if you think the juice will sting you, just wait 'til you feel the sting of when your Ma finds out...

Corn crops had ruled the region since Martha Ogle's arrival but now, though it remained king of the crops and oversaw most of their lives, more and more men moved away from the fields and into the world of wood and steel. The logging railroad had come to town. On more and more mornings, the deer was awakened by the sounds of machinery, clattering and piercing the cool mountain breeze. The corn crops still danced in the wind, but with fewer partners. Fields slowly shrank to more manageable levels since there was less and less manpower to tend them.

"When that bandsaw got invented...well, it just changed everything. Think of a steel belt strung over two wheels. Like an endless belt runnin' round and round those wheels. That's how its inventor, William Newberry, described it. Didn't work that great in the beginning. But now it's been refined and it don't snap anymore. It saws so much wood that they felled all the forests in the southeast. So now they're coming here 'cause they done run outta their own forest." Bud Ogle sighed. "So now, they're trying to take ours."

CHAPTER FOURTEEN

Turn of the Century
1900s and Logging

ETWEEN THE BANDSAW and the logging railroad and the fact that forests in the southeast were being depleted, lumber companies were rapidly pushing their way into the Appalachian Mountains. In 1901, the dawn of the new century, Colonel W. B. Townsend liked what he saw in the thickly treed slopes, and quickly established the Little River Lumber Company. A very wealthy man, he bought as much land and logging rights as possible. Another business-man, Andrew Jackson Huff, also came from Greene County to Gatlinburg during this time period, bringing his wife, Martha Whaley Huff, of the Whaley family, with him.

Both Townsend and Huff combined to bring industry and jobs to the area and they were welcomed by many of the residents. Suddenly, young men could be more than corn farmers or store owners or preachers. They could jump into the modern era of industry and they didn't even have to move to the big cities up north! They could work right here, at their home in the Smoky Mountains of Eastern Tennessee.

"We may as well join up in the logging rush. Our version of the gold rush, it's turnin' out to be." An excited Gatlinburg populace seized on this chance for more options and opportunities. They'd always been open to change; certainly they had embraced the easy sugar and other goods that Radford Gatlin's general store had brought. *If only that difficult man hadn't planted the spring crops during fall's midnight hours before winter had even been allowed its entrance. Gatlin thought we didn't want change at all. But that's not true. We just didn't want to be told to change and how to change. Wanted to have a say in our own homes and our own town. Wanted to come to those thoughts on our own. At least, we wanted to be part of the process. So yes, change can be good. When we decide it is so. So, let's decide and join up in this loggin' industry and see where it takes us...*

And so they opened up their homes to workers and many made a handsome supplemental income from the loggers who worked the forests. The many lumbermen had to eat and lodge somewhere and the Gatlinburg residents figured they may as well benefit from that need. Besides, it spiced things up a bit. Lord knows that new people meant more stories they could weave into their folklore. *Them logs are whisperin' logs. Hear 'em? They tell you a lot...speak to you...*

The logging workers told the children about the speaking logs when they came back to the cabins for their evening meal and a hard sleep. *When they're all stacked in a pile, the logs give off a sound—a tramp like someone's walking—when that happens, get ready for company because they are a'coming. Whether you like it or not. Remember what Ben Franklin says about houseguests: Guests, like fish, begin to smell after three days.* Laughter so robust the children doubled over themselves, holding their sides. *Heck, I know an uncle who smells like a fish every day. Spends all his time fishin' in every creek around these parts. The stink stays on him. Can never get it out no matter how many times he bathes. Which isn't very often. He says since he's in the creek every day, that's his bath. But it don't work. Smells worse than the fish themselves.*

The loggers laughed at the children's keen observations and continued their talk about logs that speak.

And when logs sob, you know rain's coming.

Logs don't sob! They can't cry! It's just humid and the logs crack sometimes. But now, listen here. And the children listened. *When logs sputter, you know snow is coming.*

The young adult members of the families loved to listen to the loggers tell their tales to the children, and then, loved to spin their own versions out.

"That and, for sure, when a fire made of dry logs roars up the chimney, you know there's about to be a fuss in the family."

"Not true! Our fire roars all evening and we don't fuss."

"Well now, look here...you're fussing right now and you don't even know it! I'll look for your chimney tonight. And I predict it'll be roaring...."

"Oh, it'll be roaring tonight all right if you keep talking to me like that." Squinted eyes held both furor and humor.

"Well, now, we're all workin' so hard in our fields and in the forests—dangerous work, mind—that I, for one, have not had time to fuss," one McCarter young man stated. They nodded their heads in agreement. And then...

"Heck, I don't have time to know if what we're doing is even right. What happens when all the trees are gone? When it's like a hairless 'possum's tail?" Young McCarter picked his teeth with a hay stalk and sighed. "I don't even have time to know if I'm happy or not about this whole new logging thing...."

⁂

Logging and industry were not the only acts in town. The area was now teeming with people, workers, overseers, cooks, lodgers, and now, tourists.

"Why would they wanna come here?"

"Oh you know, the loggers came, bringin' their families. So many people know about us now. Roads comin' in from all sides. But also, those authors—one of 'em is Charles Egbert Craddock. See here, Charles Egbert Craddock is really a woman using a man's name; they just found that out. Or was she just finally ready to reveal herself? In any case, Mary Noailles Murfree is her real name and she's been writing a lot. *Witch-Face Mountain...* that was one of her stories. No one ever knew she was a woman. But now, in this turn of the century era is what they call it, well, I guess society is more and more open to that kind of thing."

"Well, maybe not completely open to it...but heck. I don't care who's writin', as long as it's good writin'."

"And that other author, Horace Kephart. He wrote that book, *Our Southern Highlanders,* about all of us moonshiners." They laughed. "Oh, he did say we all drank a lot...well, guess he has a point. Some of us *do.*"

"But he also captured our way of life. Maybe described it a bit different or a lot different from what it really is...all the same, he captured it. Everyone's got a different lens. He saw us through his own lens. Someone else has another. And you all have another. But dang if they all don't see the beauty of our mountains."

They all looked out just then. The gentle peaks caressed the sky, a lone eagle slicing its way through the crevices, peering at the ever-changing landscape below. Fields, open land, forests, a growing town, roads, and over there, machines leaving a scar, and another and another across the earth. A lone deer with antlers, huge on his head, graceful in its movements, hung around almost every day, watching. Always present, recording the comings and goings of man. Now though, he watched from higher up, where the machines hadn't made it yet. Or from over there, on fewer and fewer slopes that were still untouched. Oh, these mountains, with their beasts and burdens of long memories. They hold their feelings and secrets inside. But sometimes the hurt escapes, spills down their spines, over their boulders, through their trees, and enters the history of thousands crashing into their valleys, doing whatever they please. The scars remain there forever. As a reminder.

While the mountains sat still, witnessing machines and man hacking away at their leafy coverings—sometimes an entire slope every few days—other events were occurring that continued to alter Gatlinburg and move it into the new century. Religion and places to gather remained at the very center of smoky mountain life. In 1881, right before the loggers began moving in toward the turn of the century, many of the established families had sold their land and moved to town. More opportunities, more stores, more tourists to stay at their cabins-turned-inns. The increase in visitors used Gatlinburg as a gateway to Pigeon Forge and its Old Mill that was grinding out more and more sacks of meal and flour. They were so busy at the Old Mill, in fact, that travelers had to hang around for a few days waiting for their ground goods. While waiting, people tacked notices to the mill's walls with news and gossip and other advertisements. Much of that news made its way to Gatlinburg as more and more people used the route between the two towns as they went about their business.

Between the migration into town and the travelers, the church congregation realized that they had to find a new home. Most had been attending church services at the First Baptist Church of Gatlinburg, right at the fork of the Baskins and Little Pigeon River, though some remained worshipping in their own way, churchless, but devout. This didn't quite work for them anymore; once the town expanded and welcomed guests, they wanted a "new place to sing unto the Lord." And so, the Reagans, Ogles, McCarters, and now, the Floyds, Clabos, Kears, Bohanans, Oakleys, and Bales had created their own church in 1881, which was now flourishing as the century turned and America and its Appalachian towns accelerated their crawl into the 1900s.

"Yes, we'll gather at the river.
The beautiful, the beautiful river,
Gather with the saints at the river.
That flows by the throne of God."

❧❦❧

Their new place of worship helped them through many losses and tragedies. Mary "Polly" Ogle Maples—the strong wife whose husband, David "Crockett" Maples, survived that terrible blizzard, but had to have both frostbitten feet amputated one afternoon when as much moonshine as existed in Gatlinburg was poured down his throat—had died.

"It was Polly who died first. April 17, 1885. Imagine that! Now, I don't wanna be mean, but everyone in their right mind would think he'd go first. No feet. Still gets low sometimes and looks awfully old. Injury, 'specially one like that takes a toll you know…"

"Well now, Crockett done married Lucinda King after Polly passed. She's twenty years younger, so maybe that's what's makin' him so old. Keeping up with his springtime wife!" They chuckled.

"Indeed, seems she's always pregnant…that's why we don't hear from him much." The young Ogle boys winked at one another, knowing smirks on their sunlit faces.

"Well, good for him, the ol' fella. Gotta live while you can…'cause that day is comin' for all of us. And it'll always be too soon."

❧❦❧

Indeed, the day came all too soon for a beloved neighbor.

"Sad news from over in Cades Cove. John Oliver's wife, Luraney, has gone to the Lord. She's finally with John."

"Oh, so sad to hear this!" they exclaimed, with heartfelt emotion. "They were the very first ones to settle in Cades Cove. Ever. Arrived with nothing—just a wagon with a few supplies, and she was pregnant with her second daughter at the time." They couldn't imagine being alone out here. Even their ancestor, Martha Ogle had brought her brother and family and her children—many of them grown by then. But imagine one man, one woman, and a small infant! And in the wintertime no less!

"Yessir, the Indians, helped them survive that first winter by bringin' them dried pumpkin and some other food. Bear meat, some nuts they had from their harvest... Saved their lives...they were starving. Heck, I hear John ate bark off of the trees before the Cherokee Indians came. But he made anyone he ever told to swear never to tell Luraney about that. And no one ever did. Thank goodness she went to her grave in peace."

They paused, thinking of the Cherokee and their ultimate fate. At church, they prayed for their Indian friends regularly. No matter how different the two peoples were, both still wished it would've worked out well for everyone. But regardless of intentions or whether humans sat in church, or outside on logs watching for spirits in the night, we just don't know how to be different and still share space.

"Let's see if I can recall...John Oliver died back in 1863. Yes, that was the year. February. It was so cold, and there was that huge eagle that always hung around. I saw it when I went to his funeral. It bowed its head, almost like it was prayin'. And now poor Luraney has passed...a good woman. Good people. She made the best soap and pumpkin butter in the mountains. Maybe in the whole of America."

"You know…" he thought for a moment. "John Oliver was the one that made that crossing to Cades Cove first. It was like his gateway to a completely different life. He was able to live his dream of owning his own farm. And we Ogles did the same thing here in Gatlinburg. Gatlin's Gateway. It's very much been our very own gateway to our unique way of life. Our dreams. William Ogle's dreams. No matter the name."

"And they have an eagle in the cove…we have the deer. That huge ol' stag always walkin' around us. He's so soft-footed… strange since he's so big. Maybe that deer and his offspring will pray for us when we're gone."

"Who says we'll be gone? I have a feelin' that us Ogles will be around Gatlinburg forever. Always adaptin' and leadin' it into a new era. Yessir. The Ogles will always travel through Gatlin's Gateway, and welcome lots of others through it too."

The deer heard those remarks and bobbed its head. Then he stood very still before beginning his slow, peaceful walk to his bed. Indeed, nature knows when an honest truth has settled into its very soul.

CHAPTER FIFTEEN

1910

THE OGLES REMAINED a large and steadfast family in the area and Bud Ogle was especially prominent. But it was now time to plant new seeds and make progress on the growth of the next generation. It was well into a new century in America and peace and prosperity abounded. Titans of industry continued connecting our cities and more and more people lived the urban life.

It seemed destined as well, that the outside world would also continue its encroachment on the mountain town of Gatlinburg. One did not have to move to the city to see American progress. Andrew Jackson Huff came to Gatlinburg in 1900 and built a sawmill which received a booming business from the loggers who were now permanently entrenched in the area.

The Ogles saw the progress and, as always, adapted well. A new generation was well-established, farming, working the land, tending the animals, and living the mountain life. As always, it was a toiling and tiring life, but also very fulfilling. Every inch of ground was used for growing or raising something. Mothers swept floors a million times a day and visitors were always welcome. *Where have you been? I've been waiting on you all. Come in the house, but wipe your feet and show your manners. I just finished sweeping and then scrubbing the floor with hot water I had boiling in my kettle in the fireplace. Come on now, let me show you around. Have some coffee?*

And neighbors and friends, and even logging employees now would be taken on a tour.

Here we are in the main room—we use this for cooking, sleeping, and storing everything we have. Over here, baskets, pots, plates, barrels, my spinning wheels where I make everything we wear. Even church clothes. Shoes, now, we get those at the store. But some folks make their own. Leather soles, use awls for poking holes for laces... We get cold 'round here and when the snows come, all eleven of us are sittin' right here. For days. Laughing, crying, and studying for school. A dog or two perhaps, and all the cooking and sewing equipment and supplies, all in one room for hours at a time. Thank the Lord for the Bible! Couldn't keep the patience except for that good book. Why don't we build bigger? Ah, see here, the rooms have to be kept small and low to keep the heat in...gets mighty cold in these parts.

The old cabin that began with Martha Ogle was still standing guard in its same location. It had kept watch through the early years of White Oak Flats, to Radford Gatlin's time, to the continuing logging era, and now, into the new century. It had been maintained and repaired of course, roof shingles replaced, cracks filled in; the homestead had modernized with new pens in the barns, beehives were cultivated—honey was often the only sweet a family had—and chickens ran everywhere providing eggs and sustenance for every meal.

But as the country churned forward, it could not help but nudge Gatlinburg with a stronger hand, and the new generation of Ogles could not help but see opportunity and new ways to adapt to this new world. Andrew Ogle, the great-grandson of Martha and William, and his family, were living in the original cabin and doing quite well. As he prepared the land for the spring planting and his wife was rounding up the children, the outside world was readying its next move, and the opportunity that it would offer in just a few short years would change the Ogle family's way of life and start a new, very different, chapter to their unique Smoky Mountain story.

≈≈≈

For now though, life was good. There was plenty of food, surplus was fed to the animals and sold to the markets, creating a solid income stream. Loggers paid to live on the many established homesteads, sometimes in the main cabins, but oftentimes in the weaner cabins and other structures that were available or, by now, there were quite a few homes that had been built specifically to accommodate the workers. Money was never better, yet had never really been an issue either; they didn't need much of it; grew and made and hunted everything they needed. But now, having cash to spare, they spent it on repairs—nails, lumber, saws and awls; and tools, shoes, saddles and such for the horses, coffee, sugar, tea, bolts of cloth, and other such "town goods". Candy was especially coveted and was considered a treat. Women had more jars for storing food and cans for canning, and another skillet or kettle was always helpful. Corn provided them with everything else they needed and it sat drying in corn cribs across Gatlinburg. Children played in creeks while fathers kept an eye on them when trading news at Bud Ogle's tub mill, waiting for the corn to grind. *Here's eight gallons of your corn...I'll take one as payment. What's the news? Heard Chestnut Flats folks are fightin' like never before. Too much 'shine. Scorpion juice. Well, let 'em live the way they want. The Lord will take care of all of us.*

Adults weren't the only ones trading news. The children and young adults had their own version of gossip. In fact, some of the best lessons didn't come from school and didn't come from their parents—although Lord knows they learned the most important things from their ma and pa; instead, the spirit and meaning of experiences came from each other—the youngest taught by siblings and friends. Those older brothers and sisters, who had received the slow-burning foundation of church and family, yet still embraced the flash of youth and energy and doing things their own way, were the unsung heroes of life's lessons.

∾☙☙☙

They had been playing in the creek and were still soaking wet, the cold water numbing their lower legs and feet.

"Let's move over there to the sun. Pa can still see us from there."

Men were gathered around the tub mill at Bud Ogle's place, professing to be waiting for their corn to be ground. But really, the corn was ground some time ago. In reality, the men had been ordered by their wives to take the children and go. *So I can sweep yet again! Go and don't come back with dust or mud. Shouldn't be hard...today's nice and dry.*

Not that the men minded. They could talk, get their corn ground and sip a little of the scorpion juice when their wives weren't around. Maybe a little more than they were usually allowed. After all, sweepin' took a long time. In fact, it never ended.

For their part, the children loved going over to Bud Ogle's place. Their saddlebag house was always interesting to see and they loved bouncing through all the doors, running the length of the long porch. Sweating, they could take a dip in the creek, and listen to their bigger brothers and sisters who knew everything there was to know about being grown up. But they always managed to steer the talk back toward the memories about being a kid growing up in the mountains of Gatlinburg, Tennessee.

"You'll see. It's great being almost grown to adults. Gonna get married, move into the weaner house. My own crops. But golly, growing up here in these mountains, well, there ain't nothin' better. Ah, to remember just a few short years ago, I was workin' so hard on chores, weedin' and slopping pigs and pickin' berries on the steep slopes. But it never felt like work being out in the fresh air and feelin' the wind every day. The sun. Creeks. It was like one giant playground ...."

"You should write this stuff down for us. That's what Mama's always sayin'. Write it down. Because our way of life is slowly goin' away. I myself don't know about that. But with the loggers here for a while now and lookin' around at more and more bare mountains...well, who knows how much longer we'll have all of our creeks and slopes and 'specially all the white oaks?"

"Write it down eh?" They looked at one another. "That may be the best idea yet."

And so, in the night hours, after horses were tended, cows were milked, pigs were slopped, crops were planted and harvested, berries were picked, clothes were woven, Bibles were read, schoolwork was done, trips to stores were completed, and rifles were shined, they took a breath, sat by the fire, and wrote.

"Although taught that we were put on earth to accomplish something and that challenging work was a privilege and wasting time was a cardinal sin, we still found time to play."

"We caught fireflies, played the guitar and sang, walked to church on the designated nights for prayer meeting, read or sometimes did the Virginia Reel—such fun dancing! After the day's work was done and on weekends, our house was the congregating place for most all of the neighborhood children for miles around. We nine children and all of our neighbors' children made quite a congregation. Our neighborhood activities were not all confined to our home; the whole region became our playground."

"The marble games, although fun for players, resulted in more work for mothers. Mama frequently patched the knees and seat portions of my brother's coveralls."

"We girls especially liked to jump rope and we always had several good grapevine ropes available. We invaded the woods and climbed high into trees and pulled the wild grapevines down and cut them into various sizes. The grapevines made excellent jumping ropes."

The young adults, inspired to preserve their memories and pass them down, continued to write. Sometimes formally; more often just in the form of casual lists. Regardless of form, eighty percent of the population was, by now, at least somewhat literate and young people were more excited to write than ever before since the ballpoint pen was invented in 1888 and the mechanical pencil in 1906, making writing easier and a lot less messy. No more ink splotches! And, writing was so much simpler these days with pens, pencils, and paper always available at the general stores in the area. Loggers liked to write home and so the stores always had plenty of writing supplies.

- **_Making a living_**- *we grew, raised, hunted, or gathered everything we needed.*
- **_Hogs_** *the most important source of meat—bacon, ham, sausage lard, brains, intestines, every part was used. (Except the squeal!)*
- **_Apple and Plum Trees_** *fruits were baked and dried. Our mamas made the best apple pies.*
- **_Cows_** *provide milk, butter, cheese*
- **_Chickens_** *provide eggs and meat. And feathers for mattresses.*
- **_Gardens_** *provide green beans, squash, pumpkins, tomatoes, onions, lettuce, peas.*
- **_Corn fields_** *a lot of things came from corn like bread, corn on the cob, hominy, grits, popcorn, corn pudding, and scorpion juice (moonshine). (Ma, if you're reading this, it's just what we heard from Pa. Says it's part of our history. And he don't even drink that much, for the record.)*
- **_Bees_** *make honey that we use as sweetener in many foods. That was the only sweet our family had. Maybe molasses or sugar maple*

syrup sometimes. But bees and their honey make the best sweets. Put it in our tea too. Soothes the throat.

- **_Gathering_** *gather wild greens, berries, and nuts.*
- **_Preserving_** *You have to preserve everything before winter. Dried apples, corn, beans, and jerky.*
- **_Water_** *The Ogles were fortunate because Mr. Ogle—we call him Bud—built a flume from the spring across the path to bring water to the back porch for washing clothes and faces, cooking, and drinking. Mrs. Ogle loves it! Says she has more time to read the Bible because she can start reading earlier at night. Says she can put her feet up for just a minute.*
- **_Baths_** *Imagine taking a bath in spring water. Cold! You don't bathe every day. Just on Saturday so it's before church on Sundays. Sometimes Ma warms the water in the kettle and there ain't no better feeling! That and the soap that Ma makes. But we wish we had Luraney Oliver's recipe for soap. She passed back in 1888, over in Cades Cove, but we hear she had the best soap around. Maybe in all of America. Our mamas try to recreate it, and they do a good job, but we know it's nothing like Luraney Oliver's soap.*
- **_Wood_** *Just about everything is made from wood including plates, bowls, spoons, instruments; no plastic, very little metal or glass— too expensive. Tables, chairs, bed frames, dressers, every kind of furniture in general. And of course, wood warms us and mama always has a wood fire going. Always. And our woodpile is always piled high. Always. If not, it meant someone had just died, meaning, we hadn't had time to go chop. But that didn't last long...we got back to chopping as soon as we could. Chop your own wood, it will warm you twice. Some of the best advice ever.*

- **_Chores_** *For children, gather food from the wild and from the garden, milk cows, carry and gather firewood, feed livestock, help build rock fences—fetch rocks from the creek beds, carry water. As we get older, we begin to help with Ma and Pa's chores. More help in the fields and crops and more help with the animals. Sometimes we helped them birth. We always welcome more animals.*

- **_Fun and Entertainment_** *Reading, mostly the Bible; other books were scarce, but many of us have primers for school. When we went to school. Only during summer lulls and after the harvest, when we had time. In the winter too, when we could. Singing on the porch, especially the Ogle's front porch. Older folk sit under the porch and the rest of us bring chairs or quilts to sit on the ground. Most of us children though, never sit still. Runnin' around while the banjo music is rollin' and doing anything we want while our parents sneak some special juice. We play games: who can spit the furthest, who can catch the most lightning bugs. The really little ones play with corn shuck dolls, slingshots, tops, and marbles while we all listen to the banjos and then the crickets join in. All this while that one deer watches us. We see his eyes in the moonlight. He's never far away. Folks say he protects us. Especially the Ogles.*

- **_Storytelling_** *scary, funny, or sad. Grandpa's stories are always the best. And especially after a little 'shine. The fish he supposedly caught keep gettin' bigger and bigger every time he tells the tale. And the snakes he fought get as big and thick as a bear. Speaking of, grandpas always have a bear story. And they always scare the bear off with a look. Never their rifle. Always scare 'em off with their own angry stares or a low groan. Whenever a bear sees a long, gray beard, he runs. That's the legend and I think it's true.*

- ***Going to Church*** *could see all your friends. We sing. Catch up on news and gossip. Sundays after church are visiting days, in addition to Saturday nights. Sometimes we mourn together, bury our dead. Those are the toughest days. When the tears never stop. But we also see weddings, though most girls want to get married at home. So they can drink the juice, which you can't do in church. Although we've seen some folk sneak some in. Says it makes them closer to God.*

- ***Mama's voice*** *Get washed up for dinner now. What are we having? Well, how about beans, poke sallet, cornbread and honey! Why don't you stay...you kids can pick the beans, grind the corn, gather the poke, and rob the bees, milk the cow...Pa has gone hunting- I wonder what he'll return with? Deer or rabbit? Or maybe bear? Whatever it is, we'll be mighty thankful for it.*

⤙⤚

In 1910, Andrew Ogle, the great-grandson of Martha and William Ogle, and his family were the most recent Ogles to live in the original cabin. But he would be the last Ogle to live in that particular cabin because an opportunity to sell the land had arrived, unexpectedly, but one that he couldn't pass up.

Noah "Bud" Ogle had opened a small store, amongst his many other enterprises, and had recently moved the store to town. Now, he was getting older, and his sons ran it, the mill, and the homestead, on most days. At forty-seven, he was tired, his back hurt, and his bones creaked. Mountain life was soul-filling, yet it was also very, very hard. Bending over hoes and crops, kneeling to tend animals and inspect the soil, reaching up for apples, and constant use of arms and shoulders for cutting trees, firewood and cornfields. Hauling hay, hoisting saddles on horses, climbing on roofs for shingle repairs and running to quench fires and chase grandchildren. Mountain folk used every inch of their bodies to survive in this beautiful wilderness and each had their days of glory and their great dark nights.

Bud saw the large stag deer a lot more these days. Watching, he seemed to appear almost every day, sometimes high on the mountain, sometimes hanging around the corn crib or by the banks of the creek. He was rocking in a cane-back chair this afternoon when Elijah Lawson Reagan came walking up his pathway. The apple trees were growing and had bloomed the flowers which would begin to grow juicy red apples at their centers. And the rocky terrain of his homestead gave it a peaceful aura. Sunlight had speared the trees, and rays lay in a semi-circle that embraced him on the rustic and sturdy front porch.

"Hey, Elijah. What brings you here? How's the woodworkin' business?" Bud greeted his friend and neighbor.

"Very good! Still using my hand tools. The store has all these fancy gadgets, but I prefer to make my products by hand. Gives that special something that a machine never can."

"I agree. Can you imagine electric tools?"

"I sure can't! But I admit that sometimes when it takes me hours—days even—to make somethin', the thought of getting that power from a water-wheel, installing a turbine, and generator to get power is...well, let's just say it's something to think about. For the future."

"Life is getting easier ain't it?"

"Indeed, it is." He sighed. "But will that be a good thing? If we lose our hard work ethic and ways of life—will the easy way make us lose who we are?"

"Well now, we never know what's going to happen. An easier life is not such a bad thing."

"True...it's not bad at all. Maybe it'll just take me a while to get there." And they both thought about what they would gain, or lose, when the modern world caught up with them.

And both men thought that they already knew the answer.

Though there was much progress, the people of Gatlinburg remained remote and mostly isolated, especially when compared to the growing American cities. Although the Appalachian region had its own identity and culture, it had not really been viewed as distinct from other parts of the rural south. People lived close to the land, growing crops, gathering and hunting, raising children, attending church and reading the Bible—often the only book in a household, other than children's primers and schoolbooks. After the Civil War however, "a mythology about mountain deviance emerged. Some reported mountaineers as aberrant based on exaggerated accounts of violence, poverty and ignorance. As the urban middle class became identified as the core of American society, efforts to "Americanize" other groups brought organizations such as the Pi Beta Phi into the mountain south." Word of this mythology reached the Ogles and the rest of Gatlinburg. And it reached Andrew Ogle, the current resident of the original Ogle cabin, in the form of a grand opportunity.

❧

"No, it don't bother us. Try puttin' those town folk into a corn-crib for the night, fending off bears and critters. They won't last an hour!" They laughed as they spoke about the growing interest in the town of Gatlinburg. "They likely forgot how to fire a rifle by now. Going soft there in the big cities."

"Right! Who do they think grows the food they eat? The food *they* can't even grow. Or hunt. Or even catch in a creek?"

"Lots of folks are goin' soft. That's okay for one point—we need railroads and buildings and steamboats and the men who sit in their offices to make that happen. But on the other point, they need to appreciate our place in the world. There's no way for them to build America without food. Which we provide."

"Wish they wouldn't forget so easily."

"The softies sure do have short memories."

"The only thing I say is, you're all in the right, I reckon. Love our way of life and don't want anyone messin' with it. But maybe...just maybe...we should try to expand our world. Maybe it wouldn't be such a bad thing to get more schooling. Even if we stay on the farm. Even if we're in the middle of fields all day, creeks hemming us in and the mountains smilin' down at us, we need to keep up with the modern world. It's comin' our way. And I don't know if we can stop it."

"Better to meet it when it comes our way."

"Make it work for *us*. We may be out here in no man's land, but we're still part of America. After all, the loggers came and now other bigger things are circling around our town. It's like that deer, sniffing around and decidin' where to bed down. They're sniffin' around and have been for a while now."

"I noticed. And yessir, we're definitely part of America and more and more people know it. Our nation is a mix of big cities, farms, and everything in between. It's like a quilt that Mama makes out of old peoples' clothes and our baby clothes. And even the rags from people we don't like! It's all part of one big covering."

"And, we're right in the middle. Holding it all together."

⸎

Though there were schools, there were still no public schools, the region still relying on subscription schools where parents pay for their children to attend. But in 1910, the Pi Beta Phi women's organization came to town, which would change the Ogle family - and Gatlinburg - forever.

Founded in 1867 at Monmouth College in Monmouth, Illinois, Pi Beta Phi Women's Fraternity decided to embark upon its first national philanthropy in 1910. The growing national focus on Appalachia led them to plan a settlement school in the region, and an investigation of the most educationally needy areas of the mountain south brought them to the village of Gatlinburg, Tennessee. They saw the residents of Gatlinburg as "old stock" and that the "myths about them were mixed with a tiny bit of truth".

Back in 1883, another writer, Louise Coffin Jones wrote an article: "In the Highlands of North Carolina" that Appalachia was "as unfamiliar to us as the dweller in a wheeled house on the Scythian Steppes."

"Some other author wrote that we live an almost animal-like existence!" One of the Ogle girls exclaimed indignantly.

"Goes to show how much they know about us. They never stayed here one day. Or one night when the bears don't sleep and the deer is watching over us."

"Or even asked us one question about our lives. They just look in from the outside and think they got it all figured out."

"Let's show them how we are. We're not poor. Why we have everything we need! We can make crafts that no one else can. Can make anything we need. Built houses, raised generations of children and animals, bred crops…how can anyone in their right mind call us animals! I don't see no animals building cantilever barns. Or rubbing wood nettle on bruises to make the circulation move faster. Or gettin' onions into a stomach to aid digestion and stop chest pain and frostbite, as long as it's before the black sets in. Or planting and growing acres and acres of the best corn in the country."

"Well, if they start that school they're sniffing around for, it'll be good, I reckon. For one, we'll show the world we respect learning. For another, we'll show them we're smarter than they ever thought."

In 1910, to commemorate their fiftieth anniversary, the Pi Beta Phi Women's Fraternity voted to honor their founders by providing education where no formal education had been available. And so, they began putting in motion the opening of a school in Gatlinburg, Tennessee. But first, they had to obtain land, which of course, involved the Ogle family.

"Need to persuade the Ogle family to sell thirty-five acres to us for the school. We understand it's been in the family since 1807. A long time. Let's go lay out our terms. But let's not make the same mistake that Radford Gatlin did when he came here... we must not force anything, or simply *tell* them what's happening. Instead, we must talk it out and be united in helping their family and the entire community with this school."

Despite the urge to show the world what they were made of, skeptics abounded on the Ogle's front porch on Saturday nights.

"I like how they're talkin' to us. Not pushing or pulling us like Gatlin did. And it actually does seem like a good idea... world is changin' and we need to adapt."

"They may be religious propagandists!"

"Or opportunists. We're all mentioning Gatlin again. Well, look what happened when he came to town. Just did what he wanted. And ran to court every chance he could! Dang if his name's still on the town, even though he's long gone and we couldn't stand him!"

Their skepticism was justified with what had happened before in their town—they remembered very well that it was pure angst for years! Arson charges, mischief, fighting about roads, fistfights...

"All true. But I truly think, after ponderin' it all, that this opportunity for money—to adapt and to grow our town in our own way, outweighs our suspicions."

✧✧✧

In the end, the organization did persuade the Ogle family, and the cabin and land were sold to the Pi Beta Phi Women's Fraternity, which soon started the Pi Beta Phi Settlement School.

The community even "assisted with its construction and maintenance", and, for the most part, wholeheartedly embraced this opportunity for their children. *Especially since they didn't just come in and tell us what to do. In fact, they talk about preserving our way of life. Says it's worth learning from and they appreciate our own special culture; says we are some of the true Americans. Now, I don't know about that but think on it...Gatlin came here and saw somethin'. And now, the school's doin' the same thing. We're just livin' our lives, but maybe outsiders see somethin' different. A gateway to something...*

Two years later, in 1912, the women's fraternity opened the school with thirteen students. By the end of that first year, they had 134 students. In 1921, the school acquired another thirty-five acres and expanded.

"Wouldn't it be great if this school remained here and expanded even more? I love how they combine arts and education...and they have built privies and added public health nurses and doctors. I mean, most any man can set a broken leg, provided that there's enough moonshine. But there's just some things herbs and roots and 'shine can't do. It'd be nice to get that nursing here for us in Gatlinburg."

The former White Oak Flats was now quite a bustling town in this sliver of the Smoky Mountains. Many homesteads and crops sprinkled the landscape, and the loggers remained a strong presence, but there was also a blacksmith shop, a few general stores at various strategic locations, a Baptist church, and over 600 people. And now that they had an esteemed school, Gatlinburg was attracting more and more tourists. Wiley Oakley, whom everyone called "the Roamin' Man of the Mountains," was well-known by now, making money as a mountain guide, leading city folk and such through and over the mountains. The views, they say, make everything in life understood. And Oakley...he isn't just makin' some money, he's buying up land and more land. Why he owns more land than a lot of us put together!"

Indeed, Gatlinburg was by now firmly entrenched on the map. The school expanded to include "vocational and home economics training" for the adults as well. "The school's focus on reestablishing and promoting local craft skills also helped Gatlinburg become established as an arts and crafts center." Weaving, baskets, whittling, and other such crafts were highlighted when the school's staff created a small market for these local creations.

Many of the staff spoke about what their new school was like and spread their own thoughts on mountain culture, often with a very different lens than the ones who had lived in Gatlinburg for generations.

"Phyllis Higinbotham, a nurse from Toronto who worked at the school for six years, wrote of the mountain peoples' confusion over the role of a nurse, their penchant for calling on her for minute issues, and her difficulties with Appalachian customs:"

I soon found that people weren't used to hurrying and that it takes a long time of patient waiting and general conversation to find out what they have really come for or to get a history of the cases when making a visit. I have had to get used to getting most of a woman's symptoms from her husband, and not having heart failure when a messenger comes with the news that so and so is "bad off", "about to die", or "got the fever.

Higinbotham complained that there was an unhealthy "lack of variety" in the mountain peoples' diet and that they weren't open to new suggestions. Food was often "too starchy," "not well cooked," and supplemented with certain excesses:

One of the doctors was called to several cases of honey poisoning. The men had robbed some bee gums, eaten a pound or two of each and been knocked unconscious where they stood.

"Evelyn Bishop, a Pi Beta Phi who arrived at the school in 1913, reported that the mountain peoples' relative isolation from American society allowed them to retain folklore that reflected their English and Scots-Irish ancestries, such as Elizabethan Era ballads:

Many times it is the ballad that the child learns first, no Mother Goose melodies are as familiar, and it is strange indeed to listen to a little tot singing of the courtly days of old, the knights and ladies and probably the tragic death of the lover.

When the Ogle family farm and homestead was sold to Pi Beta Phi in 1920, and especially after the next year, when it expanded, the old cabin still had a lot of life left in it. It was first used as a hospital. Then from 1922-1926, it housed a museum of mountain artifacts. Later, the cabin was moved a short distance away, where the ever-increasing number of tourists could see where it all began and wonder about a way of life that was as unique as each white oak that continued their march up the mountains, loggers hot on their tails.

The school also stood witness as the "old" Gatlinburg ushered in the new era. It saw Noah "Bud" Ogle passing away on November 16, 1913, aged fifty. The entire town turned out for the funeral, and honored yet another Ogle son, the one who built the saddlebag cabin, operated the tub mill, and cultivated a great apple orchard and managed to grow corn on rocky and largely barren soil. The one who raised seven children with his wife, who was a steadfast and strong partner to him. Now, she joined the ranks of mountain widows; men had an average life expectancy of fifty—the exact age that Noah was. Women lived a few years longer, on average, so there were always more widows continuing the farms and homesteads on their own. Thank goodness for many sons and daughters! No woman, or man for that matter, could truly do it all. Large families were always a blessing—more help on the land. More hands to hold when nature and its toils tried to take over. More souls joined together when nature and its toils, sometimes, succeeded.

One of the Oliver young men made the trip from Cades Cove to say goodbye to Noah "Bud" Ogle.

"Interesting..." John W. Oliver told the Ogle family, whom the Olivers had kept in touch with over the years. He sat down under the trees after the service, munching on a slice of bread and ham brought by the women, and caught up with the news between the two Tennessee communities of Cades Cove and Gatlinburg.

"I saw our eagle—the one that's always around." John told Bud's sons and daughters. "He never left our biggest tree on the day that Bud died. We saw him up in that tree all day long and we just knew something had happened. So, we waited for news and sadly, it came from you all here in Gatlinburg. That eagle always seems to know when something meaningful has happened. It always knows. Don't know how, but it always knows. It's like our sign."

"I know what you mean. We have a deer like that. And he was present all day when Pa passed, just roamin' around, stamping his feet at times, sniffing the air. Gettin' pretty close to the house all day long. And...almost bowing in prayer, Lowered his head and stood very still, closing his eyes. The Cherokee say that animals know. Calls 'em spirit animals. They guide and show up at times of change. Show up as spirits of our ancestors. And who knows? Maybe they do..."

෨෧ඏ

Bud had prepared well. Knowing that he had grown tired and old, Bud had subdivided his crop and orchard land amongst his children and retained only 150 acres for himself. Now, that land remained in his wife's stead, with plenty of help from the entire Ogle family, spread far and wide over the slopes of white oaks in these ancient Smoky Mountains.

The close-knit community remained at the church after the service, after the burial, and after the beloved Ogle family member was laid to rest at White Oak Flats Cemetery in the heart of Gatlinburg.

We will remember Noah Ogle. Bud, we all called him. Son, husband, father, grandfather, friend, neighbor. A valuable contributor to our mountain community. He made things better; was of a very modern mind. We all learned from him. We sure did. And, we will preserve his legacy. You know, perhaps people will come see the way he lived. The way we all lived. Oh, that's crazy talk. Why would anyone come here to see the way we live? You never know...we're gettin' more and more tourists and there's more talk about the school and how people want to know about us here in Appalachia. But we don't do anythin' special! We're just livin' just like we always lived. And lotsa folks live this way. What do we do that's so special? We live in cabins, chop wood, grow food, tend animals, roam the mountains, go to church, teach our kids, hunt, fish, play in creeks, drink a bit of 'shine, hang out on porches with our banjos, and love each other fiercely. And we love our land and mountains. I don't get it. That's what most folks do. Nothin' special. What's there to see?

The deer listened to the people talking, discussing, debating. He had spent his life watching their way of life and even if these people didn't know it yet, *he* knew that they represented the very American identity that the rest of humanity strove for. Sniffing the air, he caught whiffs of individualism, hard work, courage. Liberty and equality. The love of one's country and bravery. Deciding who they married, where they lived, how they lived. And how hard they worked equaled how successful they were. Indeed, these were some of the richest people he'd ever seen. Not necessarily in money, but in character and culture.

Which was more important. Much more important. Because he'd walked over these mountains and saw bigger towns, people rushing around, getting things done, never taking their eyes off of a sidewalk or their tasks before them. Never looking at the mountains, or at a creek as it marched down the slopes of white oaks, or an eagle flying high, or his own large brown body as it stood watching them. No one in the bigger towns ever noticed his presence. Too busy rushing from one building to the next. But the people in Gatlinburg always noticed. Always locked eyes and smiled. And always, most importantly, wondered.

The deer bedded down for the night in his nest of soft pine needles, hidden under dense brush with a sliver of a moon rising above the white oaks. Suddenly raising his head, he picked up the strongest scent of all. *My goodness, what is that? It's so strong...*

And then he recognized it. It came from the people themselves, as they slept in loving memory of one of their own, the one they had laid to rest today. A sweet, honored, and peaceful aroma of hundreds of good and loving souls, wafting on the winds, flowing through a land of paradise.

CHAPTER SIXTEEN

1920s and beyond
The Park

D OWN THE ROAD, just south of the Ogle homestead, several investors were working at "Cherokee
Orchard", a 796-acre commercial apple orchard and
ornamental nursery. Gatlinburg had never stood still, but was
now expanding like never before; it was more crowded than ever,
businesses such as the Cherokee Orchard sprang up, and they
were attracting more and more attention. The logging industry was still powerful and dominated the landscape. Residents
continued to farm their fertile lands and those who were still
arriving, too late now to claim the more fertile tracts of land,
"settled on steep mountainsides and in the area's many hollers."

Around this same time, the Tennessee Park Commission had
begun acquiring land and property for a new national park, and
people had caught onto the plan. Fighting for land had become
somewhat of a lifestyle in Appalachia and the residents knew
full well what was happening. They'd been through the Gatlin

years, the Civil War, logging. And now, the government seems to view this land as a gateway of sorts. For people who had lived on the land their whole lives, it was easy to see. It just wasn't so easy to stop.

Oh sure, I did my part. We all did. It was all in the name of good jobs! And we liked to have money. Finally. We knew it. Of course we knew it... toppling mountains of trees every day, every week. Seeing our slopes bald and brown. I had to feed my family. Yes, of course I wondered how we'd feed ourselves once the trees were gone and the jobs left. Figured I'd think about it when the time came. Or there'd be so many trees, we could just move on down the valley to slopes that hadn't been touched yet. On a clear day, you can see for miles. Surely there's enough mountain slopes full of trees... But look. There's not even a place that the critters can run to. Look around! It's bare. Like a 'possum's tail. So, yes, the park may be a good thing. A national park. We couldn't log it if it's set aside for a park; at least the critters can have their place again. The trees will grow back. And we can keep our farms and land. And culture. Don't forget the way we live. It's ours alone. City folk are sitting on concrete balconies and eating on sidewalks, while we still have our creeks, crops, gardens and barns. Front porches, our church and quilts and harvesting. Nights when all you hear is howls, or else all you hear is nothing. Nothing except the wind. Nothing except for a large stag bedding down on crunchy leaves and sniffing the air. We have our Bibles and each other and 'shine for when life gets weary. And an entire valley for when we have to just walk to get away from ourselves. Not too far though...a little distance always does the trick.

Well, the trouble is, they ain't going to let us stay if there's a park. Running folks out so they can run the critters in. Now that's a hell of a thing. Well now, wait a minute. Logging brought us jobs. Yes, and we are grateful. But it's also hard work. Dangerous. Don't you notice? More and more loggin' men on crutches. Hobbling down the aisles at church. Bottle nested in their Bible to ease the pain. Trees fallin' is just the start. Widowmakers they call 'em. When a tree topples, its limbs snag the other branches and remain there. Until they all crash down without warning. Making an immediate widow outta that man's wife. If they're lucky, it just maims them. Renders their legs and feet and necks and backs useless. Then, there's the rattlesnake bites, frostbite, axe injuries, drowning or else they're struck by lightning. And fresh men are always jumpin' off the trains to take their place.

Life went on. With the threat of the national park looming over them for the next few years, from 1926-1930, Gatlinburg "became the endpoint on a trans-mountain highway that extended through the park to Cherokee, North 66 Carolina." Visitors had thus far been manageable, but now, the number of visitors was approaching over 100,000 per year. These tourists bought crafts from the schoolchildren and their families. Weaving rugs and clothes, spinning wool, crafting large and small baskets, whittling wood—the Gatlinburg families had been doing these activities for so long! They wondered, why now? Why did everyone suddenly care, now? What did these tourists see and think?

The deer could certainly answer those questions. The dark brown beast saw inside the minds of the newcomers and visitors; was able to pick up the sweet scent of an appreciation of a very special way of life. His own antlers had rubbed against much of the vast diversity of plants and trees growing on the ancient slopes, softened by the wind, and his wise and knowing eyes had seen countless animals that were found nowhere else on earth. But mostly, the answer came when both beast and man stood on a steep rise, the trees pausing to clear the way, and the mountains came to life, stretching themselves across the whole of the earth, pleated shadows resting for just a moment before the sun revealed the entirety of its most glorious attire. It is during these moments that the special magic of the Smoky Mountains is revealed to all. Even those who are lucky enough to experience this every day of their lives. If they only looked out from their fields and cabins, smoke on their clothes from thousands of hearth fires, faces wet from refreshing creek water splashed to cool down, and tub mills and blacksmith shops and general stores and cabins bustling with the activity of hearty and God-loving human beings. If they only looked out, they would see it all. The ones who are part of the long history of this hilly, rocky, fertile, and astonishingly beautiful land. A land of paradise.

∽⦵⦵∾

Elijah Lawson Reagan had established his woodworking business in 1910, and now, in the 1920s, he had finally "harnessed the power of the water of the Roaring Fork to operate his new electric power tools." He also "built a water wheel and installed a turbine and generator which furnished power to his shop."

The Reagans were very adept at living in these mountains; they were a particularly enterprising family. Another member, Alfred Reagan, farmed some of the steepest and rockiest land in the area. On a hill that "went straight up and down", he managed to raise sheep, cattle and hogs, as well as enough corn to feed his family and even sell for a surplus. Apple, peach, pear, and plum trees rounded out this unusual farm and his wife loved color and planted "zinnias, marigolds, touch-me-nots, lilacs, violets, just a regular run of flowers." His wife, Martha Bales, wasn't satisfied though and chose to paint the exterior of their home white, yellow and blue, chosen from a limited color selection from the Sears Catalog that the postmaster brought to her and that she read every night. Even more than her Bible, she whispered with a grin.

In that house, seven children were born and raised and as they grew, they were all told about their father being the very first one to kill a bear on Roaring Fork, just outside of Gatlinburg. Of course, Reagan was too humble to tell the tale, but their neighbor, Herb Clabo, told it every chance he got:

"Alfred was quite a hunter. Best I remember, he killed the first bear on Roaring Fork. He was a tellin' me one night that I stayed all night with him. He was a great talker. He was a tellin' me about shootin' this bear, and he didn't kill it dead at the time, but he follered it on until it went on and he found it in a sink hole, where it had made it to the sink hole. It had got wounded so bad that it couldn't go on, but he said it'd just chewed laurels off, you know rhododendrons stalks off and just sort of piled them in there. He was a usin' what they called an old hog rifle, and you only shot them once till you took time to reload which was a matter of, I'll say, five minutes, owin' to, I'll say, how bad you needed to reload. He follered it on and found it in that sinkhole and shot it second time, which killed it. Fur as I know or remember, that's the only bear killed up in there."

ఞ෧෧ఞ

The growing number of tourists also saw Ephraim E. Ogle taking over his father's store around 1916. The Ogle and Company store now housed the post office and provided most of the goods bought in town until around 1925, when Ephraim passed it onto his grandson, Charlie A. Ogle, and great-grandson, Charles Earl Ogle, to continue the family tradition. Through the years the store expanded, spreading out, rambling, and jutting way beyond its original frame as new merchandise was added. "If they could find it", they could get "anything you want in the world. All they had to do was order it and ship it here to Gatlinburg, an ever-growing point on the map of Tennessee's Appalachian valleys."

But all the progress in the world couldn't stop the government from establishing the much-talked about national park. Many embraced the idea, relishing the funds they received for their land. Some, though, did not like it at all, rebelling, refusing, and then, aging bitterly on the land they were allowed to keep for their lifetimes, but knowing that after they went to their God, their land would become part of the park. *No more passing land down to the next generation. That idea is dead for us. What about their gravesites? Churches? Stores? Cabins? What would happen to their way of life? Would they continue their legacy in the town founded so long ago with the arrival of Martha Ogle?*

The deer walked all day, watching the ever-increasing activity of the humans. It was amazing that his own antlered ancestors saw just one cabin, and then, there were two, and then four, and then sixteen, and then, before you knew it, generations had passed, and now a very many healthy people were farming, building, playing, and loving in the deep embrace of these mountains. But they were also attending school, opening businesses, using technology, and welcoming many outsiders. These people were doing just fine. But their legacy, that...that was something else. It appeared to be intact, traditions ongoing and families still close-knit and looking out for one another. But who was looking out for their way of life? It was still there, yet not the same. Still there in the crops, the cabins, and Saturday nights on the porch, yet it was not the same...not the same as before. A long time, it's been. Decades ago. Life has gotten better, in many ways. *Machines! Education! Medicines and longer lives! But is life really better? I don't know what to think about that,* the deer thought. *He walked to the thicket just behind the general store, bustling with activity and sacks of goods piled up outside, waiting to be brought in. The postmaster was present, having just relayed his stories and delivered the newspapers. Then, shortly thereafter, the delivery wagon left, and now, the children scattered throughout Gatlinburg to pass on the gossip and tales.*

Yes. The deer observed. *These people were doing just fine. Look there! Children scrambled at full speed to tell stories. Just like their grandfathers! Look at the girls with bolts of cloth in their arms...just like their grandmothers and mothers. Look at the young lovers over there, holding hands and planning their futures right here in Gatlinburg. And look over there at the older farmers, hard at work. Always planting seeds. Watching them grow, tending them, protecting them if needed. Always planting seeds. Arms hooked high over their heads, stretching in the afternoon sun. Bending down to feel and sniff the soil. It was a way of life. Their way of life. And, despite the fact that it looked a bit different and more and more technology was present, their basic ways and values were alive and well.*

The deer walked back to his bed and lay down in the thick nest of pine needles, well hidden under the thick brush. He drifted off in peace with one, lone plea: *keep planting seeds. As long as they keep planting seeds.*

﹌⊙⊙﹌

"Kephart, that author, and others are supporting the idea of that national park."

"He ain't just callin' for it no more. He's yelling it from the mountaintops! Kephart and some of the businesses in Knoxville, conservationists, et cetera....they're movin' awful fast. That's all we hear about lately."

"We've seen logging, and we've seen it create jobs, but also seen it take away our land. And with it, gotta admit, some of our way of life went with it...fewer fields to tend. Far fewer trees. Tub mills, building, makin' furniture—they're all being replaced by machines and electric tools. And now, with the park, what's going to happen to our town?"

"Well, it will surely change now that Congress passed the Weeks Act allowing purchasing of land for national forests. Eminent domain they call it...They say *we want it similar to Yellowstone out west. Or Yosemite in California.*"

News had reached the residents of Gatlinburg that the government had purchased 76,000 acres from the Little River Lumber Company tracts in 1926. The park was becoming reality, and was highly anticipated by many.

But not everyone was so enthused. The residents of Gatlinburg and nearby Cades Cove lamented that their land was being taken. Oh, some were quite grand with the idea. They finally had money! They could go, buy another tract of land or move closer to bigger towns and finally retire in comfort. But many others fought with their last strength to stay on their own land. No matter if it was for the greater good, or for the rest of America and the world to experience their beloved mountains, their land and their very way of life. It was all under threat. If they moved, who would preserve their churches? Tub mills and cabins? *Even our 'Shine hollows! Will they just destroy it all? And what about the animals? What about the deer who's supposed to be the protector?*

For it or against it, or somewhere in between, it was a decision that no one would take lightly. Would, or should, they give in and embrace change? Take the opportunity? Because in a lot of ways, it was a good one. Like when the loggers came to town. One that may not come around ever again. Or, would, or should, they fight to stay on their own land, keep their own churches and cabins and crops and corncribs and their front porches?

Grand schemes and projects never happen overnight. Two years passed with the residents largely doing exactly as they'd been doing for over a century. Sure, the people were different— Shakespeare would've called them different players but on the same stage. The backdrop remained the softly scalloped peaks of the mountains, the white oaks swaying in the breeze, the yellow corn crops hiding a large lone deer walking to and fro. Rustic cabins, creeks, logs piled high and smoke from chimneys completed the scene. The script underwent slight alterations;

more players and recent happenings meant more ways to plan, prepare, adapt, and change. But what of the audience? Ah, there's the rub. *All things are ready if our mind be so.* It had come to the part of the story where enough of the audience's minds were in the right place for profound change. And that made all the difference.

David "Crockett" Maples had married Lucinda King when his first wife, Mary "Polly" Ogle had died. Lucinda was twenty years younger than her husband and she always knew the day would come when that gap widened too far. But she almost believed that her husband was immortal. His strength knew no bounds! After all, he'd survived the amputation of both feet and lower legs after frostbite rotted them. And together, they'd had eight children, the last one born when he was nearly sixty-four years old. This was in addition to his eight children he had with Polly. This was also four years after he'd killed a bear with only a knife, not having his rifle at his side while out on a walk near his homestead. Lucinda always thought her husband unlucky, but interestingly, he seemed to have good luck after the bad luck had caught him. And it always caught him, seemed to follow him even. One of his eyes grew so infected a few years into their marriage that the doctor had to remove it without anesthesia. A bit of moonshine was all he had. Same as when his feet were cut off. Except that took all the moonshine they could find. Still, *my goodness*, Lucinda was in constant awe, *Crockett just gets on with it don't he?* Everyone marveled at this strong mountain man who seemed to live in the shadows of death but managing to escape its grasp every time.

∞⊚⊚∞

It was a fine winter day, December 30, 1928, when the remaining white leaves glowed under a soft sun, clouds danced across the sky and the muted colors of the season flashed up and down each and every slope. David "Crockett" Maples' large family was by his side. Lucinda, their children, Maples' children by Polly, his grandchildren, and great-grandchildren—all great admirers of their patriarch—remained at his bedside in the large cabin. Quilts covered the bed and the fire roared. Smells of ham and biscuits wafted through the home and he opened his eyes and smiled. *Smells good,* he said.

Would you like some grandpa? Little voices accompanied thick tears rolling down cheeks.

No. Thank you. Enjoy it for yourselves. Enjoy it all. He tried to take a breath, then stopped and whispered, *I've had more than my share.* Smiling, David "Crockett" Maples left his hearty spirit and soul to his family and went to meet his God.

The cabin stood still, nobody moved. The man who walked around on wooden feet, supported by canes, who had sired this large brood of people, a true survivor—the very best of men—was gone.

The deer walked up to the homestead, smelling the sweet scent of a life well-lived. Ninety years old he was! His many legacies were moving slowly now, bowed heads heading out to share the news, to pick up the coffin, to gather food, firewood, a shovel. The ground was not frozen and so they should move quickly. The church had to be decorated. He had to be dressed. No need for his feet now, but they would go with him, just like he said he wanted. To be sure he could walk when he met God. Would take too long to crawl, he had told them with a smile and a wink. The coffin was lined with burlap—just like he wanted. Rough, able to withstand all of the things that came next.

We need to honor our grandfather. Our father, great-grandfather. You know, he made the best breakfast. Was known far and wide for his pancakes. I think we should open a restaurant. A place where travelers can eat. The park is comin'. It just is. And a lot of people will come to Gatlinburg because we will be the gateway to the national park. And they'll need to eat; the best pancakes in the mountains! We can honor him and let everyone know what a man he was….Crockett's Breakfast. Now, there's a nice name.

It would take a few more generations, but the idea remained strong within the family and finally, Kirby Smith, great-great-great-grandson of David "Crockett" Maples, opened Crockett's Breakfast Camp right outside of the park's entrance. Visitors are welcomed by a life-size statue of David Crockett Maples, the strong and sturdy mountain man, who stood up to the elements time and time again, fighting like hell for victory. *Necessity never made a good bargain*, he always said. *But then again*, he'd say, *I was never making nor accepting any bargains, only outwitting nature's deadly traps. And accepting the unacceptable.*

Progress, once begun, can rarely be stopped. In 1932, world-wide attention of this slice of Appalachia was gained when

Cecil Sharp, a folklorist from London, came to Gatlinburg after World War I and published a collection of ballads. All of this attention was not something the residents sought or even welcomed. It just meant it was more and more likely the government would take over and create the park. It was inevitable, this stirring and poking into the dusty relics of a past life.

That Cecil Sharp of London! He's like a folklorist...he came here to Appalachia after the war where the whole world fought. And his collection of ballads was published in 1932. Says things like "I sowed the seeds of love/And I sowed them in the Spring/I gathered them up in the morning so soon//While the small birds do sweetly sing." It is a nice tune...but we like our own songs. Porch songs that we sing on Saturday nights. And I take issue—as they say over there in London—with his diary. Says, "The Mitchells are a wonderful clan, living in a small narrow creek about a mile from my hotel. They are considered a very low-down lot by the richer people here who wonder why we like them and go there so often." How does an outsider know what that family is considered by us? He only gets the tourist point of view. They wonder why we like the Mitchells and go to visit so often. Heck...so often? It's our way of life! It's what we do. And we like them 'cause they're just like us.

By 1934, over 300,000 acres of mountainous land were turned over to the federal government. Congress authorized the development of public facilities such as trails, bridges, campgrounds and buildings for the national park, and these were well underway, thanks to the Civilian Conservation Corps, created to provide jobs during this uncertain era that began in October of

1929. The Great Depression they were calling it, as the years plodded on.

Despite wide support for the park, resistance ensued and was equally passionate. Opponents said nature is to be used as a resource, for food, clothing, shelter, *like we've done throughout human history!* Supporters said that democracy, philosophy and art were all contained within nature and why not set aside the most beautiful land for that enjoyment? Why not bring the wonders of America to everyone, even if John Muir, for example, wrote about it and sold books to the masses, allowing readers to simply visualize the beauty from their own humble living rooms without ever setting foot on a forest trail?

But strong opposition—the strongest from some of the residents themselves—was all for naught, for the strength lay in the federal government's determination to create the national park. The Cherokee Orchard Company couldn't even win, but they "threatened with all that they had, fighting like hell against a major appropriations bill for the park's funding if their land was taken from them". But then, they dropped their case in "1931 in exchange for a long lease on the property." Logging companies also got in on the action of resisting the national park's takeover of the lands. But despite bitter fighting and lawsuits amongst the Elkmont and other lumber companies and the Tennessee legislature, the Great Smoky Mountains National Park opened in 1934. With Gatlinburg as its gateway.

The main part of the town itself wasn't part of the park, yet many families south of the town proper finally accepted government monies for their land, some moving away, but many staying close by, in town, or buying land in all other directions.

Gatlinburg's heyday had only just begun. From a church, blacksmith shop, a school, and around 600 souls, within one year of the park's opening, approximately 40,000 visitors passed through the small mountain settlement, one and all marveling at the majesty of the mountain views, the fresh air, and friendly people. A year later, half a million visitors passed through. One of the most popular tourist spots in all of America had begun.

CHAPTER SEVENTEEN

The Park and the Legacy

O N SEPTEMBER 2, 1940, President Franklin D. Roosevelt had the great honor of formally dedicating the Great Smoky Mountains National Park. Speaking from the Rockefeller Monument at Newfound Gap, he declared it "for the permanent enjoyment of the people".

And the families of Gatlinburg took that welcoming sentiment to heart, greeting everyone from around Appalachia, the country, and the world to visit "our home. Our favorite place on earth."

Land prices skyrocketed. In the decade of 1940 to 1950, the cost of land increased from fifty dollars per acre to $8,000 per acre.

"Yessir, the park took away from us, but look at what it gave us! It's benefitted us. Why, we have more money than we ever dreamed of!"

"Sometimes, you don't know it at the time, but this is one of those times when change is truly great. It's made us rich!"

"Maybe. Maybe... That's all good. But what about our history? The way we live? Or used to live. Our way of life? We don't work our fields no more. Heck, there are hardly any fields left! Now, we have smog, concrete where there was once crops and paths and land...automobiles are everywhere! Our fresh mountain air ain't so fresh no more..."

"I agree...it ain't no more of the land that we grew up on. Less and less of it anyhow. Now, in the summer, we're all shoulder to shoulder. Our town is full up. No more room."

"We don't hardly even see the deer no more either. They still roam around, lots of tourists say they're all over in Cades Cove. And that one big one—the one who was always around—we never see him no more. At least, not as much as we used to."

"Oh, I know that one! He's so big. More majestic than all the others. Yes, he's over in Cades Cove a lot. But we seen him just the other day. Must've walked day and night to get here to the 'burg again."

The deer smelled the men's words on the ribbons of wind. Familiar scents. Comforting. They were all still around, human and beast. But not in the same way. The descendants of William Ogle didn't need the same type of protection. They were wealthy, business owners, a close-knit group who had made it in the larger world. There were so many of them! The bloodline and heritage was solid and would continue forever, no matter if they found themselves safe within the embrace of these mountains or anywhere else in the world.

The descendants of the original deer were the ones who needed protection now. *Federal law prohibits hunting and the possession of weapons of any kind within any of the national parks.* As long as they stayed in the boundaries of the park, they were safe from guns, from human progress and activity. At least, that was the intention. They had over 522,000 acres to roam, but outside of that, the land wasn't seamless anymore. It was either all national park or human habitat. There was no blurring of forests anymore, no meandering the peaks and valleys unencumbered by dividing lines and limits. Now, the deer had confines and margins. Still a very large habitat, but smaller than before. Hundreds of deer that each need 60-1600 acres of habitat depending on the particular animal. And each one needs countless weeds, fruits, grasses, and acorns to thrive.

The deer sighed, gazing out at the river that ran through town, holding his antlers high. Gatlinburg itself was certainly prospering. It even became incorporated in 1945. The little cabin that William Ogle had begun to build in his cherished land of paradise had flourished into a beloved place for so many families, honeymooners, adventurers, and those seeking a soulful lift that only the Smoky Mountains can deliver. Such a legacy here! "Gatlinburg natives owned most of the town's business interests, through the 1970s and beyond." Rel Maples, one of David "Crockett" Maples' grandsons, opened the Gatlinburg Sky Lift in honor of his grandfather. Another grandchild, Hattie, married Charles Ogle and became a businesswoman by opening a craft shop, a tourist home, and motels. Many other descendants run hotels, shops, and restaurants, all of them welcoming everyone just as the white oaks had welcomed their ancestor, Martha Ogle, in 1807. So many have passed through this gateway! Cherokees, Ogles, Reagans, Gatlins, Huskeys, Whaleys, and so many others. A gateway to a life in the land of paradise, a land shared by all, a land where an eagle can still soar, and a deer can walk all day, watching and protecting a history, a legacy, and a truly unique way of American life.

The deer blinked, settled his mind and walked out of view, slowly, making sure to fully roam his cherished territory. These are not the last days, he thought. These are the best of days. Where the past meets the future, where history lasts, legacies remain, and these cherished humans can teach others about how they lived. Cabins, tub mills, remnants of chimneys, churches, graveyards are all still here, standing guard and urging our modern world to look, listen, and honor. They whisper to you, and if you stand for just a moment, the mountains will tell you what they wish for you. "Stay close," they say, the sun filling in their peaked and pleated splendor, "but venture far."

ABOUT THE AUTHOR

CATHERINE ASTL holds a Master's Degree in English-Literature and Curriculum from Southern New Hampshire University, a Bachelor's in English-American Literature from University of South Florida, and is a graduate of the International Summer Schools Shakespeare and Literature program at the University of Cambridge, Cambridge, England. She also holds an Associate of Science Degree in Legal Assisting and worked as a civil litigation trial paralegal for 27 years before switching to her current position teaching English Literature.

Catherine lives in Wesley Chapel, Florida, where she spends time with family, reads, writes, travels, and scours bookshops to add to her personal library which is always expanding. She is hard at work on her next novel.

Printed in the USA
CPSIA information can be obtained
at www.ICGtesting.com
LVHW091126310823
756836LV00002B/249